THE BOOK OF PUNISHMENT

Widening her stance as far as the hobble would allow her, which was no more than a few inches, Natasha leaned forwards and slid her hands down the legs of the chair until she was almost touching the carpet. The muscles in her calves and thighs tautened admirably above the high gold stilettos. Her sex was now on blatant display, the tantalising crack of her sex barely hidden by the gold lacy thong.

Licking his lips, Gunter stared down at the bare smooth-skinned bottom raised so provocatively for his paddle.

THE BOOK OF PUNISHMENT

Cat Scarlett

This book is a work of fiction.
In real life, make sure you practise safe,
sane and consensual sex.

First published in 2005 by Nexus

ISBN 9780352345400

The Random House Group Limited supports The Forest Stewardship
Council® (FSC®), the leading international forest-certification organisation.
Our books carrying the FSC label are printed on FSC®-certified paper.
FSC is the only forest-certification scheme supported by the leading
environmental organisations, including Greenpeace. Our
paper procurement policy can be found at
www.randomhouse.co.uk/environment

Printed and bound in Great Britain by Clays Ltd, St Ives plc

You'll notice that we have introduced a set of symbols onto our book jackets, so that you can tell at a glance what fetishes each of our brand new novels contains. Here's the key – enjoy!

cp (traditional)

cp (modern)

spanking

restraint/bondage

rope bondage/hojojutsu

latex/rubber/leather/enclosure

fem dom

willing captivity

medical

period setting

uniforms

sex rituals

Prologue

Paris 1959

Although it was August, it had been raining all morning. Beyond the striped awning of the Café Tartuffe, cars skied crazily along the boulevard, now a treacherous black sheet of water. Women came scurrying past in sodden headscarfs, businessmen in suits under raised newspapers. A group of American tourists sheltered gloomily in a doorway across the street, glaring up at the skies in disbelief, cameras hanging forgotten from their necks. There were not enough taxis and all the most popular cafés along the Rive Gauche were heaving with customers. The deluge had taken Paris by surprise.

Mortimer finished his espresso with a grimace and glanced across at his companion. The coffee always left a bitter taste in his mouth. 'Ready, Xavier?' he murmured in French.

The older man lowered his newspaper, checked his watch in an unhurried fashion, and gave a nod.

They rose from their seats and put on their coats, leaving a small handful of coins on the table. The two men paused at the door to the café, turning up their collars against the rain, then moved out into the drenched streets. At the next corner, they took a right turn and began to head towards the Seine.

'Will there be an opportunity for me to examine the Book of Punishment,' Mortimer asked, keeping his voice carefully low, 'before we decide a price?'

'Better than that, *mon ami*. I've arranged for a young lady to be waiting for us. So you can be satisfied as to the book's merit.'

'Is she aware of its contents?'

'Of course not. But Terese is highly experienced in such matters, you need not concern yourself.'

'You've used her before?'

'Many times.'

They descended a steep flight of steps to a basement apartment, both hurrying now, eager to be out of the rain. Xavier produced a key from his pocket and unlocked the door, then gestured him inside. The room was furnished in an almost rustic style, its brown and yellow furnishings dull but functional. The homely decor seemed oddly incongruous as Mortimer considered what was about to take place in this apartment, his heart beating fast.

As they entered, a young woman who had been sitting on the sofa rose to her feet. She was probably about seventeen or eighteen, rather studious-looking, pale blonde hair coiled neatly behind her head. Her plain white blouse and black skirt gave her the prim air of a waitress in an English tea-room, though she was more likely to be earning her living as a *femme de chambre* in some third-rate Parisian hotel.

The girl smiled at both men. '*Bonjour*, Xavier,' she nodded, kissing him on the cheek. '*Bonjour*, monsieur.'

'*Bonjour*, Terese. How are you today?'

'Very well indeed, thank you.'

'I would like you to meet this young gentleman, who has come all the way from London to buy one of my books. You don't need to know his name, only that he's a friend.'

'It's a pleasure to meet you, Terese,' Mortimer said, holding out his hand.

The girl dropped his hand and stepped back, glancing at Xavier as though in confirmation.

2

When the bookseller nodded at her, she slipped out of her heels and began to unbutton her blouse as though it were a completely normal thing for her, undressing in front of a male audience. Taken aback by such behaviour, Mortimer automatically averted his gaze as she began to pull off the blouse. Then he realised how ridiculous such a courtesy must seem, given the circumstances, and forced himself to look back at her. This show was for his benefit, after all.

Terese was laying the blouse carefully over the back of the sofa, as though she did not want to crease it. Her breasts were not as large as he liked, but they were certainly memorable. He eyed her sturdy white brassière in a fascinated silence, noting the delicate frills of lace decorating the cups as she turned back to face him. Parisian girls, he thought with some amusement, clearly preferred less functional underwear than their English counterparts.

As he continued to stare, the young lady lifted cool blue eyes to his face and reached behind her back, unhooking the brassière with casual expertise.

Mortimer felt himself harden under that direct gaze. The girl was bolder than he had realised. There was absolutely no shame in those eyes. As she turned to arrange the underwear on top of her discarded blouse, her breasts swayed deliciously, small pink nipples soft but eminently suckable.

Unable to prevent himself, he began to imagine the joy of spurting across her chest, his white fluid jetting messily between her breasts so that she was forced to rub it into her own nipples or stain her blouse with his sticky discharge. Perhaps Terese would be going back to work after they had finished here, he thought, and he imagined her leaving with streaks of sperm on that severe black skirt, her hair dishevelled and her mouth bruised.

How would she explain such a disgraceful appearance to her boss? Or to her curious colleagues? It would be

3

impossible. Everyone would know what she had been doing during her lunch break, taking off her clothes for some foreigner in a darkened basement.

His excitement grew at the thought of her disgrace.

'You like Terese?'

Shaking himself out of his reverie, Mortimer glanced across at his friend and smiled. 'Of course,' he replied in English, hoping the girl would not understand. 'Though I can hardly believe a girl like her would ever consent to —'

'You'd be surprised what excites her.'

Revealing slim legs encased in stockings, Terese dropped her skirt to the floor and stepped out of it without the slightest hesitation. Having draped it over the sofa with the rest of her clothes, she sat down to undo the fiddly catches on her garter belt. She was not wearing any underwear and the gingerish mound of her cunt peeped out from between her thighs with unconscious provocation.

There was no indication on her face that she had understood their brief exchange. But a flush in her cheeks suggested she was aroused. She said nothing, though, and neither did the two men.

It was still raining heavily outside. They could hear it striking the windows at pavement level, and the sound of hurrying feet above their heads, heels clicking on stone. Yet Terese seemed as oblivious to the outside world as they were. She peeled off the stockings one by one, leaving her legs bare and gleaming white in the gloom of the basement apartment, and stood up from the sofa as though at some silent command.

'*Me voilà, messieurs,*' she murmured at last, not quite meeting their eyes.

Xavier pulled on a pair of white cotton gloves and opened a glass-fronted cabinet against the far wall. Inside were two shelves of leather-bound antiquarian volumes. At a glance, Mortimer recognised several titles

4

he had owned himself at one time or another, all of them incredibly rare and worth a fortune to the more dedicated collectors.

Today, though, the bookseller was only interested in one book, a squat leather volume with a badly damaged spine. This he carried to the table and opened it to the first page, running a gloved finger reverently over the text as he read aloud.

'The Book of Punishment. A treatise on the ancient and venerable art of chastisement, translated from the Italian by a disciple of the late Master himself. Printed for the proprietors, near Temple Bar, London, 1797.'

'The late Master?'

'He isn't named. Though that was common at the time for books of this type.'

'May I look?' Mortimer asked, staring over his shoulder at the leather-bound volume.

'*Vas-y.*' The older man smiled, tracing the words once more before stepping back so that Mortimer could look more closely at the book. 'As soon as it came into my hands, I thought of that conversation we had last time you were in Paris. Was I right to call you? Is this the book you've been searching for?'

'I think so, yes.'

'I wonder if the translator's mistress posed for these drawings? It always seems to be the same woman.'

For a long moment, they both gazed down at the yellowing frontispiece in silence. It was a glorious eighteenth-century sketch of a naked woman in some hell-like place, harried on all sides by strange masked demons, some wielding vicious-looking whips, others metal scourges and lengths of chain.

On her knees and with her hands tied behind her back, the woman in the drawing had been tethered to the trunk of a tree like a human sacrifice. The marks of the whip were visible across her full breasts, thighs and ample buttocks. Her head was turned towards a distant

5

light, her face contorted with some powerful emotion, the mouth wide open and eyes bulging. But the most awful thing about the drawing was her smile.

'My god,' Mortimer whispered, not sure whether to be excited or repulsed.

'Superb, isn't she? Look at those eyes, that tortured face.'

'Why is she smiling?'

'Because there is no division between pain and ecstasy, my friend. No way for her to experience one without the other.'

Mortimer reached for the book, keen to see more. 'Is it all right to touch the pages?'

'Of course. I just don't like to get my hands dirty.' Xavier shrugged, his thin lips pressed together. 'There are centuries of sweat and grease on these books. Not to mention other bodily fluids, I should imagine. You may want to wash your hands after touching it.'

Leafing gingerly through the Book of Punishment, using only the tips of his fingers, Mortimer was pleased to find the book in excellent condition for its age. There was the usual yellowing and cracking of the margins, even a few pages missing here and there, but most of the text was legible and, overall, intact.

His hands began to tremble as he read. The fragile pages held detailed instructions for punishments of every kind, ranging from mild reprimands for insolent women right through to rituals so bizarre as to be almost unbelievable. Some had been written out like a recipe, merely listing ingredients necessary for the punishment to be administered. Others went into obsessive detail, with several pages of fine print discussing the philosophical implications of a punishment and displaying anatomical diagrams to ensure the author's instructions were not misunderstood.

It was only when Terese moved, quietly fetching herself a glass of water, that Mortimer looked up again from the Book of Punishment. In his eagerness to examine the book, he had forgotten where he was. He had even forgotten the girl's presence.

'Time is moving on,' Xavier murmured discreetly, looking at him. 'Shall we put the book to some practical use?'

'You have anything particular in mind?'

'Well, not all these punishments can be administered without time for preparation. This one, for example, which calls for the repeated application of fresh nettles to the penitent's buttocks.' They both gazed down at page 72, reading silently through the list of ingredients to be gathered prior to the act of punishment. Xavier turned over a few more pages, his fingers clumsy in the white cotton gloves. 'Or this one. I cannot imagine attempting such a punishment indoors. The mess involved would be . . .'

'Yes, I see.'

The bookseller paused, as though trying to remember a page number, then leafed briskly towards the end of the book. His finger tapped the sketch of a girl manacled upside-down to a wheel, the expression on her face one of shock mingled with excitement. 'Perhaps I could recommend this one? It requires nothing but a feather, a thin stick or cane, and some form of restraint. All of which I can easily provide if you are interested in putting this book to its original use.'

Mortimer said nothing, tempted by the idea but not wishing to hurt the girl.

The bookseller smiled at his hesitation, opening a door in the wall to reveal a dark narrow cupboard. He lifted out an odd-looking contraption like a fold-away clothes-horse, the metal rings along its sides clanking as he dragged it to the centre of the room and laid it down, unfolding the thing to about five foot in length. Having checked that each section was clamped securely together, he produced a thick length of chain from the cupboard and gestured to the girl to come forwards.

7

Silently, Terese lay down on the frame without needing to be prompted and allowed him to lash her into position with the chain. Her face was pale but calm. The chain was tightened about her waist and chest, drawn through the metal rings at either side and secured to the frame.

Once she was comfortable, Xavier asked Mortimer to help him lift the entire frame into the air. Together, they turned it through 90 degrees until the girl was hanging upside-down. It took another few minutes to fix the frame onto metal brackets set into the basement floor, presumably for that very purpose.

The blonde hung there on the frame, hair brushing the floor, feet in the air, her lips slightly parted as she stared ahead.

Stroking the bare soles of her feet with his gloved finger, Xavier smiled down at the girl. 'Is the blood rushing to your head, Terese? It's a strange sensation, I believe, and difficult to bear. But you know why you are being asked to bear it, don't you?'

'Yes, Xavier.'

'I saw the way you looked at my young English friend when I introduced you just now. You find him attractive?'

The girl licked her lips, her cheeks a little flushed, as she rolled her eyes up to where Mortimer stood. 'Yes. No. I mean . . .'

'Come on, you want him inside you. Don't bother to deny it. Your eyes betray you every time you look at him.'

This time she did not respond. But her eyes locked with Mortimer's and the guilty flush on her cheeks deepened.

Taking an old wooden crate from the cupboard, the bookseller produced a large ostrich feather from its depths, along with a slim cane. The cane he handed silently to Mortimer. The luxurious white feather he used to stroke the girl's throat and face, circling her moist parted lips several times as though kissing her with it.

'To find another man attractive is an impertinence, Terese. You have sworn an oath of allegiance to me, or had you forgotten? I am your owner. You are my possession. Mine alone. *Tu comprends*?'

'*Oui*, Xavier,' she stammered, nodding. 'I'm sorry.'

'The book suggests that your feet should be punished for such a crime; first with delicacy, then with brutality. The punishment of cane and feather.'

The girl gave an odd choked gasp, staring from her master to Mortimer, but seemed too far gone to draw back now.

Xavier's voice grew harsher. 'Do you accept this punishment, Terese? Do you submit to me, your guide and protector?'

Her eyes were wild as she watched him walk back towards the Book of Punishment, which still lay open on the table behind them. 'Yes,' she whispered, her eyes closing as she spoke. 'I accept and submit to you.'

Mortimer thought he had never seen a girl look as beautiful and desirable as Terese did at that moment. He heard Xavier reading aloud from the book but his mind could not seem to register the words or their meaning. His entire being was focused on Terese: pale skin gleaming against the wood, small firm breasts hanging down at an unnatural angle, thighs spread invitingly apart where each leg had been chained to the frame. In spite of the way they had treated her, the girl was trembling not with fear but with eagerness. While Xavier read from the book, she began to whisper his name, her eyes opening on his dark profile. Far from dreading the ordeal ahead, she seemed to be urging her lover on.

Mortimer's hands clenched into fists at his side, no longer caring how much cash the bookseller wanted. He must own this book.

9

With an odd smile on his face, Xavier left the book on the table. 'First, the penitent's skin should be sensitised,' he told them, and drew the feather lightly across the soles of her feet. 'To prepare her for the pain.'

Terese gasped at the tickle of the ostrich feather on her skin, writhing in her bonds. But she still did not show any signs of fear. Instead, her nipples stiffened to small puckered buds and the muscles tightened in her belly and thighs. As the feather was withdrawn, she gave a shivering moan and closed her eyes as though giving in to some secret pleasure.

'Now the cane should be administered,' Xavier said, beckoning him forwards with an encouraging nod.

Mortimer glanced down at the cane in his hand with surprise. He had almost forgotten its existence. Uncertain how hard he should strike the girl, he lifted his eyes to the bookseller's face. 'Are you sure this is . . .?'

'Go ahead, *mon ami*, you will not burn in hell for this.' The man lowered his voice, finishing in English. 'But softly, this should be a gentle chastisement. The skin there is very tender.'

He was standing so close to her, he could hear her rapid breathing and feel the heat from her naked flesh.

His confidence returned abruptly. If he could not beat this girl, he did not deserve to own the Book of Punishment. The soles of her feet twitched as he raised the cane, her face a pale taut mask of anticipation. In two swift movements, he laid the stick across each upraised sole. He heard the girl's cry through a sudden rush of blood to the head. The cane had left a glowing white line across both feet, turning to a raised throbbing scarlet even as he stepped back and lowered the cane.

'Was that good?'

Mortimer glanced at the bookseller. 'I don't know. I feel . . .'

'Guilty?'

'Yes.'

Xavier laughed and clapped him on the back. 'I'm glad to hear you say that. It's never a good thing to chastise a woman without experiencing remorse. But trust me, Terese takes nothing but pleasure in this punishment. Look at her face now. Put your hand between her legs. See this? She's such a slut, she's soaking down there,' he reassured him, withdrawing a glistening finger from the girl's naked sex. 'The pain excites her.'

The girl did seem sexually aroused. She moaned as Xavier teased her feet again with the ostrich feather, its fine white fronds barely making contact with her skin. The man's laughter sounded affectionate as the feather traced a slow path along her calf and thigh, finally reaching the exposed curve of her sex: perspiration broke out on the girl's forehead; the pink tip of her tongue emerged as she licked dry lips; her cries grew more plaintive. Her cheeks were on fire and her limbs trembled as the feather teased and stroked and probed.

'Now!' Xavier ordered him, abandoning the feather and using gloved fingers instead to manipulate her sex. 'The cane, quickly!'

Obeying instinctively, Mortimer brought the cane down across each bare sole and felt the impact in his own body. He had cringed away from the idea of hurting Terese, yet now he was excited. His erection pressed insistently against the fly of his trousers. Everything inside him was tight as a coiled spring, ready to explode. It was happening just as Xavier had promised. The Book of Punishment was opening a door in his mind which could never now be shut.

His strokes were light and swift but they seemed to provide just the trigger she needed. The girl shrieked, arching her spine against the frame. Her entire body shook, her skin flushed and sweating.

'She's coming!'

With the cane still clutched in his right hand, Mortimer took a step back and stared. He watched in

11

disbelief as the girl experienced a powerful orgasm which left her flushed and gasping.

'That's incredible,' he said, shaken.

Xavier stripped off the sodden glove on his right hand. 'Perhaps you see now why I use her so often. She's insatiable, this one.'

'I need to . . .'

'Please,' the bookseller insisted, pushing him forwards. 'Kneel down and use her mouth if you wish.'

'Thank you.'

On his knees, Mortimer unzipped his trousers and pushed straight into the blonde's accommodating mouth without wasting time on any of the niceties.

It was such a relief to feel moist warmth enclosing him that he almost came on the spot. Controlling the impulse, he began to thrust in and out of her mouth, though it was a little awkward with the girl suspended upside-down so close to the ground. He did not have time, however, to unchain her and perform the act in a rather more civilised way. His need to come was too urgent.

As he felt the edge of the precipice approach and allowed the first bolt to spurt satisfyingly down her throat, Mortimer heard a cry from behind his head. He was gripping her smooth breasts, squeezing them in ecstasy as he came, and it took another few seconds for the urgency in the cry to filter through.

'Mortimer! The book!'

He wrenched himself round at the man's exclamation, still lodged deep in the girl's mouth. 'What?'

'The Book of Punishment. It's gone!'

Spraying an abrupt white arc of sperm over her breasts and belly as he rose, he apologised to Terese and stumbled across the basement, trying to pull up his trousers.

'What do you mean, it's gone?'

Xavier was standing by the empty table, his face white with shock. 'I went to check that the punishment was

12

complete ... and there was no book there. It's just vanished into thin air.'

It was oddly cold in the basement apartment. Shivering as he glanced up towards the door to the street, Mortimer pointed in sudden horrified understanding.

'The door's open,' he said, fumbling with his zip. 'Someone must have come in here while our backs were turned and taken the book. Quick, man! We may still be able to catch them.'

But all they could see in the rainy streets outside the apartment were people scurrying past under umbrellas, staring in surprise as the two men burst up the steps in nothing but trousers and light shirts.

They split up, each man walking to either end of the block in the hope of spotting someone running or even just looking suspicious, perhaps with a wrapped bundle under their arm. But there was no one. Whoever had taken the Book of Punishment must have leaped into a waiting car and sped off towards the Seine, safe as soon as they disappeared into the usual chaos of afternoon traffic.

Xavier came back towards him, breathing heavily. 'Any sign?'

'Nothing.'

The older man swore in French, running a hand through his damp hair. 'If I ever catch the bastards who did this to me –'

'Who knew of the book's existence?'

Xavier stared up and down the grey streets. 'Most of the antiquarian specialists in Paris. Maybe a handful in London and Berlin. The Book of Punishment could be anywhere by now, heading for Italy or Germany; wherever they can sell it on without too many questions.' He shook his head. 'I'll never see it again.'

Mortimer's mouth compressed to a thin line as they headed back in silence towards the basement steps. Even the thought of the lovely Terese waiting for them down there, still tied to the wooden frame, was not enough to lighten his spirits. Hunching his shoulders against the rain trickling under his collar, he remembered the glorious frontispiece to the Book of Punishment – that beautiful naked woman writhing under the diabolical lash of a whip – and knew he had to own it for himself.

'But I intend to see it again,' he said, a sudden determination in his voice. 'Now that I know what it contains, I won't rest until I've found the Book of Punishment and taken it home to London.'

1

Present Day

Dervil Badon lowered the rubber-covered paddle with a frown. The lapel of his velvet smoking jacket had become ever so slightly rumpled during Mrs Jackson's punishment session. He smoothed it down and checked his reflection in the gilt-edged mirror above the mantelpiece. Now in his late forties, yet still one of the finest masters in London, Dervil prided himself on a suave and unruffled appearance.

'Feeling any better now, Mrs Jackson?' he repeated.

The unfortunate woman bending over the bench could not seem to manage a coherent reply. Dervil had to be satisfied with a grunt and those pudgy hands clutching at her ample bottom cheeks, the flesh there rosy and quivering.

It was a sight that never failed to touch his heart.

Dervil took a few steps back, admiring the twin globes of her crimson rump. Quite a work of art, he thought. Indeed, it would be a shame to take it much further, to reach that point where her bottom stopped glowing with that beautiful cherry colour and began to look angry instead.

'I think we should stop there. It's coming up to the hour and you particularly asked to finish early today.'

'Not yet, not yet,' Mrs Jackson babbled, turning a tear-stained face in his direction. Her mascara was running, her eyes blotchy and her nose unpleasantly swollen. 'Just another few minutes, Mr Badon. We could ask the taxi driver to wait.'

Sighing, he brought the paddle down on the fleshy tops of her thighs. His mouth tightened with pleasure at the hollow whoosh of its descent and her muffled shriek as it made abrupt and irrevocable contact. Her skin seemed to flatten to a shiny anvil for a few seconds, fatty ripples spreading out across her bottom, the entire lower half of her body set into motion like a raspberry jelly.

Mrs Jackson was up on tiptoes now, almost dancing with it, as pretty as any fifteen-stone ballerina could be. The woman was nearly 60, he thought, with a certain amount of admiration. Yet there was still something wonderfully girlish about the narrow hairy opening below her clenched bottom cheeks, the dark little hole of her anus gloriously on show in this humiliating position, bent over his punishment bench to receive the paddle.

'How many times must I remind you to call me "sir" during these sessions, Mrs Jackson? You make me despair, you really do.'

'I'm sorry, sir,' she moaned.

'That's quite enough for today. Cover yourself up, you look like the cheapest sort of working girl in that position. And never answer me back like that again.' His voice grew harsh. 'Or I shall be forced to refuse any future appointments with you. Is that clear?'

'Yes, sir. Quite clear.'

Mrs Jackson scrabbled to pull her blue nylon skirt down over those capacious buttocks, straightening up from the bench with a series of groans and exclamations. She was one of those women who favoured the old-fashioned knee-length tights, grim elasticated tops biting into her flesh but leaving her pussy provocatively exposed under the pleated nylon of her skirt. Not for the first time, Dervil wondered if there was a Mr Jackson and, if so, what on earth he made of the bruising on her regularly abused bottom.

But he rarely, if ever, asked such personal questions of his clients. Once they stepped through his front door, these women had no other existence. They did not have jobs, or husbands, or children. Sometimes they did not even have names. They were simply his to punish and humiliate until their hour was up.

He leafed through his appointment book, relieved to see that the week ahead was not looking too heavy.

'Should I pencil you in for next Thursday?'

Mrs Jackson had collected her handbag from the armchair, removed a neatly ironed handkerchief from its depths, and was noisily blowing her nose. From behind the crumpled white folds of the handkerchief, she shook her head. 'I can't make it next week. I'll give you a call when I'm free.'

'As you wish.'

She handed over a folded bundle of notes secured by a rubber band, flushed and a little embarrassed as always at this stage of the proceedings. 'Thank you, Mr Badon.'

'Thank *you*, Mrs Jackson.'

'I suppose I'd better go. The taxi will be waiting.'

Dervil accompanied her to the front door, politely helping her on with her coat. An unmarked taxi cab was parked outside the large iron gates. As she emerged, the driver threw aside the newspaper he had been reading and started the engine. It was dusk and the streetlights were just coming on. The exclusive cul-de-sac was pleasantly quiet that evening, no noisy kids out on their bikes, with the curtains drawn together in the neighbouring houses.

With a final cheery wave, as though leaving an old friend, Mrs Jackson climbed into the back of the taxi and it pulled away along the empty street, taking her back to her stove, her cats, her unsuspecting husband,

17

or whoever else it was she went home to after their weekly appointments.

Turning away from the street, Dervil suddenly noticed a white Mercedes convertible parked opposite his gates. Preserving a calm expression, he halted on the threshold and waited.

Almost as soon as the taxi had disappeared, the driver's door opened and a woman slid out of the Mercedes. Legs first, long and slender in high elegant heels. Then the tall blonde straightened, shut the car door and sauntered across the road to him in an exquisite grey silk skirt and matching blouse.

Their eyes met through the dusk and he smiled at her, carefully undemonstrative. 'Good evening, Natasha. This is an unexpected pleasure. I wasn't aware you were back in England.'

'May I come in, Dervil?' she asked, the Russian accent husky. 'I have some information you might like to know.'

'Of course.'

So Natasha was back in circulation, he thought drily. That could only mean trouble. Yet there was something in her face that made him curious to know more. Too intrigued to send her away without a hearing, Dervil gestured to her to enter the house and led his former slave into the well-lit galley kitchen. With its spotlights in the ceiling and highly reflective chrome breakfast bar, the kitchen seemed the least sexually provocative room in the house.

He poured them both a strong black coffee from the percolator. 'I must admit, it's quite a surprise to see you again,' he said, keeping his tone unreadable. 'I thought I'd made it clear our relationship was over.'

She sat down on one of the stools at the breakfast bar and crossed one smooth-skinned leg over the other, the pose at once prim and inviting. Taking a packet of Russian cigarettes from her bag, she lit up without

18

bothering to ask for his permission. The cloying smell of the cigarette smoke was oddly familiar. It drifted up to the spotlights, hanging above their heads in a cloudy haze.

Natasha flicked her cigarette ash onto the kitchen floor and shrugged, not meeting his eyes.

'That was over a year ago, darling, all water under the bridge. What do you say we kiss and make up?'

'I don't think so. You were a novelty to me, Natasha,' he said, with deliberate cruelty. 'Nothing more.'

'A novelty?' Her thin pencilled eyebrows rose in angry hauteur. 'I'd forgotten what a bastard you are. I come here in a spirit of goodwill and you throw insults at me as though we were still lovers.' As she spat out the words, Natasha kept glancing over her shoulder at the empty doorway as though expecting to see someone there. 'So where is she? Where are you hiding the little bitch?'

'Who?'

'Your latest flame!' She laughed in a brittle, slightly hysterical fashion. 'Come on, don't tell me you haven't got yourself a real woman by now? Oh yes, I know that's what you think.' She tapped her chest, her eyes flashing. 'That I'm not a *real* woman.'

Dervil sighed, getting up to find her an ashtray. He handed it to her with a shake of his head. 'Now you're being ridiculous, Natasha. I simply meant it was a novelty to have a lover. You know I prefer to steer clear of emotional ties.'

'So why don't I believe you?'

'Because you suffer from acute paranoia.'

Natasha made an angry noise under her breath and stubbed out the bitter-smelling cigarette before it was even half smoked. Her hands shook as she unbuttoned the tailored jacket, pulling it open to display a pair of smooth ripe breasts, unfettered by a bra. She grasped them in both hands and held them out to him, squeezing and rolling the dusky pink nipples between her fingers.

'Look at me, Dervil. Look at these breasts. Are you going to tell me these aren't real?'

'Well, technically they're not.'

'You shit!'

Furious now, Natasha yanked up the short elegant silk skirt and opened her thighs like a butterfly spreading its wings. She was nude underneath, a pale thatch of hair covering her pussy. Her voice was a venomous hiss.

'And this?'

Dervil examined her crotch in silence, then lifted cool eyes to her face. He knew he had hurt her feelings and felt uncomfortable about that. But it would be dangerous to make the mistake of behaving too sympathetically.

'The fact that you used to be a man had nothing whatsoever to do with the end of our affair. We made a great team ... as master and slave. When we became lovers, everything changed. I wasn't ready for that level of intimacy. It was my problem, not yours.'

'That's a pretty speech,' she sneered, 'and I don't believe a word of it, Dervil.'

Yes, still as difficult as ever. Though she was right in a way, he thought ironically. Natasha looked extremely inviting up on that bar stool: breasts spilling out of her jacket, crotch exposed, those outer lips visibly glistening as though she had lubricated herself before getting out of the car. If he had not been aware how much trouble it could cause, he might have been tempted to fuck her.

Spreading her thighs wider apart, Natasha sucked two long fingers and dipped them into that moist crack.

'If you're not nicer to me,' she pointed out, a sinister purr in her voice as she changed tactics, 'I might not tell you why I'm here.'

Dervil sat back on his stool and watched her, trying to ignore the first stirrings of an erection. A memory flashed unbidden through his head: Natasha, nude except for a plastic apron, leaning over a stool after disobeying him, her bottom raised submissively for the

20

strap. Difficult though she could be at times, his relationship with Natasha had not been all bad.

'What does being nice entail? I'm really not in the mood for games tonight.'

Undeterred by his coldness, Natasha continued to play with her well-oiled pussy, skirt bunched around her waist on the bar stool, breasts gleaming under the bright spotlights. The expression on her face was speculative. 'Do you still have that little French whip?'

'The martinet? Of course.'

Her eyes became dreamy. 'Do you remember, darling, how we used to play together in the evenings after you had finished with your last client? The martinet always left such cruel marks on my skin. I would pretend I was a disobedient cabin boy and you were my captain. It was so romantic.'

'What is it you wanted to tell me, Natasha?'

'Not so fast.' Her fingers moved rhythmically between her open thighs. 'You want to know? Punishment first, information later.'

It had been one of his few mistakes in life, Dervil told himself sternly, becoming involved with this woman. She might have been born a male, but that was merely a hiccup of nature. Natasha had always possessed the guile and sensuality of a woman; now she had the body to match. It was fortunate for her that she came from such an influential family in Moscow. Without that background, she could have spent her entire life trapped in a man's body.

Nevertheless, he was quite curious to know what information had brought her all the way back to England. It must be important, because she knew him too well to risk wasting his time with trivialities. No, this was not a bluff. It was not her style to lie. Her duplicity lay in other, more subtle directions. Yet it was clear she would not part with any information until her desire had been satisfied.

21

'OK, fine.' Not bothering to disguise his irritation, Dervil pushed his now cold coffee aside and stood up. 'Come along then, we'd better go through to the studio. Unless you expect me to chastise you with a fish slice?'

The studio was warm and brightly lit, the windows kept locked and heavily curtained. In his previous house, he had converted the spare bedroom into a small dungeon, complete with chains hanging from the walls and a forbidding black paint job. But when he moved into the cul-de-sac the dungeon scene had seemed old-fashioned, and he had opted for a smart modern look. One client, a successful dentist, had remarked how similar it was to her own surgery: whitewashed walls, clean surfaces, linoleum flooring and glass-fronted cabinets stacked with shining instruments.

Dervil switched on the air conditioning and began to clean Mrs Jackson's sweat off the bench with an antibacterial spray. It felt odd, the two of them together again in the punishment room after more than a year. But not so odd that he could not keep his cool. Regardless of the history between them, he was determined to treat Natasha with the impersonal courtesy he extended to his paying customers.

Having ordered his unexpected visitor to kneel in the centre of the room, hands clasped behind her back, he unlocked one of the instrument cabinets and thoughtfully studied its contents. She had requested the martinet. Not his favourite tool for such occasions, and certainly never to be recommended during the warm-up period.

Dervil removed a pair of smooth black leather gloves from the bottom shelf of the display cabinet, pulled them on and turned back to face her. Natasha had been watching him in silence, but when she saw the gloves she began to whimper.

In an impassive voice, he ordered her to shut up and strip. The absence of other instructions was deliberate.

Soon he was rewarded by the amusing sight of his former lover struggling to remove her skirt in a kneeling position. 'Pull it up over your head. And stop making that ludicrous noise. Anyone would think you'd never taken your clothes off before.'

The tight skirt caught on her too-large breasts, leaving an ugly red mark as the zip snagged her skin on its way past. By the time she was free of it, Natasha was flushed and panting, her dignity gone.

Standing before her, his swollen groin on a level with her mouth, Dervil tilted her head back so he could look down into her painted face. 'So you feel the need for punishment, do you? Why is that, Natasha? Have you been a naughty girl since we last met?'

Her lips trembled, a mixture of eagerness and apprehension in those blue eyes. 'Yes, sir.'

'What exactly have you done?'

'I . . .' She hesitated, flinching away as he stroked her cheek with one leather-clad finger. 'I had to go out to work when I went home to Moscow. To pay back the money I borrowed for the operation.'

'You worked as a prostitute? That's disgusting. I hope you're ashamed of yourself.'

'Yes, sir,' she whispered, hanging her head.

'Look at me when I'm talking to you,' Dervil said sharply. He raised her chin and slapped her on the cheek. Not too hard, but it was enough to make her gasp. 'So you returned to Moscow and worked as a whore. Was this on the streets or in a brothel?'

'Both.'

'Tell me about the first trick you turned on the streets.'

Her eyes filled with quick tears of humiliation. She did not shy away from discussing her past exploits, though, meeting his gaze directly as she spoke. 'He was a sailor. Big and stocky, built like a pig. I hated the look of him. He took me down one of the back alleys behind

23

the bar where I was touting for work. It was raining hard that night, my dress got ruined. I had to kneel and suck his cock.'

'He spunked in your mouth?'

She shook her head. 'In my face.'

'You allowed some sweaty sailor to shoot his load in your face? Did you even know this man's name?' When she shook her head again, Dervil gave a derisive laugh. 'I hope you were well paid for that little slip from grace.'

'I didn't get paid at all,' she whispered, her face hot with shame. 'I felt like such a fool. He just pushed me to the ground after he'd finished and walked away without paying. All the other sailors were gathered round, laughing at me. There was nothing I could do.'

He slapped her face for a second time. Slightly harder this time, to demonstrate that he was still in control. 'Stupid whore! So you gave it away for free?'

'Yes, but I was more careful the next time,' she stammered. 'I asked for the cash up front.'

'Another sailor wanting his knob sucked?'

Natasha winced at his deliberate crudity, an angry look on her face as their eyes clashed. 'He was a wealthy man, actually, a butcher. I used to visit him at lunch-time when the shop was closed. We had sex in the cold store. He liked to . . .'

Dervil prompted her confession with another slap, sharp enough to sting and leave her gasping. 'Liked to what?'

'Tie me up and bugger me.'

He could not help smiling at her delicious candour, gently stroking his leather glove down her cheek before slapping her again. 'I bet you really enjoyed that, didn't you? That was always your favourite position when we were together, as I recall. Bent over with your wrists lashed to your ankles and a cock up your dirty little arse.'

'Yes, yes,' she burst out, trembling all over, raising

her face towards him as though urging him to hit her harder.

'Tell me about it.'

Her cheeks were mottled red now, heavily flushed across each cheekbone. She could scarcely speak, her voice a series of odd little snatched gasps between slaps. 'It was awful, awful. He never even bothered washing his hands before fucking me. There was the smell of blood everywhere and tiny gobbets of meat all over my thighs and arse.'

'Yet you kept going to visit him, didn't you?'

She did not bother to deny it, nodding and staring blindly over his shoulder as he continued with his taunts.

'Once or maybe as often as twice a week, I imagine,' he said, his tone deliberately insulting. 'You must have been sick of his smell, the filth on your body afterwards. Raw meat under your fingers and blood in your hair. But you couldn't stop visiting him, giving him that shapely little bottom to abuse. I expect you even began to dream about him in the end, this man and his carcasses. Because you were addicted, weren't you?'

Her head was rolling between his hands now, backwards and forwards, her neck lax as he repeatedly slapped one cheek and then the other.

'No,' she argued, but only weakly.

His hands dropped to his sides. He knew that look on her face; he had her under his spell at last. There was nothing he could not demand now. She was locked too deeply into the past and its debauchery to resist him. Her eyes were glazed as she stared past him at the cabinet with its gleaming array of fine leather instruments and metal tools, all designed to enforce discipline and increase pleasure.

'What information do you have for me, Natasha? Tell me the truth. I need to know why you came here tonight.'

'The Book of Punishment,' she whispered. Her eyes drifted up to his face, still wide open, unfocused. 'It's up for sale.'

The Book of Punishment? Of all the things she could have said, that was the one name he had not anticipated hearing on her lips. Momentarily stunned into silence, Dervil stared down at her for a few tense moments. Could she be telling the truth for once?

'For sale? Where?'

'Amsterdam.'

He was finding it hard to breathe. 'Why wasn't I informed immediately? How long have I got until the auction?'

'Forty-eight hours.'

'Christ, I don't believe this.' His manner suddenly crisp, he stripped off the leather gloves and slapped her for real. 'Snap out of it, Natasha. I don't have time to play any more games with you tonight. This is important.'

She put a hand up to her cheek, a sullen pout on her lips. 'You bully. What did you do that for?'

'Sorry, but I needed you to come back to reality fast. Why didn't you tell me about the Book of Punishment straight off? You know I've been after it for years . . . as have most of the eminent collectors in the field,' he added drily, and glanced at his watch. 'If you leave now, you could be in Amsterdam before midnight.'

'Me?'

'Now don't argue with me, Natasha. Put your clothes back on and stop sulking. We're talking about Amsterdam, for god's sake. It's not as though I'm sending you to the North Pole.'

She pulled on her grey silk jacket, fastening it with difficulty over her large shiny breasts. Her voice was low but menacing, like an angry wasp dashing itself against a window. 'Why do I have to go? I just travelled all the way from Russia. Do you have any idea what sort of a hellish journey I had, darling?'

'Why are you being such a nag all of a sudden? I thought you were in love with me.'

'Well yes, I am,' she said jerkily, grimacing at her smeared lipstick and mascara in the mirror.

'Then you should want to help me.'

'But you don't love me in return,' she said in a plaintive voice. 'All you do is treat me badly.'

Dervil drew a sharp irritated breath and turned to snatch the martinet down from the display cabinet. 'If you bend over right now and I give you twelve lashes of the martinet, will you take that as proof that I love you?'

She nodded with instant joy, throwing aside her skirt and bending submissively to touch her toes.

'Excellent.'

He aligned the whip above her buttocks with the cool eye of a professional, noting the old scars of former beatings, able to recognise not only which instruments had been used but even how many strokes she had received.

'Because I need you to get to Amsterdam tonight, find out who the vendor is, and make a respectable offer for the Book of Punishment before the bidding closes. Is that understood?'

'Oh yes, master,' Natasha gasped, a triumphantly pained smile on her face as the first lash of the martinet landed across her buttocks.

2

It was still raining heavily outside when the bell jangled noisily above the shop entrance. The tall man in the doorway stared around himself for a moment, his eyes moving along the rows of bookcases with their neatly arranged spines and labels, lips pursed in a silent whistle. His voice was deep and humorous, the accent definitely American.

'So this is the infamous Mortimer's Bookstore,' he murmured, then looked at her. 'And what is your name, young lady?'

'Indigo,' she said hesitantly, clicking on the computer file to close it and getting up from the pay desk. 'Mortimer was my father. But he died last year, I'm afraid. I run the bookshop now. Is there anything in particular I can help you with?'

'Erotica.' The large Texan with the snakeskin boots grinned at her, shrugging the rain off his shoulders as he closed the shop door behind him. 'Dirty books, ma'am. That's what your bookshop is famous for and that's why I'm here.'

'Of course, sir. If you'd care to follow me?'

Conscious of his eyes on her legs, Indigo led the large Texan with the snakeskin boots to the back of the bookshop and up a narrow flight of steps to the first floor, where their specialist collection of erotica was discreetly housed.

'Much of our older stock is antiquarian, mainly erotic works from the eighteenth and nineteenth centuries. But since my father's death I've started selling new publications, with an emphasis on modern fetishism. What are your particular tastes?'

'I'm not sure, Miss Indigo,' the Texan drawled, looking her up and down with a lascivious smile. 'What exactly have you got?'

She knew he could see her nipples through the clinging material of her blouse, but did not particularly care, and raised her arm to indicate the various bookcases. She had been doing this job too long to feel any embarrassment. 'This area is devoted to bondage and sadomasochism. The shelves on the other side contain various sub-genres such as traditional CP, modern CP, spanking and pony girls.'

'Pony girls?'

Indigo tried not to smile at his ignorance. She pointed to a poster on the wall, depicting a curvaceous blonde pony girl in full regalia, her breasts outlined by a sturdy harness. 'Submissives who dress up as ponies, with cute little tails and full leather harnesses. Surely you must have pony girls in the States?'

'Oh yeah, I expect we do,' he grinned. 'Just not in the circles I move in, unfortunately.'

'Well, you can check them out here. And if pony girls aren't to your taste, you'll find more specialised fetishes on the lower shelves of each section.' Coolly, she began to list the more popular ones. 'We stock books that feature shoes, rubber, adult babies, watersports, coprophilia, bestiality —'

'What if I want to buy one?'

Indigo pointed to the pay desk behind her. 'We can take payment for erotica right here; to ensure your privacy is respected.'

'You've thought of everything, haven't you?'

Indigo lifted a hand to flick the dark fringe out of her eyes and saw his gaze linger on her breasts under the tight red blouse. From beneath lowered lashes, she considered his physique in return. She had not had time that morning to finish masturbating before she had to rush off to catch the train, something which always left her aching and dissatisfied.

'We like our special customers to feel comfortable here, yes.' She perched on the edge of the desk, provocatively swinging her bare legs as she watched him. 'Take off your coat, make yourself at home. As my father used to say, you're amongst friends now.'

The Texan gave her a slow smile, shrugged out of his jacket and began to look around. 'Thank you, Miss Indigo. Thank you very much indeed.'

He picked out a novel from one of the shelves of contemporary erotica, smiled over the cover photograph of a semi-naked girl in handcuffs, and read a few pages at random.

She pretended not to be interested in what he was doing, flicking through some sales figures that had been left on the pay desk as she waited for him to make a selection. But her eyes kept sliding back to the man's face, watching his lips move silently with the words, his eyes narrowing, his whole body beginning to tighten as the erotic literature worked its spell.

'Can you recommend this?'

Indigo tried to identify the novel he was holding up. 'I'm sorry. I can't quite see the . . . What's the title? Who's it by?'

He brought it closer so she could see the glossy cover text with its revealing photograph. At last, she recognised the novel. And the look on his face, a smile she interpreted as lust disguised as friendly interest. It was a pity about his long drooping moustache. She had never been one for moustaches. But as long as that was the only thing drooping, she could probably handle it.

He was standing right in front of her now, using the book as an excuse to invade her personal space.

'Oh yes, that one. Actually, I haven't had a chance to read it yet. But she's a good writer, I've read some of her other books. That's her latest. It only came out a few months ago.'

'Could I ask you a favour, Indigo?'

'A favour?'

The Texan flicked through the novel, presumably trying to find the chapter he had been looking at before. 'Would you read some of this book aloud to me? Not much, I promise. Just this short passage on page 90.'

She took the book from him, feeling his fingers brush hers. Her face was getting rather hot now, and so was her pussy. It had been rather a long time. But she hated looking desperate, even with a stranger. 'You want me to read aloud to you?'

'From here,' he pointed, 'down to there.'

'That's a new one on me. Reading aloud to the customers. I'm not sure that I've got time to –'

'You told me you liked the customers to feel special. That you and I were friends now.'

'Well, technically that's true, but –'

'You're not being very friendly now, are you? Though perhaps that's how you prefer to operate.' The American raised his eyes again, searching her face. 'Keep the bastards in their place. Stay on top of the situation.'

'That's not me at all.'

'Good.' His hand slammed emphatically on the desk, making all the pens in the wire container jump. 'Because that's not me either. Now I want you to do what you're told, Miss Indigo.' He jabbed a finger towards the book in her hand. 'Read me that passage. Read it out, good and loud.'

What on earth had possessed her to wear such a short sluttish skirt today? And to sit up on this desk like a whore, right at his groin level, showing the man everything she had? Knee-length black leather boots, bare legs right up to her crotch, and nothing but a flimsy lace thong between him and glory. A more inviting pose she could hardly imagine, unless she hooked both hands under her thighs and spread herself wide for the bastard.

Shivering with barely concealed delight, Indigo smoothed down the page and began to read aloud.

'The man with the whip strode towards Alissa and lifted his black lash on high. There would be no reprieve for her this time. The whip came down with a crack like thunder and she screamed, her whole body shaking with fear and pain . . .'

She glanced up, aware that the man had moved closer, was standing right between her legs now.

'Go on, don't stop,' he said urgently.

Her heart beating fast, Indigo bent her head to the book again, tracing her finger along the short passage he wanted her to read in case she lost it in her excitement.

'Writhing helplessly against the manacles, Alissa watched his hands strip the dress from her body. Her breasts spilled out, reddened by the whip, and he slapped them until they stung. His laughter echoed about the high-ceilinged room. "I hate you," Alissa cried, half delirious with pain and the creeping awareness of an excitement she could no longer control. He bent and kissed her vilely, crushing her lips beneath his. "No, no," he hissed against her mouth. "I am your husband now. You must love me, Alissa. Do you understand? Love me as I love you." '

His hands were on her thighs, pushing the short skirt up to her crotch. 'Cheap worthless smut.'

'It is pretty bad, isn't it? I thought she was quite an accomplished writer, but that really stinks.'

'Shut up.'

'Sorry, I thought you wanted to discuss it.'

'I told you to shut up, didn't I?'

His hand flashed out and he slapped her face almost casually, just as the man in the novel had slapped Alissa's breasts. She sat there like a statue on the edge of the desk, too shocked to move. Light and sharp the Texan slapped her, two slaps for each flushed cheek.

'I'm in charge here, lady. Is that understood?'

Taken aback by his change of mood, she licked her lips, then began to breathe hard as his finger played with the waistband of her thong, slipping beneath to manipulate her prominent clitoris. The flesh there was slippery. Unable to control her own excitement, she gave a low moan and knew that it had betrayed her.

He grinned, enjoying himself. 'That feels good, doesn't it? Would you like me to get down and lick it?'

Indigo nodded slowly, watching his face.

But he withdrew his finger with a derisory laugh, slapping her thighs further apart and stepping between them. 'Well now, you're a greedy little thing. Didn't your daddy ever tell you the customer should always come first?'

His hands dropped to her blouse and he undid the buttons, exposing her breasts in the red lacy bra. She arched her back towards him as the Texan pulled up the bra and squeezed her breasts together. Her eyes closed on a wave of illicit pleasure. She ought to be pushing this man away, calling for help from her assistant Chloe. This was not how she behaved with her regular customers. But she had been feeling bored all week, only too ready to indulge in a wicked little session like this with a stranger from the other side of the Atlantic.

Large calloused thumbs pressed into her nipples. 'I think you need to be bent over this desk and fucked till you're sore.'

'Aren't you going to spank me first?'

Her teasing whisper appeared to take him by surprise. It had been intended as a hint, a nudge in the right direction. She found straight sex a little boring. But the Texan in the snakeskin boots did not seem to have understood her hint.

'No,' he said slowly. 'I was just planning to fuck you.'

She dropped her eyes to the leather belt looped around his jeans, deciding to try a different approach.

'But maybe you need to push me down over this desk first, give me a few licks of your belt. To make sure I behave myself.'

The man hesitated, his gaze moving slowly over her exposed breasts, the bunched-up skirt around her waist, the black lace thong stretched over a damp and eager pussy.

'My belt?'

Suddenly, the American seemed to have understood. His eyes lit up and he dropped her hand, then unbuckled the thick leather belt on his jeans and looped it sturdily around his wrist.

'If it's OK with you, it's OK with me. Better bend yourself over that desk then, Miss Indigo,' he said with a grin, 'and we'll see how you take to this fine Texan leather.'

Flushed with excitement, she jumped down from the desk without the slightest hesitation and bent over, gripping the sides of the smooth wood. His hands fumbled with her skirt, finally managing to yank it back up over her hips and expose the damp thong. She felt cool air on her bottom and sighed with anticipation, resting her face against the desk as she waited to be struck. She had got out of bed that morning in an embarrassingly horny mood and this was exactly what she needed: a firm belting to warm her up and possibly a thick cock up her pussy afterwards.

The thick leather belt whistled through the air, exploding across her buttocks with a loud crack.

She jumped up at the impact, her mouth flying open on a gasp, her cheeks filled with heat. 'Oh . . . yes . . .'

'What's that? You want me to stop?'

Unable to manage a coherent reply, Indigo shook her head and settled back down across the table with her bottom raised invitingly in the air. Her pussy, lush with warm fluids, contracted with pleasure as the first wave of pain dissipated.

Grinding her breasts against the wooden surface, she enjoyed the familiar tingling sensation as her nipples stiffened until they were almost painful. The Texan might seem inexperienced at belting women but he was learning fast. Another few strokes like that and she would be able to stick two fingers up her pussy and bring herself to orgasm with no trouble at all.

She writhed pleasurably under the next two lashes of his belt, her face hot as she fought the desire to masturbate. In her experience, it was always better to wait until the pain was almost unbearable. But in the end it was no use. Her desire won as Indigo reached between her legs and pushed her fingers inside the slick opening to her pussy, delighting in the gorgeous wetness of her arousal.

The Texan must have seen her masturbating, because he swore under his breath and laid the belt on harder. 'You're really enjoying this, aren't you? I've never seen a girl so . . . well, maybe once or twice when I was at college . . .' He made an abrupt noise and stepped closer, hauling her legs up by the ankles and holding them together in the air while she kicked furiously to escape. 'Have you ever had your legs tied up like this? Roped like a steer?'

'*What*?'

'It don't hurt much worse than a beating, ma'am.'

To her immense relief, her assistant Chloe chose that moment to put her head round the door to the erotica room.

'Didn't you hear the phone, Indigo?' she began cheerily enough, then stopped in confusion when she saw what was happening. The blonde's face went a particularly bright shade of scarlet, her voice a high astonished squeak as she took in the scene. 'Oh . . . I'm so sorry! I didn't know you had . . .'

'What is it, Chloe?' she asked hurriedly, trying not to look too flustered as the Texan released her legs and stepped back from the desk.

'There's an urgent phone call from Amsterdam. I think he said his name was Roland. Should I take a message?'

'Erm . . . yes, absolutely.' She dragged her skirt down and began to rebutton her blouse with trembling fingers. 'Thanks for letting me know, Chloe. I'll just finish dealing with this customer, then I'll be right with you.'

Once Chloe had disappeared, the man with the snakeskin boots gave a deep sigh and looked at her with disappointment in his eyes. 'Damn, I was really getting into that.'

He bent his head, looping his belt reluctantly back onto his jeans. 'I suppose that was your boyfriend on the phone,' he added, 'wanting to know what you're up to?'

'Who, Roland?' She laughed, putting a quick hand on his sleeve to demonstrate she was still interested. The telephone call could wait. This couldn't. Her pussy and bottom were aching for more punishment; it was a terrible admission of weakness, but Indigo had never been much good at refusing pleasure when it was so blatantly on offer. 'He's just an old friend. I'll ring him back in a while. After all, we still haven't found you the right book.'

The Texan's eyes widened and his smile slowly returned. 'That's true enough, Miss Indigo. You got any books on roping cattle?'

'I don't think so. Would straight bondage be OK?'

Her backside still sore from the Texan's belt, Indigo threw herself down behind the desk in her office and stared at her message pad. Grabbing a quick sip of coffee, she put down the pad and dialled a number in Amsterdam. It rang only twice before being answered in deep male tones.

'Roly?' she said softly, glancing up to check that the office door was closed. 'It's me, Indigo. Sorry about the

36

delay. I was . . . erm . . . tied up with a customer. What have you got for me?'

'I've found it.'

Her hand tightened on the phone. 'The Book of Punishment?'

'That's the one,' he agreed flatly. 'I heard a whisper last week that it might be in Amsterdam. By the time I got here, the Book of Punishment had come out of hiding. It went up for private auction this afternoon. Three bidders in the race so far.'

'Three bidders?' Indigo could scarcely contain her fury at this information. 'Why haven't I been asked to put in an offer? Everyone knows how badly I want that book.'

'Probably because it's out of your league, baby.'

'What's the vendor's name?'

'Look, you asked me to let you know when the book came back onto the market. It's out there now but it's going for crazy money. So you want my advice? Forget about the Book of Punishment. It was your dad's obsession, not yours.'

'I still want a crack at it, Roly. It meant so much to my father, I'm not prepared to let it drop that easily.' She thought for a moment, glancing at her watch and making the necessary calculations. 'If I catch the first flight out to Amsterdam tomorrow, could you get me a meeting with the vendor?'

'Listen –'

'No, you listen to me. I don't care what the price tag says, just get me that meeting.'

'OK, OK. I'll try and arrange that for you.' Roly paused, his voice becoming sly. 'Though you haven't forgotten our little deal, have you? This information isn't free. I expect to get paid in full, no excuses this time. You know what I'm saying?'

She smiled, perfectly well aware what he meant. 'Roly, if you help me find the Book of Punishment, your cock is going to get well and truly sucked. And that is a promise.'

3

Indigo found the Café Jamaica without too much difficulty; as Roly had informed her, with a smirk in his voice, its glowing red and blue neon sign shone out in the darkness beyond the canal, easily visible as she left the waterfront and made her way past an array of open shop windows, each one displaying a semi-naked woman seated on a stool or bent over in some provocative pose intended to entice passing custom onto the premises.

This was definitely the coffee shop where she would find Roly, whose love of all things Jamaican was notorious. Right name, right street, and reggae music was blaring out through a grimy bead curtain across the entrance.

Indigo took a deep breath and pushed through the rattling beads into the thick sweet smell of cannabis.

Allowing her eyes to adjust, she took a few moments to glance around the dimly lit interior: there were men leaning on the counter, smoking large reefers and drinking cups of aromatic coffee; low wooden tables surrounded by cushions where young people lounged in the darkness; and a heavily tattooed woman in her thirties whose shaven head glistened as she stood polishing glasses behind the counter. This woman's head swivelled as soon as Indigo stepped through the bead curtain; the blue eyes assessed her with rapid expertise, then slid back to the glass in her hand, no doubt dismissing Indigo as another curious tourist looking for a toke.

She spotted Roly almost at once. The book dealer was hunched over a table in one of the darkest corners, his back to the door, but the matted shoulder-length dreadlocks made him instantly recognisable.

To her surprise, though, Roly was not alone.

There was a woman kneeling on cushions at the same table, an exotic-looking blonde with exceptionally long legs, hair swept back from her forehead to reveal such theatrical make-up she might have just stepped off a stage.

They seemed an odd couple, Indigo thought, her eyes narrowing on the woman's face. Could this be another buyer for the Book of Punishment?

The blonde certainly looked as though her tastes might run to the delights of sadomasochism. She was barely covered by a short rubber skirt, for a start, and her full breasts had been squeezed into a rubber halter neck, like the skirt in midnight blue. The long tanned legs were impressively muscular, and made even longer by a pair of high platform heels, fastened with thong straps around sturdy ankles. Her lipstick was deep crimson, lined with an even deeper red to accentuate the fullness of the lips. Below extravagant green and silver eye-shadow, kohl provided the final flourish to a face which was almost too striking to be real.

Oh yes, she was precisely the sort of woman Indigo could imagine with a whip in her hand, torturing businessmen at the weekends in order to earn a living, or perhaps – Indigo's smile broadened at the picture in her head – bent over for a sound paddling at the hands of some possessive lesbian.

As Indigo watched, the blonde stroked Roly's cheek before removing a reefer from between his limp fingers.

Sucking smoke into her lungs in an exaggerated fashion, she leaned across the table and whispered in his ear. Then she rose to her feet, more statuesque than ever now she was no longer on her knees, and blew him a pouting kiss over her shoulder as she sauntered from the café.

Indigo tried to step back into the shadows, suddenly unsure of herself, but it was too late. Roly had seen her and was getting to his feet, a sleazy smile on his lips as he noticed she was alone. With a sinking feeling in the pit of her stomach, she realised that backing out of their arrangement was no longer an option. In a moment of weakness, she had agreed to suck his cock if he could find out anything useful about the Book of Punishment. Now they were almost face to face, the idea of even looking at his cock made her feel nauseous.

However, it would do her reputation no good at all to back out of their agreement. Even if sucking his cock made her retch like a dog, she would have to go through with it.

The book dealer came lolloping towards her, yanking at the loose dirty jeans that had settled too low down on his hips.

'Indigo!' he greeted her loudly, oblivious to her embarrassment as heads turned in their direction. 'Glad you could make it after all, I'm going to enjoy showing you Amsterdam. Care for a quick toke before we get down to business? This place is incredible. They sell every kind of weed under the sun.'

He went to kiss her on the lips but she turned her head at the last second and he caught her cheek instead, his breath reeking of cannabis, lips unpleasantly moist against her skin.

'Not my thing, I'm afraid.'

'OK,' Roly shrugged. He slipped an invasive arm about her waist as though they were lovers and pulled her close. 'I tell you what though, the mushrooms here are superb. Have you ever tried mushrooms? They really blow you out, the first time. How about I grab us a bag for later?'

'No thanks,' she told him, and coolly extricated herself from his arm. 'Shall we go?'

40

The book dealer followed her out through the rattling bead curtain onto the street, stumbling over the step and swearing.

It was almost dark outside. Indigo looked up at the stars, a pale new moon high in the sky. She took a few steps away from the café and pushed the loose hair back from her forehead. There was a thin film of sweat over her face. Why had she agreed to meet him there? It was a relief to stand out here on the pavement and breathe fresh air again.

'Spoilsport,' Roly muttered irritably, but he did not attempt to change her mind, pointing her further away from the waterfront. 'Come on then, the hotel's this way.'

'You managed to get me a meeting with the vendor?'

'Sort of.'

Indigo frowned. 'What does that mean?'

'I'll explain when we get there. Not on the street, yeah?'

Roly tapped the side of his nose and glanced from side to side as though afraid their conversation might be overheard. When he caught her staring at him, he slid his hands into his jeans pockets and looked away, the watery blue eyes shifty.

'Who was that woman you were talking to?' she asked abruptly. 'Was that the vendor? Or is she another buyer?'

'Natasha?' Roly squirmed, clearly disturbed by her questions. 'She's just an old friend. Nothing to do with the Book of Punishment. But she's pretty ... um ... sexy, isn't she? You wouldn't think she used to be a man, would you?'

'A man?'

'Straight up.' He laughed nervously, watching her, and she had the impression he was desperate to change the subject. 'Had the operation about three years ago. Chop, chop.'

Indigo raised her eyebrows, thinking back to what she had seen in the café, the statuesque blonde with her full breasts bursting from that tight rubber top.

'She's very convincing.'

'Oh, it's all real enough underneath. No padding. She had the whole lot done. Tits and everything. I had a squeeze of them once. It's amazing what these cosmetic surgeons can do. You wouldn't know the difference.'

They turned again, this time down to the right, into a broader street bordering another canal, red neon signs glowing in the windows and reflected in the water, most of them advertising live girls and lap-dancing. Here it was harder to walk along the street without constantly knocking into other people; the crowds were much thicker, men clustered in groups around each display of naked female flesh or wandering along the street in a leisurely fashion as though window shopping.

The book dealer stopped in front of one of these neon-lit buildings, indicating the upstairs windows with a jerk of his head. 'Right, this is the place,' he muttered, not meeting her eyes any more. 'Now follow me and stay close. You'll be fine so long as you keep your mouth shut.'

The stairs at the side entrance were narrow and starkly lit by a single unshaded bulb, under constant attack by moths. Indigo wrinkled her nose with distaste. There was a strong smell of cabbage and sausages emanating from somewhere above, presumably some kind of kitchen. At the top of the stairs was a reception area: a fat man stood behind a counter there, and three girls in skimpy outfits were seated on stools with folded arms and crossed legs. All of them stared blankly up at a small television mounted on the wall.

Indigo glanced at the television screen, curious to know what they were watching so attentively. It was some sort of game show: semi-naked women wrestling in mud amidst bursts of rapturous applause, with an

MC with a microphone and a tartan bow tie watching from the sides and occasionally commenting on the action in what sounded like badly dubbed Dutch.

The fat man nodded at Roly without speaking and slid a key across the counter, not even bothering to glance at Indigo as he turned his attention back to the mud-spattered women on the screen.

Entering the small bedroom they had hired, she was relieved to discover it was rather less grim than anticipated: Roman blinds at the window, a double bed draped with what appeared to be clean sheets, a large wicker chair in one corner, and even delicate blue irises in a vase on the bedside cabinet. The room stank of stale sweat and semen, it was true, but Indigo made a point of pulling up the blinds and pushing the window as wide as it would go, allowing the warm evening air to circulate.

'So,' she said crisply, turning to face Roly. 'This is where we're meeting the vendor, yeah?'

Roly shifted uncomfortably under her gaze, taking a tobacco tin and lighter from his back pocket. He threw himself down on the sagging mattress and began to roll a joint, his fingers clumsy.

'It's not that simple, Indigo,' he said, pausing to cough behind his hand. 'I did what I could for you, because we're friends and I never like to disappoint a friend. But it was too late. By the time I got hold of the vendor and told him you were interested in making a bid, the book had already gone.'

'Gone?'

'Been sold. To some private collector from Switzerland.'

Indigo stared at him in silence for a moment. She did not know what to say. There was a slight flush in her cheeks and her stomach ached; she was angry, and perhaps a little tearful too. After all these years of searching, trying to respect her father's last wishes to find and own it, the Book of Punishment had been sold to somebody else without her even having a chance to inspect it. It had slipped back into the oblivion of private ownership, as it had done when her father lost it. Now she might never find the book again.

'What was the final price?'

Roly shrugged indifferently, moistening the cigarette paper with a practised flick of his tongue. 'More than you could have raised at such short notice. I told you, the Book of Punishment's out of your league. But there's no need to go home empty-handed. I can get you almost anything on the same subject. For instance, I can lay my hands on a good second edition of Masterton's *Excrucio* at half the market price. Fully intact in its original binding.'

'I already own a first edition of the *Excrucio*.' Her voice was taut. 'You said you could get me the Book of Punishment. That's why I came up here with you.'

His smile made her skin creep. 'Correction, baby. You came up here because we had an agreement.'

'If you recall, that was in exchange for helping me get my hands on the book. Unfortunately, you didn't come up with the goods. So no deal, Roly. You won't get your cock sucked tonight.'

The thick sweet fragrance of weed filled the room as he lit the joint and dragged on it heavily. Oddly enough, the book dealer was still smiling. He did not seem in the least perturbed by her defiant attitude, which worried her. She was alone with him in a hotel-cum-brothel in a foreign country. Roly might be a hideous flabby toad but he was still considerably larger than her. She might find it difficult to fend him off if he decided to force the issue.

He held out the joint. 'You look all strung out. Have a drag on this.' When she shook her head, Roly sighed and fumbled in his jeans pocket, producing a torn and grubby piece of paper which he waved in her direction.

'Know what this is? It's the address of that private collector in Switzerland. I had to call in some serious favours to get it, but I wanted to honour our arrangement and help you find that book. Do you know why, Indigo? Because I don't like to see you disappointed.'

Her heart racing with sudden unexpected hope, she bent to take the paper from his fingers. But he was too quick for her, snatching her wrist and pulling her down onto the bed beside him.

He stuffed the piece of paper back into his pocket, shaking his head at her in mock disapproval. 'Not so fast. We've got some unfinished business first.'

She hissed with irritation, wriggling sideways on the bed in an unsuccessful attempt to escape, but his grip was too tight.

Roly smiled again as he watched her struggling, so close now she could see unpleasantly yellow stains on his teeth and almost feel the grate of stubble against her skin. 'You wouldn't want to see me disappointed either, would you?'

Gritting her own teeth as she realised the futility of her position, Indigo managed a terse 'No.'

'Then you'd better keep your side of the bargain, baby, and start sucking.'

She groaned inwardly. What could have possessed her to agree to such a disgusting proposition? Yet she did not want to pass up any opportunity to locate the Book of Punishment, however remote, just in case it disappeared again from the open market. She was going to have to suck his cock and there was no feasible way to wriggle out of the arrangement.

Roly unbuckled his jeans and rummaged about inside his flies. To her dismay, his cock was still perfectly flaccid; he pulled it out, a fat white slug lying motionless on the grimy denim, and gestured to her to kneel beside him.

Indigo stared down at his penis with a bad taste in her mouth. It looked dead. This was going to take more effort on her part than she had anticipated. She took his penis in both hands and squeezed it, though without much enthusiasm, hoping to massage it back to life without having to use her lips.

Impatient now, he gripped the back of her head and forced her down into his lap. 'Suck it, baby. That's what we agreed and that's what I plan to get. A nice slow suck from that well-educated mouth of yours. Plenty of tongue too, yeah? Give me the works, a proper ream job, right round my arse and balls.'

Flushed and angered by such deliberate crudity, Indigo bent to slip the flaccid penis into her mouth. Thoughts of revenge flitted briefly through her head but she ignored them, knowing she could not afford to reject his offer. To her relief, after a couple of strong sucks, his penis began to stiffen and expand. Fumbling to release his balls, she felt Roly help her, shifting on the mattress as he dragged his jeans down to knee height and angled the hairy thighs further apart. In this position, the smell of sweat was almost overwhelming. Yet she did not draw back, determined to fulfil her obligation, sucking rhythmically on that ever enlarging cock while she cupped and stroked his testicles with both hands.

The dealer moaned, pulling her head closer. 'Yeah, that's great. You suck like a real pro, Indigo. I can get you top dollar for that mouth in Amsterdam. You only have to say the word.'

Unable to supply any sort of intelligible reply with her mouth full, Indigo had to be content with what she hoped was a scathing grunt as she continued to suck. She ignored the nagging warmth between her own thighs. She had agreed to do this and she would go through with it. Right to the bitter end. But she did not have to enjoy it.

As though reading her thoughts, Roly slid a hand inside the loose linen dress and squeezed one of her

46

nipples, tightening his grip until she gave a stifled cry of anguish. To her chagrin, he sounded almost amused. 'You're hating every minute of this but it's still turning you on, isn't it? If I'd known you liked it rough and ready, I'd have fucked you years ago.'

Furious now, she sucked even harder at his cock, as though hoping the end might come off in her mouth. Certainly something was about to come off. He was rigid, the mushroom-shaped head pinkish now and pulsing between her lips as though eager to explode. The sooner this ignominious task was over, she thought, the better for both of them. His hands were all over her breasts, both nipples now embarrassingly erect beneath his fingers; it would only be a matter of time before he worked his way down to her pussy, which was sticky as a beehive and aching to be rubbed.

'Hey girl, slow down before there's an accident,' he said, letting go of her breasts. 'Suck my balls like I told you . . . and the rest.'

With a grimace, only too aware what he meant by that, she let his penis plop wetly from her mouth and leaned sideways into an awkward crouching position between his thighs.

Roly laughed at her obvious lack of enthusiasm. He rolled onto one side, turning his hips in to the mattress at an acute angle, and pointed back at his anus with one stubby finger. 'Come on, don't be shy. I want to feel your tongue right up my arse.'

'Is that really necessary?'

'I'm afraid so, yes.'

Flinching at his derisive tone, Indigo lowered her head between his thighs until her mouth was level with those flabby bottom cheeks. She stared at them in silence for a moment and wondered whether it would be possible to please him without debasing herself any further. The likelihood seemed remote. There was only one way for her to go from here and that was down.

The hair on his buttocks looked smooth and silky, so thick it obscured the dark puckered entrance to his anus. Though not quite enough to render it inaccessible, she thought grimly.

With reluctant fingers, she parted his cheeks and licked tentatively at the coarse flesh. Her tongue ran several times along the outside of the crease before she gathered the courage to dip inside, flickering around the anal opening without actually entering it.

'You tease!' he groaned, pushing his hairy backside into her face. 'Do it properly like we agreed. Fuck my arse with your tongue. Clean me out down there.'

Indigo shut her eyes tight and let her tongue penetrate his anus. Inside, it tasted nutty and perhaps slightly sweet, not as horrible as she had expected when he first suggested it. Surprised and a little curious now, she slipped her tongue further inside and started to explore the warm moist channel of his rectum. She half expected him to pull back at such a deep intrusion. But the book dealer writhed about on the mattress like a girl enjoying her first experience of cunnilingus, muttering something she did not catch but could tell was clearly intended to be encouraging. So she kept pushing onwards and upwards, her face nuzzling into his bottom.

A few seconds later his buttocks clenched, convulsing against her mouth, then she heard him moan in quiet desperation.

With a suspicious tongue, she probed around inside the narrow channel. His muscular rectum seemed slicker now, almost as wet as her own pussy had become, the smooth fleshy walls slimed with a mess that she could only guess at.

'Fantastic, fantastic,' he gasped as her head rose abruptly. He gripped his swollen penis in one fist and directed it towards her lips. 'Now suck me off and make sure you swallow the lot. They charge extra if you leave spunk on the sheets.'

The fat purplish head was back in her mouth before she could argue. With a desperate thrust of his hips, Roly rammed it down her throat, the reason for his urgency soon becoming apparent. She had barely adjusted her position to accommodate his full length, tilting her head back and letting her jaw go slack, when the penis in her mouth stiffened and began to jerk as he reached orgasm.

Indigo gagged on that first hot rush of semen, the dark nutty smell of his anus still in her nostrils as she dutifully squatted there to swallow. But at least it was over now, she told herself. She had performed the task and not humiliated herself by letting him see how excited she had become. Her pussy might be wet and aching but she had not once given in to the temptation to touch herself. That was surely an achievement under the circumstances.

His sperm was not too horrible to swallow, though it did taste a touch salty. Belatedly remembering not to soil the sheets, her lips formed a leak-free ring about his cock until it had finished jetting down her throat.

Afterwards, he rolled away with a satisfied smile and yanked up his jeans. 'Yeah, that was worth the cost of the room. I knew you'd come across in the end, given a little gentle persuasion. You're that sort of girl though, aren't you?' He laughed. 'Hard to fuck, but always willing to suck a bloke's knob if he asks nicely enough.'

'Bastard,' she managed to say, collapsing back onto the sheets, his semen still thick in her throat.

'You loved every minute of it.'

'In your dreams.'

He paused and turned to examine the bed, frowning as he pointed out a damp patch beneath her knees. 'But what the hell's this? I told you to be careful. If that's spunk . . .'

'It can't be spunk! I did exactly what you said and swallowed the whole bloody lot.'

Sniffing the stain suspiciously, Roly stared back up at her with a half-angry, half-fascinated expression on his face. 'This smells like pussy juice.'

'Rubbish!'

Indigo sat up with flushed cheeks at his accusation and pulled the thin linen dress to her waist, exposing her pussy, barely concealed by a white lace thong. Aware of his scrutiny, she bent to investigate with her fingers, dragging the thong to one side and probing her moist puffy lips in the forlorn hope of proving him wrong. But the glistening sheen of excitement was only too visible as she parted the lips of her cunt and craned her neck to peer at the pink flesh inside.

'Oh shit,' she muttered.

'You horny slut.' His eyes gleamed with appreciation. 'Licking my arsehole turned you on so much, you dripped on the sheets.'

'I'm sorry –'

He gave her an amused slap across the breasts, mesmerised by the way they bounced up and down. 'Don't waste my time with apologies. The damage is done, look at the mess you've made. In fact, you might as well finish off now, get the sheets as wet as you like.'

'W – what?'

Roly took her hand and pushed it hard between her thighs. 'Come on, don't pretend. I can see you're dying for a wank.'

'Right here? In front of you?'

He crumpled the torn piece of paper in his fist, laughing at her expression of outraged desperation.

'Think for a minute. You can walk out of here tonight with this address in your handbag, or you can walk out of here with nothing but my spunk in your belly. So stop whining and start rubbing, OK? It's a sad fact, but there are few things I like better than watching some dirty little girl frig herself after I've spunked in her mouth.'

'Ugh, you're sick.'

'Yeah, whatever.' Roly lay back on the mattress, waving the paper in front of his face like a miniature fan. 'Give that famous tongue of yours a rest and let's see what you're like with your fingers for a change. Then maybe you can have this address.'

OK, Indigo thought furiously, watching his smug face and wishing she could smack it – if you really want to watch, that's what you are going to do.

With a gesture of defiance, she dipped two fingers in her sticky pussy and used her thumb to press down on the taut bud of her clitoris. After keeping her hands clear for so long, it felt glorious to touch herself at last, to let some of those filthy thoughts loose and really indulge her imagination. Not even looking at Roly, she pulled the thin linen dress over her head, grabbed a breast in her free hand and squeezed. Like squeezing a Spanish orange, she thought. Hard enough to hurt, tight enough for the juice to start flowing. And the nipple came erect too, instantly alert, taut against her palm.

Gasping and moaning, she pushed her fingers deeper inside her cunt and twisted them. Brutal was how she liked her solo sessions. Brutal and uncompromising. Noisy too, unfortunately. She was no sweet little girl rubbing her pussy and sighing like a princess in a fairy tale. He could stare all he wanted. There was nothing half-hearted about the way she fucked herself.

Oh Jesus, four whole fingers in her cunt. Now she was rocking. Another inch or two and she would hit the knuckles.

Hair all over the place, cheeks flushed, her whole body swayed to the rhythm of that strategically placed thumb. Right on the clitoris, pressing down hard, hard, hard; grinding the tender flesh until she squealed like an excited pig, helpless to stop herself. She did not want the conniving bastard to think she was putting on a show for him, but she simply could not control the volume of her groans.

Indigo wanted sex. No, she craved sex. Like a baby craves its mother's milk, she thought with a sudden rush of excitement, crying aloud and burying her face in the cool sheets. She did not want to suck or kneel or bend to have her backside smacked again. What she craved tonight was deep ruthless penetration from a man with a really stiff cock. Perhaps in her bottom too.

Oh yes, that would feel good. Being forced onto her stomach on the bed or perhaps over that large wicker chair in the corner; legs akimbo; everything on show from the waist down; her face red with desire and embarrassment; that tiny opening between her bottom cheeks stretched by some huge swollen penis; the sheer thrust of it, bruising and burning the delicate skin there, penetrating her anus; spurting its seed deep inside, trailing a thin white streamer of sperm down her thigh.

At last she was coming, lost to all reason, thrashing about and gasping for air like a fish on the deck of a boat.

Once it was all over and her cries had eventually died away to a few comforting sobs of pleasure, Indigo managed to sit up again and start rearranging her hair. Her pussy stung viciously; it felt as though someone had been using sandpaper on it. There was fresh bruising on one breast and both inner thighs. And she could not seem to focus properly. It was with trembling hands that she reached for her dress and dragged it back over her head again, finding it quite difficult to get her arms in the sleeves, her co-ordination was so shot.

'Christ, Indigo.' Roly threw the torn piece of paper down on the mattress beside her, shaking his head in disbelief. 'Take it, just take the address. You deserve it after that performance. Do you always fuck yourself like that?'

'Pretty much,' she agreed, still breathless.

'You had me scared there. I was beginning to wonder whether I should call an ambulance.'

Indigo laughed and got to her feet, slipping back into her heels. She crossed to the only mirror in the room, a dirty cracked glass on the wardrobe door. She checked her reflection, the charming disarray of her hair, the flushed cheeks, feeling more like herself now that she had climaxed. After months of torpor, such an uninhibited orgasm had given her new strength, loosened muscles that had been far too tight and put a more forceful spring in her step.

'So the Book of Punishment is in Switzerland?' She glanced down at the address in her hands and paused for a moment, her smile dry. 'Of course. How stupid of me. I went there with my father in the summer of '91, to see a man about a book.'

4

'You're sure that's the right address?'

It was nearly midnight and Dervil was not in any mood to play games with Natasha. He was exhausted after a particularly difficult session with a lady from Tring. She came to him several times a month, always wore school uniform and insisted on calling him 'Headmaster', even though she was at least 65 and suffered terribly from varicose veins. It was such a predictable part for him to play, he rarely enjoyed their meetings. Being able to administer the strap to the coarse cheeks of her derrière until it was scarlet and throbbing only ever partly alleviated his boredom with the role.

Natasha blew a smoke ring towards the ceiling and shrugged, a touch of impatience in her sulky voice.

'If that's what I wrote down, yeah. You can't expect me to remember every little word that was said to me in a coffee shop in Amsterdam.' She snorted derisively. 'I was pretty high at the time, you know.'

'Yes, you told me.'

The Russian transsexual tapped the address she had given him with a false pink fingernail. 'So that's where the man lives who bought the Book of Punishment. You know him, yes? He's a dealer?'

'In a manner of speaking.'

'Then it's easy. We go there and do business with this man, bring the book back to England.'

He raised one eyebrow, looking at her. 'We?'

'Of course, we. You can't go to Switzerland alone, Dervil. It's not possible. You need a woman with you.'

'For what?'

Natasha licked her lips, leaning forwards to gaze at him with eager smouldering eyes. 'For womanly things.'

'Oh, those.'

'And to drive the car.'

Dervil nearly smiled at her naive candour, but stopped himself in time. It was never wise to encourage Natasha in her obsessions, even though she had almost persuaded him to take her along on this occasion. She was right, after all, he thought drily. He had indeed decided to go by road, and two drivers were always preferable on long journeys, especially one that might involve traversing the odd mountain range.

'Don't be impertinent or I shall have to punish you,' he warned her sternly, pocketing the address before she had a chance to take it back. 'What makes you think I'm driving to Geneva anyway? It would be much easier to fly.'

'Because you get sick in planes, darling.'

'There's always the train.'

'And in trains.' She did a silent impersonation of someone retching violently. 'But never in the car.'

He did smile then, turning away to hide it. It was a pity he could not feel the same way about Natasha that she felt about him. But that was life. Littered with brutal inconsistencies.

Dervil picked up the strap he had left on the table after his last client and weighed it thoughtfully in his hand. It was thick brown leather, well oiled and flexible, custom-made by a famous London firm with a reputation for supplying some of the cruellest instruments of punishment in the world. There was sweat caught in the fine stitchwork, but whether it was his or Mrs Halliwell's, he could not be sure.

He wiped the strap and turned to face his former lover, his voice deliberately harsh. 'Put out that cigarette and stand up.'

'But darling –'

He brought the leather strap down on the table with an incredible crack, pleased to see the woman jerk as if she had been shot and leap immediately to her feet.

'Do what I tell you and don't answer back. It's only been a year since I sent you away, for god's sake. Have you forgotten everything I taught you?'

'I'm sorry.'

'Silence!' he thundered.

Dervil walked around her, inspecting her with a master's eye, tugging at the creased leather skirt until it hung straight, adjusting the seam in her sheer stockings, even kicking her feet apart to make balancing in those ludicrous heels more difficult.

'Hands behind your head,' he instructed her coldly. 'Shoulders back, tits out.'

From the trembling lip and glint of excited fear in her eyes, he could tell Natasha was more than ready to take this and more brutal treatment. That was why the beautiful transsexual had agreed to go to Amsterdam at such short notice, after all. In order to please him, just as she had pleased him in the past; in the hope of meriting exactly this sort of punishment.

'You must learn to control your tendency to answer back,' he told her. 'Such behaviour is wholly inappropriate in a submissive. Or do you feel you've grown beyond that status? Perhaps you've had some experiences since we parted that make you think you're in control here.'

She stammered a denial.

'Because I want you to forget that idea.' Dervil stood behind her, considering for a moment how he should do this, in what position he should punish her and how hard. 'Do you remember this particular strap, Natasha? It's always been one of my favourites.'

'Aunty's strap,' she whispered, turning her head slightly to look over her shoulder at it.

'Face front! I did not give you permission to move. Are you trying to provoke me into losing my temper?'

Mutely, she shook her head. But he knew the Russian too well to believe her. She loved the power of provocation, using it in subtle ways to increase the sexual tension between them. She was often deliberately slow to assume the correct position, would dart glances at him during a punishment instead of keeping her eyes lowered, and frequently said more than required when asked a question. What she wanted from him was a reaction, anything to spark off an explosion between them.

'Yes, I thought you'd remember the strap. Of course, I'm disappointed that you failed to bring me the Book of Punishment,' he continued, positioning himself behind her. 'But at least I know where it is now. Which is why I'm prepared to be lenient with the strap. Seven strokes only, as punishment for your failure. Though you could try to reduce that to five, if you wish.'

She nodded, not yet daring to speak again.

'When discussing the Book of Punishment, did Roly give you the names of any other interested parties?'

'Crustau.'

He frowned, turning that information over in his mind. 'Gustav Crustau? A real bloodhound but too cautious with money to play for such high stakes. He's unlikely to keep up the pursuit. Who else?'

Natasha hesitated. 'A German . . . I don't recall . . .'

With the skill of long experience, Dervil accurately measured the distance between her bottom and his hand, and brought the strap down at precisely the right speed to make her hop on the spot and hiss at the unexpected pain.

'Name?'

'Hoffman . . . Gunter Hoffman.'

He smiled as she groaned beneath her breath, knowing the sudden blow had aroused her. 'I didn't know old

Gunter was still alive. He could be dangerous if he's serious. Definitely one to watch. Who else?'

'Only one more,' she managed. 'A woman. But I don't know her name. Please don't hit me!'

Ignoring her soft breathless plea, only too aware that these hesitations were deliberate, intended to heighten her own excitement, Dervil administered another blow to her backside. The strap gave a satisfying crack as it contacted her leather skirt, no doubt leaving an angry reddened patch on the skin beneath.

She was dancing on tiptoe now, taller than him in her high black heels, her breath coming in short gasps. 'No, wait. I remember now, her name was a colour. A blue colour. Violet . . . or was it Lilac?'

'*Indigo*?'

His hand had frozen in mid-strike, eyes narrowing in disbelief as he realised who she must be talking about.

'Yes, that's it!' she squealed, her face flushed with relief. 'That's what Roly said her name was . . . Indigo.'

'Indigo,' he repeated in a mutter, lowering the strap and turning away to hide his reaction. So Indigo was also on the hunt for the elusive Book of Punishment. Not that he should be surprised; her father had been obsessed with the book. The same desire must run in the girl's blood.

He had only met Indigo on a handful of occasions, mainly at book fairs around Britain and once in Frankfurt. A beautiful girl, if you could forgive a too wide mouth and eyes that had held his just a fraction longer than was comfortable for a dominant. Rather petite for his tastes, about five foot four at a guess. He preferred his women taller than that, taller and a little more pliable. There was something too spiky about Indigo, the sort of bristling feminism which made his hands itch to hold the girl down and smack her bottom hard.

It might be rather amusing to cross swords with a young woman like that, he considered. He had often visited the bookshop off Charing Cross Road when her father was alive, but it had always felt awkward with Indigo in charge. Who wants a sharp-tongued minx like her looking over your shoulder while you're browsing books on submissives?

Dervil smiled wryly. Indigo had never struck him as the type who could be persuaded to play the game in return for a sale, which was a pity. Though she might change her mind if the Book of Punishment was at stake; perhaps even turn her hand to the ancient traditions of punishment and reward, regardless of ethics.

The possibility entertained him. How far would she go to get her hands on the book? Her father had never turned down an opportunity to indulge his perversions. It would add a certain frisson to the chase, making it part of his mission to discover if Indigo really was her father's daughter.

His erection was becoming uncomfortable at the thought of forcing Indigo to bend for a beating, of watching her skin glow beneath his hand or the cruel weight of a paddle.

'Drop your skirt,' he said urgently, rubbing at the thick brown strap until the leather was warm.

The skirt fell to the floor in a soft rustle of material and Natasha stepped gracefully out of it. Dervil let his eyes linger on her body for another few moments, appreciative of how lucky he was. Master of all he surveyed in this place, his own private dungeon here in the London suburbs. Natasha's buttocks gleamed above the black tops of her stockings, an inviting target.

He stepped forwards, bouncing the strap on his palm. 'I'm glad you remembered her name, Natasha. Very glad indeed. Now bend over and touch your toes, there's a good girl. It's time for your reward.'

5

The logo above the first-floor buzzer read *Sticky Fingers Inc.*, with a blue icon of a video camera beside the name. Indigo smiled drily to herself. Heinrich had clearly expanded his company since they had last met, to include other areas of the pornography business. The place reminded her of a vast greenhouse, all glass and metal supports at the front, while the rear of the building resembled a concrete car park.

Indigo hit the buzzer again, this time leaning on the bloody thing until a man finally answered, his voice almost lost in crackle and hiss. 'I'm here to see Heinrich,' she said in German, loudly and with more confidence than she really felt. 'I've got an appointment. The door seems to be locked. Could you let me in?'

To her surprise, the disembodied voice replied, 'Push the door and come up,' without any attempt at an argument. There was another buzzing sound and the door in front of her unlocked. She pushed as instructed and climbed the clanking metal stairs to the first floor, where the door to Sticky Fingers Inc. stood ajar as though she really had been expected.

Inside the office, it was chaos. Men erecting massive lights like satellite dishes, girls wandering about with mobile phones clamped to their heads, a tall wiry-looking man shouting at a girl on her knees by a monitor, and acres of coloured cables running every-where. Beyond them all was the calm blue of the lake, seen through the glass windows at the far side of the office.

'And who are you?' a grey-haired woman with a distracted expression asked abruptly in German, stopping to stare at her.

'I'm expected,' she said firmly.

The woman consulted her clipboard, frowning. 'Are you Melinda? The English model?'

'Yes,' Indigo lied.

'Well, you're incredibly late.' She switched to English and pointed impatiently through a doorway into another chaotic-looking room. 'The dressing room is through there. Didn't you bring your own clothes? Oh never mind, we should have something in your size. Though you're shorter than I expected. You'd better hurry up. The shoot starts in less than twenty.'

'Is Heinrich here?' she asked, catching at the woman's arm before she could disappear.

The woman looked confused. 'You know Heinrich?'

'I need to talk to him about a book.'

'He's never in this early. Maybe later, after lunch, if he's not too busy. I'll tell him you want to see him.'

Indigo hurriedly shook her head, frowning. That was the last thing she wanted. 'Please, there's no need. I'd prefer to surprise him. My father knew him; he's an old friend of the family.'

'I see,' the woman said politely, though it was clear she did not see anything but was in too much of a hurry to bother with English girls and their eccentric behaviour. 'Well, better go and get into costume. If you need to ask anything, that's Georg over there in the red baseball cap.'

It was Indigo's turn to look confused. 'Who?'

'Georg,' the grey-haired woman repeated, giving her a withering stare as she moved away with her clipboard. 'The director.'

OK, she was not imagining things, Indigo thought, clutching her handbag and heading resolutely for the dressing-room. That's why the place was in so much uproar. They were planning to shoot some sort of film here. A pornographic film, presumably.

And she had just volunteered to play a part in it herself by pretending to be Melinda, whoever the hell she was.

To her relief, although the dressing-room floor was strewn with discarded clothes and shoes, there was only one other person in there. A red-haired girl of about her own age was standing on one leg in front of the wall mirror, swearing loudly as she struggled to squeeze into heels at least two sizes too small for her. She was not wildly attractive for a porno actress, Indigo thought, assessing her at a glance. But she was pretty enough in her own way, with bold green eyes and a slightly lopsided mouth. Well-padded hips barely fitted into a black rubber skirt, her breasts swinging free above a tidy waist.

The girl turned as Indigo made her entrance, wide green eyes flashing with annoyance. 'Are you here at last? Thank god for that. I was beginning to think I'd have to go through with this damned thing on my own.'

The girl sounded American. From somewhere in the Midwest, to judge by that drawling accent. Indigo smiled and unslung her bag, then dropped it to the floor and held out her hand with a friendly smile.

'Sorry I'm late,' she said brightly. 'Got the wrong bus to the wrong *Strasse*. Story of my life.'

The girl grunted, taking her hand reluctantly. The green eyes looked her up and down. 'You must be Melinda. I'm Eloise.'

'Lovely to meet you, Eloise. Is there any coffee round here? I'm dying for something hot and wet.'

'On the table over there.'

'Thanks, darling. This is an absolute life-saver.'

Indigo poured a generous amount of strong black coffee into a polystyrene cup, glancing at the other girl in the mirror. The American girl was watching her in return, unblinking. She was not stupid, so Indigo would have to be. She kicked off her shoes and took a sip of coffee, her voice deliberately high and vacant.

'Which scene are we doing first? I'm so scatty, I completely forgot to bring any clothes, so . . .'

'Rubber first.'

'Oh yeah. The rubber scene. Is there any –?'

Eloise pointed to the floor where a black rubber suit lay in a tangled heap, inside out and barely recognisable as clothing. 'That should fit you. It was too tight on me.'

'Cheers.' Indigo picked up the two pieces of rubber and tried to make sense of them. 'This bit goes over the head, yeah?'

There was an odd silence, then Eloise giggled. 'I don't know,' she admitted, coming forwards to help her. 'I put my leg through that hole. But you're probably right, that may be why I couldn't get into it.'

After struggling into the strange rubber outfit – a black miniskirt and bra top, both so tight they almost cut off her circulation – with the help of some talcum powder she stood still while Eloise sprayed her with a can of rubber shine. Minutes later, her hair had been slicked back from her forehead with thick industrial gel and her eyes made-up with a dramatic black and silver eye-shadow. She glanced at herself in the mirror. She looked like an alien from a science-fiction movie. The rubber glistened around her hips and chest, moving in perfect harmony with her body like a second skin.

'What size are you?' Eloise handed her a pair of high heels in grotesquely shiny black plastic. 'These might be a bit loose.'

'I'd prefer those suede ones with the ankle straps.'

Eloise laughed drily. 'Sure, who wouldn't? But you can't wear suede shoes on a shoot like this. The acid would ruin them.'

'Acid?'

'In your pee.'

Indigo stared at her for a moment, frozen in the act of slipping her foot into one of the high plastic heels. 'Pee?' she repeated mechanically, her mind working at a furious rate. 'You mean . . .'

'This is a watersports movie, honey. Georg's speciality. His *Dolls with Umbrellas* won an award last year. Didn't your agent tell you?'

'Um . . .'

'Look, just relax. Do whatever Georg tells you and you'll be fine. He's a great director, one of the best . . . keeps his hands to himself, never screws the girls unless they ask him. All you need to remember is to drink as much cola as you can before they start shooting. Trust me, that stuff will make you pee like a racehorse!'

'Thanks for the tip.'

'Don't sweat it, honey.' Eloise wriggled into a transparent plastic bra top and rearranged her breasts until the nipples were almost popping out. 'It's a dirty business and we girls have got to stick together.'

They were called to the set by a spotty-faced youth in cut-off denim shorts and a T-shirt that read DOWN ON YOUR KNEES AND SUCK. He grinned over his shoulder at both girls as they followed him, indicating with a jerk of his head where they should wait for the shoot to begin. They trotted out under the hot lights, Eloise gulping from a large bottle of sugar-free cola every few minutes. The floor of the set had been covered with a see-through plastic groundsheet which slipped treacherously under their high heels. The two girls waited in silence, adjusting each other's clothing and hair, preening like a couple of birds of paradise.

It had seemed like a joke up to that point; but suddenly Indigo was nervous. Especially now that she knew peeing or being peed on might be required of her. When she had told the grey-haired woman she was Melinda, it had merely been a way of getting inside the place. She had not expected to be forced into continuing with the pretence. It was a little too late to admit the truth now.

Watersports might not really be her scene but if this gave her an opportunity to get closer to the Book of Punishment – which might very well be somewhere on these premises – it was worth accepting the gig. So she was about to star in her first blue movie. Taking her clothes off, peeing herself, that sort of thing. How hard could it be?

Georg was a thin man with sparse receding hair under his red baseball cap and a ginger goatee. The director asked each of them to turn around so he could check their glistening rubber outfits, then nodded with apparent satisfaction.

'I think,' he told Indigo calmly, 'you must be the one to pee first. Into the other girl's face, yes?'

'Ugh.'

He motioned Eloise to lie down beneath her. 'We will practice this. How you say it, a dry run?' There were a few sniggers from the watching crew and Georg waved an indulgent hand in their direction. 'Ignore those fools, they don't know anything about art. All they want is to see naked girls piss and lick each other clean. It's so boring, so predictable. But we will not be boring today.'

Kneeling beside Eloise, the director positioned the sturdy redhead on her back, knees up and slightly apart to reveal a moist shaven pussy. His hands worked quickly and delicately, tilting her throat back and rubbing at her nipples through the bra top until they stood to attention, stiff flushed peaks pressed hard against the transparent plastic. He spoke quickly, his tone matter-of-fact.

'Eloise, you will come into the room and find ... whatever her name is ... crying. You comfort her. You kiss. You stroke each other's tits and cunts. Then she says "I need to pee" and you lie down. She straddles your face and *splash*! Lots and lots of piss all over the place, as much as you can. Yes?'

Indigo nodded hurriedly as he glanced in her direction, but could not help biting her lip, her cheeks very pink.

'You have not done this before?' He frowned, squatting back on his heels as he looked her over, taking in every detail of her almost nude body. 'But I ask the agency for a girl with plenty of experience. Why do they send you?'

'It's OK,' she said firmly. 'I can do it.'

'You are sure? Because it's only one take. No reshoots.'

'I understand.'

Georg placed a hand on her midriff and slid it down over the shiny rubber miniskirt, pressing hard and watching her face for a reaction. When she failed to flinch under the pressure, he sighed. 'Eloise, could you pass me that bottle? Here, drink cola. No, finish the whole bottle. Your bladder needs to be full, full, full. Otherwise it will not be good pissing.'

She managed a few deep gulps of the disgusting fizzy drink and shook her head. 'That's fine, I really don't need any more.'

'More, more. Come on.'

Indigo gagged and spluttered as the director pushed the plastic bottle back between her lips, cola spilling liberally over her chin and down her cleavage. Her temper flared at the unnecessary force and she took a step back, nearly turning her ankle in the ludicrous six-inch heels they had supplied. 'Hey, for god's sake! Watch what you're doing.'

'You want to leave here? You don't want to do this movie? Because we can easily get another girl,' he told her sharply, 'a girl who likes to piss and isn't afraid to fill herself up for the shooting.'

'Yeah, yeah,' she muttered but complied, draining the bottle in a mutinous silence while he watched. 'OK, it's all gone. Happy now?'

'Ecstatic.'

She handed him the empty bottle as proof that she had completed the task, wiped her sticky face with the back of her hand, and turned away so he would not hear her biting remark, 'I'm so pleased.'

A sudden blow to the backs of her legs made her stagger, and she almost overbalanced as she collided with Eloise. The taller girl steadied her, a warning look on her face as their eyes met. Indigo turned to see the empty plastic cola bottle swinging from Georg's fist. That was what he had used to hit her, she realised, aware of a dull aching just below her bottom. She rubbed at the backs of her legs, staring at the film director with new respect. It had been a legitimate exchange, there was nothing more to say. Georg had tried to impose his directorial authority on her, she had been insolent, he had taken his revenge.

'So I'm meant to be crying when Eloise walks in,' she said quietly, sitting on the sofa and putting her hands to her face. The last thing she wanted was to cause a scene. 'Like this?'

'That's perfect.'

Georg turned and walked away. The watching crew dispersed to their various positions, preparing for the shoot.

The redhead crouched down beside her, pretending to be fiddling with one of her heels. 'You certainly know how to take a situation to the wire,' she whispered to Indigo, glancing over her shoulder to check no one was listening. The nearest member of the crew was adjusting one of the arc lights behind the sofa but his swarthy face was absorbed in the task; he was not paying them any attention. 'You were so rude, speaking to Georg like that! With any other director, you would have been in serious trouble. They don't like it when the girls answer back.'

'I'm a human being, not a pissing machine. All I wanted was to be treated with a little respect.'

'All you got was a slap.'

Indigo shrugged. 'That doesn't bother me. But perhaps next time he won't be so quick to push me around.'

The other girl looked unconvinced but she stood up, straightening her skirt with a nervous gesture. 'I think we'll be starting any minute. You know all your moves, yeah? Don't worry about pissing into my face. I've had it done hundreds of times before, it's not a problem. There's a towel over there, just hand it to me at the cut.'

'Sure thing.'

They took up their positions, Indigo on the sofa and Eloise waiting outside the door. The arc lights gave off such an intense heat, her make-up was running into her eyes and she could feel sweat trickling between her breasts and thighs. The rubber did not help, the tight black skirt sticking tackily to her skin as she tried to cross her legs.

Georg gave the signal and Indigo sank her face into her hands, shoulders shaking as she made muffled crying noises. Eloise walked in and sat down beside her, giving her a sisterly hug.

'Darling, what's the matter?'

'I'm just so upset,' she moaned, putting on a whimpering voice. 'Please help me, I don't know what to do.'

The redhead kissed her gently on the cheek. 'Shh.'

'Hold me, I need you to hold me.'

Obeying in silence, Eloise drew her closer and gently stroked her hair for a moment.

'Kiss me properly,' Indigo whispered in her ear, more daring, and sighed as Eloise bent her head in response.

As their mouths met in a passionate kiss, Indigo felt the other girl's hand moving on her bare thigh. What had Georg wanted now? Oh yes. She let herself fall back onto the sofa and the hand crept higher, pushing beneath the tight rubber skirt to find her pussy. It was slick and willing down there, opening like a sea anemone at the touch of those slender fingers. Her breathing began to speed up.

Indigo closed her eyes and let the girl's creeping fingers explore her more intimately, uncrossing her legs to allow her greater access, to let them see her properly, all the way up inside, acutely aware of Georg and the crew on all sides of them. The camera lens burned into the flesh of her pussy like a sinister eye, the powerful overhead lights leaving her skin flushed and overheated. She could imagine the crew's penises stiffening in their jeans as they stood around the set, watching the two girls kissing and fondling on the sofa.

The rubber skirt had wrinkled about her waist now, her actions even more whorish as she raised her legs, still encased in smooth black plastic and pointing slightly in towards each other as though she were a gauche schoolgirl, and placed her heels on the sofa. It was a provocative pose and one she often adopted during an encounter with multiple partners; designed to confuse and arouse the onlooker, it suggested both innocence and depravity. Which would you prefer? she seemed to be saying. The choice is yours.

Her pussy was not shaven like Eloise's, fine dark curls covering her mound in a neat triangular strip. But then she had not expected to be displaying herself to a roomful of strangers today. Not to mention the thousands of men who might buy or rent this film worldwide, able to pause her filthy behaviour for moments at a time or press rewind as often as required until they shot their load into a tissue or the soft accommodating mouth of a girlfriend.

The redhead used two fingers to spread her pussy lips apart, bending to kiss and lick at the fleshy hood of her clitoris until Indigo found herself gasping and writhing under that clever tongue without needing to act. The other girl was clearly experienced at lesbian sex and needed no lessons in how to arouse a woman at short notice.

Eloise flicked her tongue backwards and forwards over her clitoris until the intense sensations became too powerful and Indigo begged her to stop, grasping a handful of the girl's slick red hair and trying to pull her away.

But the other girl did not respond. She just kept on licking and flicking and curling, that subtle tongue moving like a snake's between her pussy lips.

Suddenly Indigo felt that familiar cramping in her belly that accompanied orgasm and she threw back her head, crying aloud as the first wave hit. For that instant, she forgot about the circle of watching men, the camera film storing every obscene image of her body and face as the climax peaked, even the girl whose fingers and tongue had brought her there, and she writhed like a wild thing in the grip of pleasure.

'More gasping, more groaning,' a man's voice urged her, breaking into the fantasy that she was alone with Eloise. 'We need to hear it.'

Her eyes flickered open and she stared directly across the room into Georg's bearded face. The director gestured to her to make more noise, crouched opposite the two girls like some sort of sexual coach, taking occasional sips of his coffee as he watched her climax.

'Keep your legs wide apart, the camera needs to see everything that's going on.' He grunted with satisfaction as she complied. 'Now, Eloise, I want you to stick your fingers up her cunt. Not like that! Do it properly, fuck her with your whole hand. Yes, yes. Let me see your faces, really hear the groans. I want to feel your pleasure.'

Those fingers were fantastic, pressing right up inside her, but the knuckles stung a little. The discomfort served to heighten her excitement, turning her mind to a rougher type of sex. She wondered what Georg would be like in bed, which position he preferred and whether he would hit her first, the way he had done earlier with the plastic cola bottle.

Then Eloise clamped her mouth again over the taut mound of Indigo's sex and she climaxed for a second time, clawing at the other girl's shoulders, her thighs and buttocks twitching into spasm. Her bladder was screaming to be emptied, so full it was ready to burst, but she clenched down hard on those internal muscles and somehow managed to control it.

'Now,' Georg prompted her as the climax subsided, 'it's time for the pissing. Tell her in a loud voice.'

'I need to pee,' Indigo said, pulling Eloise away.

'Louder.'

'I need to pee!' she almost shouted, struggling to get up from the damp sweat-stained sofa. 'Right now!'

'Down on the floor, Eloise. Beg her to do it in your face.'

Eloise wriggled beneath her, drawing her knees up exactly as the director had instructed her, to ensure the camera could see her exposed pussy.

'Piss in my face,' the redhead gasped, raising her shoulders off the floor so that her face could also be seen clearly. The position must have put an incredible strain on her back and stomach muscles, yet she held it without weakening. 'I want you to piss on me. Make me swallow your hot piss.'

Straddling the unfortunate girl's face, high up on the black plastic heels, the skirt a mere inch of rolled-up rubber about her waist, Indigo had no problems at all following the director's instructions. She bent her knees slightly to get the correct position, aware that her buttocks must be on full show to the men behind them, her sex still pulsing deliciously from her orgasm. As soon as she relaxed those tightly clenched muscles, her pee came flooding out in a lovely golden stream, hitting poor Eloise straight in the face and cascading over her hair and shoulders onto the floor. The smell of fresh urine was so strong, and the sight of her peeing over another girl's face so striking, that she caught an intake of breath from every man in the studio and knew she must have done a good job.

She might not be a professional actress like Eloise, but she had carried out the director's instructions as closely as she could and she could tell Georg was pleased with her efforts. That bulge in the front of his jeans was a bit of a giveaway, she thought.

'That's great,' Georg was saying, on his feet now, applauding her performance as he came nearer. 'But don't stop yet. It's working so good, I think we keep rolling. Eloise, it's your turn to pee now. You're going to pee into her mouth while she kneels in front of you. Tell her you can't hang on any longer, you have to go right now or you're going to burst.'

'I need to pee too. I'm going to have an accident.'

'Now look desperate, put your hand down there and grab yourself. That's good. Hop up and down, like you can't wait.'

'It's spilling, it's spilling!'

'That's beautiful.'

'Please let me pee on you. I need to pee in your mouth.'

Indigo obeyed the director's frantic signals and knelt beside the red sofa, a little unsure about what was coming next. She did not have long to wait to find out. Eloise came level with her mouth, a red-headed goddess towering above her on those high plastic heels, and pulled up her own rubber skirt.

The smell of that shaven juiced-up cunt was fragrant and intense. It made her want to come again just staring at her, so close to her face.

'Oh god.' Eloise pulled Indigo's face into her crotch, a little groan of excitement and desperation accompanying the sudden move.

Then the neat shaven lips were spurting urine into Indigo's face, hot fluid streaming into her open mouth and down over her chin and throat, the smell and pungent taste of it making her gag and retch as she tried in vain not to swallow.

'Swallow it, swallow it!'

Against every instinct, Indigo opened her mouth a little wider and obeyed the director's insistent command.

God, it was vile stuff. She managed a few reluctant gulps before the flow came to a halt and she was able to stop swallowing and lick the swollen lips clean. Her tongue dived inside after that, circling the sweet hooded bud of her new friend's clitoris and tugging on it like a nipple, sucking and tugging in the hope of obliterating the taste of urine with the scent of excited pussy.

But just as she was getting used to the taste, Georg shouted 'Cut!' and there was a violent round of applause from the watching crew.

'Is that it? Have we finished for the day?'

Georg laughed, throwing them both a towel and perching on the arm of the sofa while they cleaned themselves up. 'No, we shoot again after lunch. This time wearing the maids' outfits. Meanwhile, there's cheese and baguettes and plenty of wine if you want it. You can lie down in the dressing-room if you need to sleep. You'll be called back after the siesta, at about 3:30.'

Smiling suggestively at the bearded director, Eloise hitched up her skirt and rubbed the towel over her soaking pussy. 'How did that scene go, honey? God, it really turned me on, peeing into her mouth like that. I can hardly wait until after lunch for some more action.'

'Maybe you don't have to wait,' he murmured, watching her.

The other girl's face was flushed with arousal. She threw the towel aside. 'I'm going crazy here, Georg. You want to fuck me in the arse?' she asked bluntly, abandoning the subtle approach.

'Yes.'

'Wonderful,' Eloise said, and they disappeared together into the dressing-room, her scarlet-tipped fingers unzipping his jeans before they were even through the door.

Knowing precisely how the other girl was feeling, her own face still glowing with embarrassment at what she had just done, Indigo tried not to look round at the hungry faces of the watching crew. She had caught the occasional interested glance since filming had stopped, and knew that two or three of them had been furtively rubbing their groins during the shoot itself.

If she chose, she could have several cocks up inside her during the next hour or so, either at the same time or separately. The mental image of bending to take one cock in her pussy and another in her mouth, and perhaps even a third in her bottom for a really dirty little siesta, was enough to make the tell-tale juices trickle down her inner thighs.

But that was not why she had come here. The whole point of impersonating an actress and starring in this blue movie was to find Heinrich's office and hopefully the Book of Punishment.

Indigo slipped out of the studio, smoothing the rubber skirt back over her hips and muttering something about finding the bathroom. This was no time to go all weak-kneed at the thought of a stiff cock. That sort of activity could wait for a more convenient time. The Book of Punishment could not.

She began to search the rest of the building for Heinrich's office and, after opening a few doors in error and having to apologise to the surprised occupants, at last found a door bearing his name.

Knocking softly, she waited for his voice. But there was no reply. Either he was not in the building yet or he had slipped out for some reason. Perhaps to have lunch, she thought, glancing up and down the corridor before cautiously trying the door. To her relief, it was not locked and she was able to enter his private office without any difficulty.

She walked across to the mahogany desk and stared down at a framed photograph of a slender silver-haired woman in a neat grey suit: presumably Heinrich's wife. Scanning the rest of the desk impatiently, she saw no books in evidence, only reams of paper and tedious-looking document folders. She raised her eyes to the shelves of antiquarian books which lined his office and sighed. The Book of Punishment could easily be among this collection of faded leather spines. But it would take some time to check every title.

Would she be able to recognise Heinrich if he walked into the office now? Her father had known him well; they had been old friends in the book world. Yet she herself had only met the Swiss book dealer on one occasion, a day lodged firmly in her memory because it was the first time she had ever seen an erotic publication. She had not been particularly young – perhaps seventeen, perhaps a little older – but her father had always kept her away from that side of his life, careful not to introduce her to such dubious pleasures before she was old enough to appreciate them. Like most teenagers, she had known about dirty magazines, and even seen the odd blue movie at sleep-over parties. But she had found centrefold photographs boring and the acting in those movies predictable. The revelation that books on the same subject existed, books which captured the imagination and left her pussy wet with feverish anticipation, changed her entire outlook on sex.

Still a virgin at that time – though admittedly an expert at hand-jobs and back-seat sucking – reading those first few erotic volumes had left her eager to experience real penetration.

It was Heinrich she had fantasised about most in those early years. He was the man who had slipped her a copy of Tesney's *Bound for Eternity*, advising her not to show it to her father. When she flicked through the book in front of him, cheeks growing hot with embarrassment as she guessed a strongly erotic content from the illustrations, Heinrich had smiled in a less than fatherly way and given her his personal phone number in Geneva.

'Call me anytime you want to talk. I know how hard it can be, finding out about sex for the first time.'

After that private conversation, whenever she lay in bed reading Tesney's classic tale of two bondage-loving vampires, it had been an imaginary Heinrich who fingered her unused pussy and anus, pushing her down into the pillows to mount her roughly from behind.

Her father had never found out what Heinrich had given her: a lifelong taste for the obscene in literature. But he had watched her grow from a gawky teenager into a seductive young woman who knew what she wanted and was not afraid to pursue it.

For it was only a few months after reading *Bound for Eternity* that she had given herself to the owner of a small second-hand bookshop off the Strand, in return for several shelves of tatty Victorian erotica, some genuine, most not. A balding good-natured man in his fifties, he had appreciated the precious gift of her virginity, smiling as he wiped the blood off his cock. And she had been happy to do it, relieved to discover that taking a man's cock inside her and feeling his spunk trickle out afterwards like warm treacle was every bit as horny an experience as it had seemed in the books.

That had been the start. Now she felt that finding the Book of Punishment would bring her full circle, back to her father's obsession with antiquarian erotica, an obsession which had filled her own head with the same love of ancient leather bindings and gloriously filthy illustrations.

Indigo traced a finger along the spines on Heinrich's shelves, reading their faded gilt titles as fast as she could, pausing occasionally when she could not resist checking the condition of a rare book or flicking through a work she had never seen before.

Not all the titles were legible: those she had to take down from the shelf and open, leafing gingerly through coloured endpapers to read the title page, itself often heavily foxed and gossamer-thin. No one had said anything to her about the condition of the Book of Punishment, so she was not sure what she should be looking for, except that it was an original, a first edition. It was enough, she supposed, to own a copy of such a rare and unusual work. Though it would be a massive bonus to find it in good, or even excellent, condition.

She was so engrossed in one book which came complete with several folding illustrations that she did not hear the door to the office open and gently close at her back.

'Looking for something, my dear?'

Startled, she spun round to see Heinrich himself standing behind her. She would not have recognised him but for the way he held himself, and the secret smile on his lips. When they had met in the early '90s his hair had still been dark, and there had been a tremendous vitality in his face and body that had excited and scared her at the same time.

He was silver-haired now, a tall and distinguished gentleman in a dark pinstriped suit, a white rose thrust jauntily through one button-hole. In his hand was a vicious-looking walking-stick with a silver top cast into the shape of a naked woman on all fours. With the stick, he gestured casually to the book in her hand.

'That's an excellent Rutland, my dear, all the fold-outs completely intact. Do you own a copy?'

'No.'

'I could sell it to you if you like. A special price for a very special friend.'

She slid the nineteenth-century volume back onto the shelf, trying to hide her trembling hands. 'I'm not interested, sorry. But you're right about one thing. I did come here to buy a book.'

'The Book of Punishment.'

'You have it?'

Heinrich smiled, coming further into the office. 'You English are so curiously persistent. Just like your late father.'

'I'm determined to buy the Book of Punishment, Heinrich. Name your price, I'll consider anything.'

'How foolish of you.'

Indigo came round the desk to stand in front of him. Her heart was racing at a frightening speed but she refused to give up. She fumbled with the rubber bra top, yanking it off to expose her firm breasts, the nipples springing to attention under his steady gaze. Her hands dropped to her hips and she stood before him, back straight and breasts thrust proudly forwards above the tiny black rubber skirt.

'I'm serious. You can have me bent over this desk if you want. But I'm not leaving here without the book.'

'Ah, my lovely Indigo.' Heinrich gave a deep sigh, leaning on his stick and considering her bare breasts with no change of expression. 'At one time such an offer would have had me drooling all over you, fingers in your pants and my cock stiff as a poker. But look at me, I'm too old for that now. Straight sex no longer has the same appeal. I'm afraid you will have to offer me something a little more ... unusual ... if you want me to divulge the book's whereabouts.'

'Unusual?'

Heinrich lifted the walking-stick and stroked it tenderly down the rounded curve of her bottom in the rubber skirt. 'Perhaps perverted might be a more accurate description of my tastes.'

'I see.'

He smiled like an old wolf, his lips lifting away to reveal a row of sharp off-white teeth. 'I doubt it, my dear.'

6

'How do you feel, Indigo?'

'Like my chest is being flattened.'

'But still comfortable, I hope. The straps aren't digging into your ribs or restricting your breathing?'

Sitting upright on the bed, Indigo managed to roll her shoulders and take three deep breaths in quick succession. She exhaled in an exaggerated fashion, lips pursed, and shook her head.

'They're tight. But it's not a problem.'

'Excellent.'

'What exactly are the straps for, Heinrich? And why do I have to wear this hideous outfit over the top?'

'Don't worry about the straps, they're for later. The hideous dress is actually a rather beautiful Victorian-style nightdress which is intended to cover the straps so they don't show. Is there anything else you need me to explain?'

Indigo was beginning to suspect what the old man intended and was feeling a little freaked out by the prospect, but she had come such a long way that she was not about to give up simply because she disliked the rules of the game. No, she was willing to do whatever it took to get her hands on the Book of Punishment.

'Who else knows about this discreet little dungeon of yours, or is it common knowledge?'

'Only a handful of my staff know that this place exists. It's my own private indulgence; I keep it locked at all times and only I have the key. Apart from the cleaners, of course, and they don't care what I get up to so long as I keep paying their wages.' Heinrich smiled, a touch of cynicism in his voice. 'One of the rewards for being such a successful businessman is that people stop asking you questions and are merely content to lend you money and watch it grow.'

'So if I were to scream . . .?'

'Nobody would hear you. Nobody would come.'

'I just wondered.'

'Now, if you could slip these onto your eyes,' Heinrich continued, calmly passing her a double-ended plastic vial containing two contact lenses, 'we can move on to the teeth.'

'Teeth?'

As he watched, she bent her head and, with an unfaltering hand, inserted a soft plastic lens into each eye. Her vision blurred with tears but it was not impossible to see. She blinked a few times, trying to get used to the discomfort.

'Well done,' he murmured approvingly. 'I'm glad to see you're not the squeamish type. Yes, teeth. I had my own incisors made specially, of course, so they're a perfect fit. But I always keep a spare set here for my lady visitors. They won't be as convincing as custom-made teeth but I think we can probably get a reasonable match. Just don't play hard to get, huh? You might end up choking on them.'

She tried not to recoil in horror as Heinrich passed her an open attaché-case lined with blue velvet and displaying what appeared to be two sets of shiny teeth, top and bottom. Except they're not real teeth, she reassured herself firmly. They looked more like her late grandmother's dentures. Her hand hovered over the gleaming white selection for a moment, unsure what to do.

'How do I . . .?'

'Take one and try it on.'

Conscious of his penetrating gaze, Indigo fumbled for one of the sinister white sets and slipped it over her real teeth before he could accuse her of losing her nerve. The false teeth wobbled slightly at first, feeling odd and clunky in her mouth. After a few minor adjustments, though, they managed to stay in place even when she rolled her jaw experimentally from side to side. She did the same with the upper jaw, then waved the case away and ran her tongue over the sharp white teeth.

'They feel really . . .' She hesitated, staring at herself in the mirror opposite the bed. Thanks to the coloured lenses, her eyes had become brilliant green slits on a black background, and now she appeared to have real fangs in her mouth. 'Weird.'

'Yes.'

'Are you trying to turn me into a vampire?'

'No,' the old man laughed, turning to rummage through one of the other cases behind him on the bed. 'Or rather, yes. But you're not meant to become one yet. I have to bite you first, then you become a vampire. That's how it works.'

'Bite me?'

He flashed her a quick smile, lips drawn back to display those wolfish incisors again. 'In the neck.'

'Seriously? Because I don't think . . .' Her voice tailed off as she realised he was holding up a small plastic bag containing something red and squidgy. 'What's that?'

'Blood.'

Her eyes widened on his face. 'Whose blood?'

'Some unfortunate pig's, I should imagine. Definitely not human, my dear, so you can stop looking at me as though I were Hannibal Lecter. I believe this is what they used in Elizabethan theatres when they needed gore for a stage fight. This little packet tucks in there, under the lace neck of your nightdress, and when I sink my fangs into your sweet flesh . . .'

'Oh my god!'

'Blood everywhere. The dress will be quite ruined. I hope you don't mind. You look so fetching in it.'

'Heinrich,' she asked bluntly, 'are you mad?'

'Not at all. I merely idolise the concept of the vampire. They're such romantic creatures and yet there's nothing sentimental about them.' He pointed up at the complicated system of wires and pulleys above their heads. 'That's my real triumph, up there. I had this rig made to my own specifications. It's perfectly safe. Everything is controlled with this little remote.'

'You built all this, just so you could fly?'

'Naturally, my dear.' He exposed the fang-like white teeth again and spread his arms in a theatrical manner, half serious, half self-mocking. 'For I am the demon vampire, master of the undead, and you are my virgin bride. Does the prospect excite you?'

Indigo stared up at him, surprised by the hot seep of moisture from between her pussy lips. She had expected to find this amusing, a way of humouring the old gentleman in return for the Book of Punishment, but instead she was becoming aroused.

'Yes.'

Heinrich raised his eyebrows, clearly delighted by her response. 'Really?'

Dragging the heavy white folds of her Victorian-style nightdress up to her waist, Indigo examined her bare pussy. It seemed a little puffy down there, the lips pinkish and swollen, as though she had already been fucked. Using just two fingers, she expertly stimulated her clitoris to an erect quivering bud, dipping once or twice into her tight pussy for lubrication. To her satisfaction, her pussy was soon nicely wet and open for business. Spreading her whole palm over her cunt, Indigo rubbed hard at the responsive flesh, imagining the older man sinking his fangs into her unprotected neck as she used the heel of her hand to firmly manipulate her clitoris.

While Heinrich watched in silence, she continued to masturbate like that for several minutes, drawing her knees right up to her chest and bringing herself to an intense orgasm. Her short high gasps of pleasure were not faked, and the answering bulge at the crotch of his black leather trousers soon told her they were both ready for sex.

'It certainly looks like it,' she murmured.

Heinrich leaned forwards without speaking and inserted one long finger into the hot pulsing crack of her pussy. It moved sensuously inside, exploring her eager flesh at its leisure. Even through the blurred vision of her contact lenses she could see his face tighten with instant fascinated lust.

'Yes,' he breathed, withdrawing his finger to examine the thick creamy streaks of pussy juice. 'The cunt cannot lie.'

He raised his head and their eyes met. Suddenly Indigo was a teenager again, fresh-faced and ripe for corruption, remembering with a shiver how he had slipped her that dirty book during one of her father's sales trips to Geneva, how she had been so eager to surrender her virginity to him, how she had enjoyed all those fantasies of crude animalistic sex that usually involved him buggering her while she ground her hips against the bed.

Without meaning to, she let her thighs fall further apart. The smell of her excited pussy was unmistakable now, as was the blatant invitation for the older man to fuck her. Yet still Heinrich did not respond, did not lean forwards and cover her body with his own, merely watching her with those strange predatory eyes.

He stood up from the bed, breaking the spell. 'Not yet, my dear. Be patient, and you will see how prolonging the wait only increases your pleasure.'

His hands went to his groin. Unlacing the leather thongs which kept his trousers fastened, he released his cock. Fully erect, it sprang out proudly from his body, the swollen purplish tip shiny with pre-come. Below its thick stalk, a pair of massive hairless balls hung loose.

Indigo stared up at this vision with greedy eyes, her sex twitching as if it longed to be entered. So here at last was the penis she had craved as an inexperienced seventeen-year-old, imagining how the beast would grow as she sucked on it, never having seen a real penis before and only able to guess how its satisfying girth might feel in her mouth, how it would spurt hot seed down her throat at the glorious moment of climax. Now it seemed those early fantasies were about to come true; Indigo could barely contain her excitement.

Nevertheless, not wishing to disobey the demon vampire, master of the undead, she lay back on the bed in her high-necked virginal nightdress and waited as instructed, rubbing her damp thighs together, her face flushed and impatient.

'When the time comes,' he promised, reaching for the remote control, 'you will fly through the air like a vampire bride with your own blood streaming down your breasts.'

One of the buttons on the remote control controlled the lighting; the overhead spotlights went out and the room was lit by a dull luminous glow from panels set into the walls at intervals. Through the semi-darkness, she watched Heinrich position himself at the far end of the narrow room which served as his dungeon and private studio, then ascend in a whirr of machinery until he was suspended only a few feet from the ceiling. His face, bloodless and sinister, was lit by a single projector light, hidden up there amongst the pulleys, playing flickering images of fire and drifting mist across his features.

His penis, now monstrously erect, jutted out below his belly like a spear. An eerie music began to play, a high fluctuating note which made her neck prickle with apprehension as she lay there, waiting for him to strike. At that moment, the illusion he had created felt very real: the virgin asleep on the bed, innocent and unprotected, and the vampire master, poised in the dark air above her. Even though it was a charade, she still wanted to scream, to beg him to stop before it was too late, but her lips seemed frozen together.

With a terrifying gesture, Heinrich spread his arms wide and the black cape draped itself around them like the wings of a giant bat. His fangs glistened as he tilted himself into a horizontal position, the head of his exposed cock pulsing with urgent desire. He cried aloud in some language she did not understand, the words guttural and commanding. And as he did so, the pulley wheels turned again and he was flying high across the ceiling in a flicker of red mist and flames.

Finding her voice at last, Indigo screamed.

Heinrich was on top of her an instant later, his great black wings blotting out the light and his breath hot in her face.

She caught the flash of sharp white fangs and tried to throw herself from the bed, but strong hands gripped her by the shoulders and pinned her down as he sank his teeth triumphantly into her throat. She heard a distinct pop as the concealed bag of pig's blood burst, and felt wetness begin to spread across the high white lace neck of her nightdress and down into her cleavage.

'Now you are mine,' he told her, his voice muffled against her throat, and he pulled back to reveal lips and teeth smeared with sticky red blood. 'Mine for all eternity.'

His head bent again and he sucked at her neck, exactly as though he were drinking her blood for real. His penis pressed hard against her hips and she felt him reach down and pull up the heavy material of her nightdress to lie between her naked thighs, groaning and slurping there like a drunkard.

Her breathing quickened as she imagined what might come next. Her sex felt like an open gash under his belly, aching to be entered and used. The torture was exquisite.

Leaning back to admire his handiwork, Heinrich took a moment to examine her strange transformation from virgin to vampire. His voice was thick with arousal. 'Isn't that a beautiful sight? You're a creature of darkness now. Fly for me, my bride. Spread your wings and let me see you fly through the air.'

His hand clenched on the remote control and Indigo felt a powerful tugging around her waist and ribs. Above them, the machinery whirred and clicked.

Suddenly she was being lifted clear of the bed and into the air, her cry one of excitement as well as fear. For a moment, she flailed helplessly, terrified of falling. Then slowly she realised that it was safe – she was held there in perfect security by the hidden belt and wires. There was nothing to fear. Her need to climax was even more urgent than before, her thighs rubbing restlessly together, her pussy dripping with lush fragrant juices. Suspended high above the bed, she tore at the blood-stained dress and moaned with pleasure as her breasts sprang loose. She grasped them in both hands and squeezed, revelling in the warm slimy feel of her flesh, her nipples stiff and proud.

From her elevated position, she looked down and saw Heinrich still crouched on the bed below her. He was staring up at her as he masturbated, his body hunched over like some sort of malignant demon, massive cock straining in his fist as his orgasm approached. Lost in his fantasy, he clearly believed she was his vampire bride, flying above his head and eager to join him in the world of the undead. Briefly, she allowed herself to believe it too. If it helped them both get off, she thought drily, where was the harm?

'Come to me, my master,' she cried, lifting her nightdress to reveal the dark triangle of her sex. 'Let me take your vampire seed inside me.'

Heinrich needed no further encouragement. His left hand fumbled for the remote and he too rose towards the ceiling, rampant erection poking out from beneath his belly. She grasped it with greedy fingers, drawing their bodies closer together. The slippery purplish head jerked into her palm, rigid and pulsing, a streak of pre-come glistening across the slit. There would be no time to enjoy him inside her, she realised with a stab of frustration. The vampire master was almost ready to come, poised right there on the edge of orgasm.

Holding his cock firmly against her pussy lips, she masturbated him with smooth rapid strokes. Heinrich's face was darkly flushed now, his breathing erratic. She worked him expertly, pressing and lodging the head of his cock deeper and deeper between the moist lips of her sex until they were almost fucking in mid-air. The wires shook ominously above their heads, the steel pulleys creaking under their combined weight.

Then Heinrich gave a great cry and shot his full load against her pussy, spunk drenching the open lips and dripping liberally down her thighs.

Dropping his wilting penis as soon as it had finished pumping its come, Indigo stuck her fingers up inside her sex, deliciously hot and slimy with sperm. It took only a few hard rubs before her pussy contracted into an intense orgasm. Crying with pleasure, she sunk her own teeth deep into his neck, their bodies locked inextricably together for a few dizzying seconds before Heinrich hit the remote control and they were lowered in a tangle of leather and bloodstained lace.

'That was amazing,' she gasped as they collapsed together on the bed, rolling onto her back to stare up at the wires which had held her so securely in mid-air. 'Though I still don't believe in vampires.'

Heinrich managed a weak smile as he sat up, tucking his penis back into his trousers. 'But you do still want the Book of Punishment, my dear?'

'Naturally.'

'It's no longer in my possession, I'm afraid. But I can

tell you where it is if you wish to make an offer. I sold it to Herr Wolfmann, a dealer with a large private residence on the other side of the lake. He's holding a party tonight and I believe my nephew Christian will be attending. He could escort you there, if you wish to meet Wolfmann and come to some sort of arrangement.' Heinrich dismantled his blood-streaked fangs and stood examining them with apparent fascination. 'But you won't have much time to lay your hands on the book.'

'Why not?' she demanded.

'Because Wolfmann bought it on behalf of a third party,' he said coolly, sliding the teeth into his pocket, 'who arrived from London only this morning. His name, I believe, is Mr Dervil Badon.'

7

The man's gnarled fingers played the old-fashioned metal dial like an instrument, turning it first one way, then another, listening to each click with an air of reverent absorption. Finally the combination was complete; the heavy metal door creaked as it swung open beneath his touch. With a sigh of relief, Wolfmann reached into the depths of his safe and withdrew a rectangular object wrapped in plain brown paper. This he caressed for a moment with loving fingers before handing it reluctantly to Dervil, who was standing behind him.

'The Book of Punishment,' Herr Wolfmann murmured, stepping back to watch his client examine it. 'The first and only genuine edition. It was banned on grounds of public obscenity, of course, within days of the initial publication. There were 250 illegal copies printed in Paris the following year, but they were not true to the original and lacked illustrations. I have seen several of those in my time, easily spotted by their inferior boards and lack of ridging to the spine.'

'But this is genuine? Not a counterfeit?'

Wolfmann made a wry face, as though hurt that his professional expertise could be doubted even for a second. 'I spent the better part of last night examining this book, Mr Badon. It is indeed a genuine first edition, printed in the year 1797.'

Dervil unwrapped the brown paper coverings, his hands trembling and a fine sweat on his forehead as he considered what he held in his hands. The wrappings fell away to reveal heavily embossed eighteenth-century leather boards and a gilt spine which appeared, apart from the odd crack at top and bottom, to be intact. In all his imaginings, he had never expected to find the book in such good condition.

'I can hardly believe it's mine at last,' he admitted with a laugh, placing the book on Wolfmann's desk and turning to the title page. He traced the text lightly with his fingertip and began to read aloud. 'The Book of Punishment. A treatise on the ancient and venerable art of chastisement, translated from the Italian by a disciple of the late Master himself. Printed for the proprietors, near Temple Bar, London, 1797.'

The dealer was smiling. 'Mild foxing to the titles and some interior pages. Otherwise in fine condition for its age.'

'Good god,' Dervil said softly, leafing through with his fingertips and discovering a depiction of some hellish dungeon, dozens of naked writhing bodies chained together. Standing above them on platforms stood male guards, wielding vicious bullwhips and with unmistakable erections poking out from their medieval-style hose, as though aroused by the cruel lashes they had inflicted on the bodies below. 'No wonder the authorities banned it.'

'There are others further in, even more obscene and diabolical. Keep looking, if you wish to be shocked.'

Excited by the potential uses of such a book, Dervil continued to glance through its yellowing pages, barely able to read any of the fascinating text which accompanied each illustration as he discovered increasingly intricate and vile depictions of suffering and sexual arousal. He felt his own penis stiffen, staring down at one unfortunate young woman being used by three men at once, while a fourth man branded her buttocks with an elaborate W – presumably for 'Whore', he mused, admiring the artist's keen eye for detail. Her face was a pale oval of pain and ecstasy, thick dark hair streaming unbound about her shoulders and naked spine. A few pages further on, the same young woman was shown hanging upside-down from a bar, arms secured by ropes behind her back. A swarthy-faced hunchback appeared to be applying some sort of threshing flail to her buttocks whilst another knelt to feed his penis into her obedient mouth.

The similarities between these scenes and his own life as a master were too striking to ignore. Though his own style of administering punishment seemed almost tame in comparison, he thought drily.

Wolfmann was at his shoulder, watching the changing emotions on his face. 'Is it everything you expected?'

'It's grotesque.'

'But you still wish to purchase it?' Wolfmann pressed him, a note of uncertainty in the older man's voice. 'We had a gentleman's agreement. The book was to be paid for on collection. Otherwise I would never have procured such an expensive item on your behalf.'

'Stop sweating, Wolfmann,' he said lazily. 'Now that I'm satisfied as to the book's authenticity, the money will be in your account by close of business today.'

The dealer looked relieved. He removed the Book of Punishment from Dervil's hands and wrapped it in plain brown paper again, then slid it back into his safe with an apologetic smile. 'In that case, you will not mind if I hold onto it until then. Just in case there are any problems at the bank.'

Dervil was more than a little irritated by the man's untrusting attitude but he shrugged, not bothering to argue. He had seen enough for now. He was content to wait until the transaction was complete before seeing the rest. By this evening one of the few remaining copies of the original Book of Punishment would be in his possession, to read and consult whenever he wished.

'I hope you will grace my little celebration tonight,' Wolfmann continued, closing the safe and concealing it behind a garish modern oil painting which consisted of various indiscriminate blobs and swirls. 'It's to be a fancy-dress party on the theme of punishment. I can arrange for you to hire some suitable costumes if you wish. There'll be quite a few dealers and collectors from Geneva there that you know. It should provide an amusing diversion for you and your ... um ... lady friend.'

'I'm sure Natasha will be delighted,' he replied.

When he left the dealer's house, Dervil decided to take a taxi back to the hotel and collect Natasha for lunch. They paid a brief visit to the bank, to be reassured by a tall bespectacled clerk that the money would be electronically transferred into Herr Wolfmann's account by the close of business, and then strolled on into the tourist areas of the city. The streets were much as he remembered: well kept and pleasant, if a little hotter and more crowded with holiday-makers now that it was summer. It had been late autumn the last time he travelled to this part of Switzerland. He knew what he was looking for and eventually found it: a small family-run restaurant where Dervil had dined a few years before, with a rather different woman on a separate book-buying mission.

Feeling a touch nostalgic, he insisted on a table outside on their cool shaded veranda looking down towards the lake, and ordered the same meal: an iced borscht soup, followed by roast lamb with sauerkraut. For the first time since Natasha had told him the book was on the open market again, Dervil allowed himself to relax.

He raised his wine glass in a toast, smiling across the table at Natasha. 'Here's to my acquisition of the Book of Punishment. It's costing me a small fortune, but what a prize!'

'When do I get to see it?' she asked, sipping at her own wine with a petulant expression.

'Patience, Natasha. Once it's safely in my possession, you can try every punishment in the book if you desire.'

'I do desire,' she nodded and grimaced, poking a fork into the sauerkraut piled high on her plate. 'What is this muck? Are we really supposed to eat it?'

Dervil grinned, forking a liberal amount into his mouth. His voice was indistinct. 'If you'd prefer to bend over and have your arse stuffed with it, I'm happy to oblige.'

'Pig!'

'We make a good team, don't we?' he murmured appreciatively, then paused, seeing a dangerous familiar glint in her eyes. 'Though not in a romantic sense, of course. You haven't forgotten this is strictly a business trip, have you?'

'How could I forget? You tell me often enough, you bastard!'

'Better to be honest about it,' he shrugged.

'One day,' she threatened him in that thick Russian accent, lowering her voice to a whisper as though afraid the hovering waiter could hear what was being discussed, 'I hope you meet a woman who makes you as unhappy as you have made me. Then you will be sorry, Dervil Badon.'

He laughed and tossed back the last of his wine, looking down to meet the hurt in her eyes without a single shred of remorse.

'There isn't a woman alive who could make me unhappy. Do you know why, my darling? Because I was born without a heart.'

She shivered superstitiously, her nipples visible under the thin silk of her blouse. 'My god, don't joke about such things!'

Dervil shrugged and clicked his fingers for the waiter, suddenly bored with the conversation and eager to move on.

His tone was sharp, deliberately final. 'Who said I was joking?'

* * *

The party thrown in his honour at Wolfmann's turned out to be an even tamer affair than Dervil had feared. In the end, he provided his own costume, black leather jeans with a sombre black shirt, chosen deliberately to complement Natasha's gold sheath dress, a dramatic ensemble which barely concealed the hobble he himself had fitted to her shapely legs before leaving their hotel for the evening. Although it had been amusing at first to watch the beautiful transsexual shuffling along behind him like some overgrown Golden Labrador, it was rather less entertaining to encounter a roomful of Swiss book dealers and collectors in similar attire.

Clutching a motley assortment of crops, straps, and decorative studded paddles, the other guests stood about Wolfmann's spacious living-room, nodding politely to each other, all of them desperate to appear relaxed in their leather harness wear and full rubber body suits.

Dervil lifted a glass of wine from a passing waiter's tray, resigning himself to several hours of unremitting boredom. Some of the younger women in the room were attractive, it was true, but did he really have the energy to initiate any of them into the joys of submission?

Spotting an old acquaintance across the room, he made his way towards him, amused by Natasha's geisha-like shuffle at his back. 'Gunter? I didn't expect to see you at this sort of party.'

'I made a special effort in order to congratulate you.' Gunter shook his hand with surprising warmth. 'The Book of Punishment! It's all over town that you finally managed to acquire it. You must be pleased.'

'You wanted it for yourself, I believe.'

'I couldn't match your offer. No matter. Have you had a chance to examine it yet? Was it worth the price?'

'Every penny.'

The older man glanced over his shoulder, a smile flickering on his thin lips. 'And who is this vision?'

'How remiss of me. Please allow me to introduce you to Natasha, a colleague of mine from London. Natasha, this is Gunter, with whom I've been doing business for nearly twenty years.'

Gunter kissed her hand in gallant fashion and exchanged a few words with the blonde, his eyebrows rising steeply at her thick accent. 'Is that a Russian accent?'

'Natasha is a Muscovite by birth, but a Londoner by choice. You find her attractive, Gunter? Since you seem to be alone, why not take her as your companion for the evening?'

'Oh, I couldn't!'

'Too tall, too Amazonian for you?'

'Nothing like that, she's stunning. But what about your own pleasure this evening? I can't simply . . .'

Dervil smiled, ignoring Natasha's silent fury. He took her hand and placed it in Gunter's. 'I insist. Think of it as a consolation prize, my friend.'

'You're too kind.'

'I find it entertaining to see Natasha in the arms of another man. A little whim of mine. No need to worry about her running away, either. She's been hobbled, as you can see.'

The older man nodded, already admiring the cruelly restrictive hobble beneath her dress which prevented Natasha from moving her feet more than a few inches apart. He drew the tall blonde closer and slipped an arm about her waist, having to look up at her in spite of his own height, his expression benevolent, almost fatherly.

'What has that brute done to you? It seems an act of wickedness to hobble such a beautiful creature. Though I must admit, it lends her a certain vulnerability which is extremely fetching.' Gunter's voice dropped to a whisper as he leaned forwards to caress her cheek. 'Am I too old to please you? What do you think, *meine Liebling*?'

'I think whatever my master tells me to think,' Natasha replied submissively, but much to his amusement her eyes flicked to Dervil's face as she spoke, an angry glitter in them.

Gunter laughed with delight at her response, pinching her cheek as though she were an overgrown baby. 'Obedient as well as beautiful. I am even more in your debt, Dervil.'

'Feel free to use her as you wish. Test her limits, see how far you can take her before she breaks.'

'Yes, indeed.' Gunter hesitated, glancing down at the rubber-covered paddle in his hand. 'I brought this because of the theme, but it seems a little harsh on first acquaintance to . . .'

Responding to Dervil's silent gesture of command, the transsexual turned and bent over a low-backed chair. Grasping the hem of her gold dress in both hands, she drew it shamelessly up over her thighs and hips to expose a sturdy-looking bottom. Beneath the rustling shiny material, she wore nothing but a gold sequinned thong, its narrow strap sinking deep into the crevice between her buttocks, and the hobble, a cruel instrument of restraint holding her ankles firmly together.

Widening her stance as far as the hobble would allow her, which was no more than a few inches, Natasha leaned forwards and slid her hands down the legs of the chair until she was almost touching the carpet. The muscles in her calves and thighs tautened admirably above the high gold stilettos. Her entire crotch was now on full and blatant display, the tantalising crack of her sex barely hidden by the gold lacy thong.

Licking his lips, Gunter stared down at the bare smooth-skinned bottom raised so provocatively for his paddle. Yet still he did not take advantage of her submissive posture. 'Is she always this . . .?'

'Eager?'

Gunter nodded.

'Almost invariably, I'm afraid. It's a real weakness in her nature; I have to chastise her for it all the time. Now use that paddle, Gunter, and make her squirm. Perhaps you'll find out why I paid so much for the Book of Punishment.'

Dervil watched in amused silence as the older man took up his position behind Natasha and weighed the paddle dubiously in his hand. Conversation across the room gradually died away, all eyes turning to the curious spectacle near the veranda windows: the broad-shouldered, statuesque blonde bending for a paddling from mild-mannered Gunter. During their exchange, Natasha had not altered her obedient stance by a single inch nor uttered a word in protest. Now her knuckles turned white as her grip tightened on the chair legs, her face a little flushed, no doubt aware that the punishment was about to begin. She had been through this before, after all, with many different men and in far more embarrassing situations than this. But Dervil supposed that experience could never quite remove the sting of that first blow, nor the fear of it.

'Is she ready?'

He raised his eyebrows at Gunter's hesitant whisper. 'You are in charge here. You should merely begin.'

Nervously clearing his throat, Gunter leaned forward to peer into her reddened face, hanging upside-down over the chair. 'Are you ready, my dear?'

'Yes, sir.'

'Um . . . right. Excellent.'

Gunter raised the paddle and, after another momentary hesitation, brought it down smartly on her up-turned bottom.

Much to her credit, Natasha let out her breath in an explosive hiss but did not move. The paddle, which had landed rather awkwardly on the left cheek, had left behind a dull red stain as though wine had been spilled under the surface of the skin. Taking a step backwards,

97

Gunter stared down at that stain in consternation for a moment. It took an encouraging nod from Dervil for him to raise the paddle and bring it down again, this time on the other cheek.

Admiring the symmetrical flush spreading across her left buttock, Gunter gave a strangled whoop of excitement and struck her once more. This time, the rubber-covered paddle landed squarely across both buttocks with a loud and comprehensive thwack, making the hobbled Natasha hop on the spot in an undignified fashion and curse beneath her breath.

With a frown, Gunter let the paddle drop to his side. He glanced over his shoulder at Dervil. 'Too hard?'

'Not at all,' he said, becoming a little impatient. 'She's just getting warmed up. Keep going, you'll spoil the rhythm.'

'I do apologise.'

Gunter continued with the punishment as instructed, counting methodically in German between each stroke, his gaze focused on the quivering flesh beneath the paddle.

Natasha was holding onto the chair legs with grim determination, her breathing ragged and her eyes shut tight, no doubt surprised by the older man's strength but too proud to admit her discomfort. The bunched-up material of her gold dress was a superb foil to the pale skin of her thighs, the muscles clenched hard as she tried to keep her balance in spite of the restrictive hobble.

Tearing his eyes from her reddening bottom, Dervil saw with some amusement that a small crowd had gathered around them, intrigued couples and single men settling on sofas and chairs to watch the action. At each rhythmic stroke, more than a dozen pairs of eyes swivelled from the paddle swinging in Gunter's hand to Natasha's prettily flushed bottom, their muttered approval indicating a morbid fascination with this lesson in domination.

Gunter himself appeared oblivious to his audience, concentrating instead on the reddish mottled buttocks raised towards him in a gesture of penitence. He took his task seriously, that was clear, no longer paying any heed to the cries and moans of the blonde as he paddled her bottom with an almost professional dedication. Not that Gunter was unaffected by such feminine submission, Dervil noted cynically. There was a sheen of sweat on the high domed forehead and a growing bulge in his trousers. It would not be long before the paddling stopped and turned to something more intimate.

As his gaze swept the room, Dervil encountered a pair of sharp determined eyes fixed on his face.

He frowned, his own eyes narrowing; there was something familiar about the girl in black rubber, watching him so intently from across the room, yet he could not quite remember where he had seen her before. At that moment, the girl glanced hurriedly away, no doubt realising that he had seen her staring.

Dervil was amused by such a pretence of shyness, assuming that it was a pretence. He allowed his gaze to linger deliberately over the ripe breasts spilling from her bodice and those muscular thighs which promised every man in that room a wild and energetic ride, especially if the girl was on top. Though young woman would be a more accurate description. She was far too self-assured to be a teenager. The young man beside her was not much older, a scrawny boy in an ill-fitting leather body suit. She had barely looked at her companion since he had spotted them. They were not lovers, he thought shrewdly, noting the physical distance between them. Brother and sister, perhaps?

He clapped the older man on the shoulder. 'I think she's probably had enough now.'

'Are you sure?'

'Natasha would never admit it herself. But she's beginning to weaken. Look at her legs, they're shaking.'

99

'Yes, what a fool I am.' Gunter helped the transsexual blonde to sit down on the low-backed chair, his tone solicitous. 'Can I get you something to drink, Natasha? Some more wine, or a glass of warm brandy, perhaps?'

'Just give her some space. She'll be fine. Tell me, who's that dark-haired girl over by the buffet table? The one in black rubber. She seems vaguely familiar.'

Gunter glanced across the room, wiping his sweaty palms on his trousers. His thick eyebrows shot up in surprise.

'That's the delightful Indigo. Surely you must remember her, Mortimer's precocious little daughter? Though he didn't take her around the book fairs that often, I suppose.' He paused, sounding curious. 'She must be here with young Christian, Heinrich's nephew. Seems a little odd, though. I wasn't aware they were such good friends.'

'Christian? That's the boy with her?'

'That's right. He's in the book business too.'

Seeming a little impatient, Gunter adjusted the overt bulge in his trousers. It was obvious he was still aroused and eager to relieve himself. The older man's glance returned to Natasha, who was slumped in the chair where he had left her, unable to get comfortable because of the cruelly restrictive hobble.

The gold dress was still bunched about her waist, the expensive material crushed and crumpled after the indignity of her punishment. Her matching thong glistened under the spotlights, barely hiding the full lips of her sex beneath. It was a decadent sight, and one which even Dervil – who had only brought Natasha along on this trip as entertainment for his business colleagues – could not help but find arousing.

'What do you think, Dervil?' Gunter asked hopefully. 'It's been several minutes now since I stopped paddling her. Will Natasha have recovered enough yet for . . .?'

'Oh, I should imagine so.'

'Thank god. I didn't think I could wait much longer.'

Straddling her flushed face without further hesitation, Gunter unzipped his trousers to produce an impressively rigid erection. This he pushed into Natasha's slack mouth with a few muttered words of encouragement.

The blonde blinked and gasped at the sudden intrusion, but soon fell into an obedient rhythm, sucking and clutching at his groin with exhausted hands. Luckily for her, she did not have to keep up that performance for very long. Dervil watched with a stab of envy as Gunter groaned and pulled her closer, his hips working fiercely as he came in a sudden rush, pumping sperm down the transsexual's throat. She was swallowing now, struggling a little, those long manicured nails trying to prevent the pulsating penis from suffocating her as it emptied.

As he finished, Natasha pushed two fingers past the tight gold lace of her thong and began to simulate a fucking motion. Her hips were right on the edge of the chair seat, rocking violently back and forth, that cruel hobble preventing her from opening her legs any wider, her whole body tilted with an almost drunken glee to receive the older man's semen.

She was making a familiar keening noise under her breath. The eyes of the audience were riveted on her tantalisingly concealed sex, those fingers working beneath the thin gold lace of her thong. Not that Natasha cared what they thought, crying out in sudden uninhibited orgasm. Her back arched impossibly and both hips lifted right off the chair until she was supported by nothing but her neck, cradled low on the chair back, and her high gold heels. In spite of her restricted position, Natasha continued to rock herself back and forth, extending her orgasm for as long as possible, her wrist a blur between her thighs, fingers shoved crudely in and out, up and down, the hobble still holding her legs together at the ankle, her face sticky with sperm and saliva as Gunter stared down at her in disbelief.

Perhaps he ought to have warned Gunter in advance, Dervil thought wryly, amused by the expression on his old friend's face. There was never anything half-hearted about one of Natasha's orgasms. Especially when she was able to climax in public like this, playing to a fascinated audience of innocents and BDSM wannabes.

Dervil turned to fetch himself another glass of chilled white wine, conscious of a growing stiffness in his own crotch, and came face to face with the dark-haired girl who had been watching him from across the room.

So she was Mortimer's daughter. What had Gunter called her? The delightful Indigo.

His eyes skimmed her figure in the black rubber suit, her breasts even more enticing close up, her waist charmingly slender. Yes, she was certainly sexy enough for any man to want her, and those were the eyes of a shrewd and intelligent young woman. Quite a powerful combination. And there was no sign of her young companion in the leather body suit.

'Hello,' he murmured.

The promising mouth curved into a brilliant smile. 'Hello,' she replied, coming even closer, too close really, so much shorter than him that she had to tilt her head back to meet his eyes. Indigo looked enchantingly innocent and rude at the same time, he thought. He glanced down and saw a nipple peep outrageously over the edge of her black rubber suit, breasts brushing against him as she swayed on high black heels.

Before he could mention the Book of Punishment, which he knew perfectly well she must have come here to obtain, the girl lifted a cool hand to stroke his cheek. 'I know who you are,' she murmured. 'You're the devil.'

'It has been said.'

'I enjoyed watching your friend just now. She certainly likes to be hurt. Though I was a little surprised you didn't join in.'

'I wasn't in the mood.'

'Wrong place?'

'Wrong girl,' he smiled. 'What's your name?'

She shook her head, her lips glossy and parted as she watched his face. 'No names.'

'If that's how you want to play it –'

'Can we get out of here?' she interrupted him.

'Right now?'

'I need you to hurt me,' she muttered urgently, leaning into his chest. 'Hurt me properly.'

Dervil stared down at her, his smile dying. Was the girl drunk? 'I beg your pardon?'

'Don't you want to?'

Dervil hesitated for a moment, glancing down at her svelte body in the tight black rubber. So that was her game, he thought. To sell herself in return for the Book of Punishment. It wouldn't work, of course. He had no intention of parting with it, no matter how delicious the offer. Yet he still found himself nodding, his mouth oddly dry at the prospect of marking her smooth white skin.

'Yes.'

'Come on, then.' Her hands trembling, the girl tugged at his sleeve. 'Let's go somewhere more private and you can hurt me as much as you want. Because I like it. Being hurt, that is.' She looked away, a slight colour in her face, her voice dropping to a whisper as they left the room together. 'I really, really like it.'

8

However much Indigo might tell herself that being dominated by Dervil Badon was a necessary subterfuge, a legitimate excuse for sneaking away from the party and searching Wolfmann's office, she knew it to be a lie. Well, a partial lie. She did need to find the Book of Punishment, assuming it was still on the premises, if only to check its authenticity before making a rival bid. But being hurt by Dervil was not a necessity. It was more of a bonus really, a combination of business with pleasure.

Third door to the left, Christian had whispered as they parted company at the buffet table. Wolfmann's nephew was a helpful boy, she thought. If a little submissive for her tastes.

'Do you always move this fast?'

She flashed Dervil a flirtatious smile, silently counting the doors along the corridor until they had reached number three.

'Only when I'm horny,' she admitted, not entirely lying, and tried the door handle to Wolfmann's office.

To her relief, his office was not locked. Pulling Dervil into the unlit room, she nudged the door shut with her foot and backed away from him in the darkness. She ought to have been excited. But now they were alone together, her initial plan to seduce Dervil and escape with the book was beginning to feel dangerous.

'Does that bother you?' she asked.

'A little.'

Her pulses jumped. 'How sweet!'

'I'm hardly that.' His voice was dry. 'Where's the light switch in this place? I can't see a damned thing.'

Indigo felt her way cautiously to the desk, a dark solid mass in the far shadows, until her thigh struck its edge. It was safer when he could not see her properly but there was no point putting off the inevitable. They had not come in here for a game of chess, after all. After fumbling for what felt like a desk lamp, she managed to switch one on and smiled at him through the soft intimate glow.

'Better?'

'Much,' he nodded, taking a quick glance around the room. 'Though I doubt Wolfmann would appreciate us using his private office to play master and slave. I think we ought to find another room.'

Hurriedly, Indigo unzipped the tight rubber bodice to her waist and felt her breasts spill out. His hand on the door handle, Dervil turned back to face her, his eyes fixed with sudden intent on the exposed flesh. She felt nervous under that gaze, butterflies dancing in her stomach, aware that she was playing an extremely dangerous game with this man. Yet she dared not let such an opportunity slip. If she was ever to get his sexual attention, it would be now.

Grabbing a breast in each hand, she squeezed them until the nipples began to tauten and rise up. Her pussy responded at once, contracting and moistening as she met his eyes, eager to have this man inside her even though fucking Dervil Badon was not an essential part of her plan. This was meant to be a simple beating, she had to remind herself, designed to distract him from her real objective.

'Wolfmann's too busy with his guests, he'll never find out. Let's do it right here, on the old man's desk.' Pushing various papers and documents carelessly off the desk, Indigo hoisted the rubber miniskirt to her crotch. Her smile was deliberately provocative. 'Should I bend over? Or would you prefer me on my knees?'

105

'My god, you're incorrigible.'

'What do you want to use?' Her eyes rapidly searched the dimly lit office. 'There's a walking-stick over there. Too hard?'

Dervil had been watching her with his arms folded, dark eyes amused but still wary. Now he glanced sideways at the sturdy-looking walking-stick in the corner, shaking his head.

'Definitely too hard. I don't want to cause you any damage, just hurt you. Perhaps my shoe would be . . .'

'Is that the best you can offer me? Your shoe?'

For a moment it felt as though she had pushed his patience too far. Dervil's eyes narrowed on her face and he came closer, unfolding his arms in what seemed like a threatening manner. He did not strike her, though, reaching out to stroke one of her breasts instead. She almost flinched away from his touch, only stopping herself with an effort. But it was too late. He had spotted the tiny involuntary reflex and was frowning.

'Perhaps,' he said meditatively, 'a hands-on punishment might be more appropriate.'

'Hands-on?'

Dervil was gaining control of the scene, his hand closing around her breast to cup it, undeterred by the way she had begun to shiver. He was a hard man to manipulate, she realised, lowering her eyes so he could not read the expression in them. For a moment, he weighed the sensitive flesh in his hand as though it were a fruit he was planning to buy, and stroked her nipple with long uncompromising fingers, leaving her whole body aroused and tingling. Then, silently, he examined her: the high black heels and muscular calves, the way the rubber skirt had been hitched up to expose her pussy in the skimpy black thong, her flat midriff and the firm globes of her breasts, and finally her head, bent to conceal her humiliation, dark fringe falling across her face.

106

'That's right. In my experience, which is considerable, there's only one remedy for a pushy submissive. What you need, my dear, is a good old-fashioned spanking.'

Before she could protest, he sat down in the high-backed leather swivel chair behind the desk. His eyes were so dark, she thought he really did look like a devil as he leaned back against the beautiful green leather and smiled. Crooking a long finger, Dervil beckoned her towards him. 'Come along, don't keep me waiting.'

Trembling and awkward, Indigo felt she had no choice but to obey. She approached him with nervous anticipation, used to being spanked but not entirely certain what to expect from a man like Dervil Badon. He was too unpredictable to second-guess. Sure enough, as her thighs met the leather arm of the chair, his hand curled about her wrist and jerked her forwards across his lap. With his erection pressing hard against her belly, she lay there face-down in his lap, her legs splayed wide as a frog's and her pussy damp with excitement. She was completely at his mercy like this, and she stifled a cry in her throat as the firm hands moved, adjusting her position.

What was he going to do to her? she wondered feverishly. And how much would it hurt?

She felt his fingers move down the taut ladder of her spine, tracing a line to the hollow of her back then curving across her bottom. The rubber skirt was yanked higher, exposing her smooth buttocks, embarrassingly bare except for her thong. His hand slid, dizzyingly slow and intimate, over the full cheeks and even into the cleft between, where the thong had sunk itself, and eased a finger beneath its tight strap to probe her anus.

She squirmed and moaned at his intrusion, wishing the bastard would hurry up and get it over with, spank her until her cheeks glowed red. That would at least distract her from this urgent need to have sex with him.

'Eager little thing, aren't you?'

His dry remark touched a nerve. Was her eagerness that obvious? She stopped squirming and lifted her head, staring back up at him for a moment, her mouth compressed with determination. 'Actually, I was just wondering how long it would take you to start. My bum's getting cold down there.'

'Why, you impudent . . .'

She gasped as he slapped her once across both buttocks, her pussy contracting in instant arousal. God, she was ready for this. More than ready, in fact. Her heart had begun to hammer under her ribs, her whole pelvis liquefying with anticipation as she waited for him to strike again. Dervil Badon had a reputation for being one of the most competent and professional dominants in the business. It excited her to think she was about to discover whether or not that reputation was deserved.

He leaned forwards, his voice harsh in her ear. 'If you're trying to goad me into hitting you harder, let me advise you not to bother. I've never been known for having a light hand.'

'Oh goody.'

This time he spanked her three times in quick succession, high on the less fleshy part of the buttocks, sharp enough to sting. 'Keep that up and you'll make me angry.'

'You mean,' she gasped, 'you might lose your temper?'

'Little chance of that, I'm afraid,' he said bitingly, but changed tactics and targeted the soft bouncing flesh at the top of her thighs, his hand heavy in spite of his denial.

There was a real sense of warning behind the swift flurry of blows; perhaps he was losing his temper after all, she thought. Not that she cared. Harder was what she wanted, harder was what she craved. Her hands clenched tightly into fists and she stuffed them against her mouth, her face flushed with an almost intolerable desire. Oh yes, she thought, this man knows what he's doing. His tormenting hand came down first with a cupped palm, then flat against her skin, cruel and viciously stinging, then suddenly gentle again, designed to leave her aching for more.

God, she needed to come. Her hips jerked helplessly, each slap pressing her deeper into his lap where she could feel that formidable erection swelling his trousers. The spanking was not enough, not nearly enough. Surreptitiously, she wriggled one hand beneath her belly, pushed the thong to one side and started to rub at the moist gash of her sex. Her gasps were soon punctuated by cries of pleasure, her bottom raised higher for his slaps.

'Harder,' she moaned, deeply flushed and almost incoherent as her orgasm approached. 'Harder.'

Dervil gave an odd croaking laugh, his penis rearing hard against her stomach. He was just as aroused as she was, that was obvious. Yet still he held back, refusing to give an inch. 'I'm sorry? I didn't quite catch that.'

'Please!'

'Oh yes, I enjoy hearing you beg. Can you do it again?'

'Please,' she hissed over her shoulder, hot and sweaty, her pride gone. She rotated her hips under his forceful hand, desperate to come now, to rub herself to orgasm as Dervil Badon spanked her, as she dangled over his lap with her moist lips open and her legs spread like some sluttish rag doll. 'Please, please, please!'

His slaps intensified, then suddenly his finger was back there, at the entrance to her anus, pushing inside and penetrating that dirty little hole with complete disregard for her dignity.

Her face flushed crimson with shame. 'Not in there . . . stop it . . . oh my god, you filthy . . .'

But she did not really want him to stop. In her head, of course, Indigo was already imagining how it would feel to be buggered by this man. Not merely fucked, but bent over and sodomised until her legs could no longer support her and his spunk was trickling out of that well-stretched hole. She knew how it would play out between them in her perfect fantasy. Her thong would be tugged right down to her thighs, exposing her pussy and the narrow opening of her anus; she would be thrown forwards across the hard walnut desk, cooling her hot face against the wood; his swollen penis, cruel and urgent now, would be released from his trousers; then she would feel his hands dragging her buttocks apart, as he guided himself into that tiny burning orifice between her cheeks and stretched it wide open. The rhythm of his thrusts, like the regular rise and fall of his hand on her bottom, would bring her closer and closer to orgasm.

Indigo screamed with pleasure as she came at last, pressing all three fingers deep inside her sex, the muscles in her wrist aching as she tried to imitate the thrusts of a penis, her pussy bumping against Dervil's trousers with every jerk of her hips. Everything seemed jumbled up in her mind, her head whirling with filthy impossible images, Dervil somehow thrusting into her pussy and anus at the same time, his breath hot on her neck, sperm oozing out of both passages afterwards to leave her sticky and trembling and gloriously sated.

Dervil withdrew his finger from her anus and pushed her off his lap, watching as she tumbled to the floor. 'Do you ever do anything by half measures?' he asked, the dry words barely registering as she swam back to reality through a hazy mist of pleasure.

She lay on the floor at his feet for some minutes, trying to recover her breath, her skin pink with exertion, her hair dishevelled and almost covering her face. The thick woollen rug felt rough against her nipples, with the rubber skirt still hoisted around her waist. Being hurt by Dervil Badon was a wild and incredible

110

experience, just as she had suspected it would be when she saw him across the room, taking in his expression of cruel disinterest as his girlfriend was paddled until her bottom was cherry red. And he was the new owner of the Book of Punishment, a fact which had made their encounter tonight even more exciting for her.

Indigo rolled onto her back and stared up at her tormentor, everything on deliberate provocative show. 'Aren't you going to fuck me?'

Dervil shook his head, yet she could not believe he was not tempted. 'I'm afraid not. We came in here to play a game, a delightful game which I enjoyed immensely. But now the game is over.'

She said nothing, but her jaw tightened at his rejection.

'I think you'd better tidy yourself up so we can rejoin the others,' he continued, standing up and adjusting the bulge in his trousers. His voice was calm and level as he gazed down at her, his eyes moving dispassionately over her barely clothed body. 'Don't think me ungrateful. You're a beautiful girl and I appreciate the offer. But if you imagine this little charade is going to soften me up, make me hand over the Book of Punishment without so much as a whimper, then you don't know me at all.'

'Sorry?'

'I'm not a fool. I knew who you were as soon as you walked into the party tonight.' His eyes met hers as he said her name with cool deliberation. 'Indigo.'

Red-faced and breathless with embarrassment, Indigo scrambled to her feet and dragged the two sides of her corset back together to hurriedly zip it up. Seeing his eyes drop to the moist crotch of her thong, she wriggled the rubber skirt down to her thighs with some difficulty. Damn the man, she thought unevenly.

One of her high heels must have fallen off during the spanking; it was lying on its side, sad and forgotten beneath the desk. After hopping towards the desk in an

111

ungainly fashion, she bent to slip the shoe back onto her foot, horribly aware of the man's sardonic gaze.

So her plan had failed. Dervil Badon not only knew who she was, he had even guessed why she had begged him to hurt her and chosen this particular room to use. There was a sinking feeling in the pit of her stomach. It was disappointment, mingled with a very real fear of how he might try to punish her. Under the circumstances, it was probably best to admit her deception and slip away from the party before he had a chance to get his revenge.

She straightened and turned to face him with a shrug. 'So you know who I am. That's not a big problem, is it? Yes, I want to add the Book of Punishment to my private collection. But you can't blame me for that – it's a fantastically rare book and my father spent most of his life searching for it. Or did you expect me to give up and go back to London without even trying to get a look at it?'

Dervil had been watching her in silence. Now he smiled, inclining his head as though acknowledging the truth in what she had said. 'I suppose not. But you'll forgive me if I don't trust you, Indigo. I've just parted with an obscene amount of money for the Book of Punishment and I have no intention of risking my investment for the sake of a quick fuck.'

She could barely manage a reply, her cheeks scarlet with humiliation. 'Actually, sex with you was never part of my plan.'

'So you did have a plan?'

'Not really, except that I needed to get inside this office.' She lowered her eyes to the floor, finding that direct gaze too intimidating. 'My original idea was to sneak out of the party at some point and search Wolfmann's office, just to find out if the book was genuine. But then your friend got herself paddled and it turned me on so much, I couldn't help myself. I'm a

112

submission junkie, you see. Can't get enough of it. Everything we did tonight, the spanking, the orgasms, it was all real.'

'I'm relieved to hear it.'

She hesitated, licking her lips. 'But you do have it with you? The Book of Punishment?'

'It's in this room, yes.'

She lifted her eyes to his face then, barely daring to breathe. 'Could I . . .? Would you allow me see it?'

There was a black leather attaché-case standing beside the armchair. Dervil slid the case onto the desk, produced a small bunch of keys from his pocket and unlocked it.

She peered over his shoulder, her heart racing. Inside the case was a sturdy brown paper parcel, about the thickness of a book.

'Here it is, the elusive Book of Punishment.' He handed her the parcel in silence, his smile ironic as he watched her turn it over in her hand to weigh and examine it. No doubt he knew how many years she had been searching for it and how dearly she would love to slip the brown paper wrappings off and see what lay inside. Yet it was equally clear that he had no intention of allowing her that pleasure. 'But that's as close to it as you're going to get, my dear Indigo. Unless you care to visit my home once we get back to London and pay for a full session with me. You never know, I might use one of the punishments in this book on you. That would be poetic justice, don't you agree?'

'Couldn't I just take a quick look?' she pleaded.

Dervil laughed and removed the parcel from her hands to replace it in the attaché-case. 'I'm afraid not. In fact, I rather think it's time you were leaving.'

'Leaving?'

'There's nothing worse at an SM party than an uninvited guest, unless it's an uninvited guest who gatecrashed with the express intention of committing theft.'

Her cheeks flared with hot colour. 'How dare you? I'm not a thief, Dervil Badon.'

'Don't insult my intelligence, my dear girl. We both know why you came here tonight and it certainly wasn't so you could enjoy my hand on your backside.'

He seized her arm in a steely grip and dragged her out of Wolfmann's office and down the hall towards the living-room. She did not bother to struggle, knowing it to be useless against his superior strength. The party guests appeared to have grown more risqué since they left, the lights turned down low while various spankings and canings took place around the spacious living-room. Dervil paid no attention to them, stepping across a writhing couple on the floor then throwing Indigo onto a leather sofa in front of Wolfmann.

Sweating heavily, their host lowered the cane he had been applying to the buttocks of a curvaceous redhead and stared at them, adjusting his glasses with a bewildered expression.

'What's this?' Wolfmann demanded, frowning down at her prostrate figure. 'Indigo?'

'This little fool came here tonight to steal the Book of Punishment. Luckily, she's almost as incompetent a thief as she is a liar.'

Wolfmann inhaled sharply. 'So the book's safe?'

'Still under lock and key in your office. But the question remains, what to do with its would-be thief?'

As she tried to rise, Dervil held her down on the leather sofa, kicking her legs apart to leave her crotch exposed. It was obvious what he wanted: to humiliate her in front of everyone in the room. One of the watching men spoke in heavily accented German, stepping forwards as though keen to participate in her public humiliation.

'I think what this girl needs is a good man,' he told the fascinated onlookers, 'up her arse!'

There was brutal laughter on all sides and Indigo shivered, fearing for a moment that the man might be allowed to carry out his threat. The prospect of such a barbarous punishment both horrified and excited her. To be sodomised right here in public, buttocks raised up on display and some anonymous stranger forcing his cock between her sore cheeks, was a possibility which touched every perverted nerve in her body and left her trembling with aroused apprehension.

She was smothering against the smooth black leather of the sofa, and twisted her head round to stare furiously up at Dervil Badon. 'This isn't funny, you bastard. You know perfectly well I only wanted to examine the book, not steal it.'

Wolfmann laid his cane twice across her buttocks, watching with satisfaction as her body jerked under the strokes and she cried out. She had not expected him to strike her; the pain caught her off guard. Angry at herself for losing control so easily, she buried her face in the leather sofa again and tried to muffle the hoarse sound of her breathing. But it was too late; she had already made herself look ridiculous. The man's laughter stung almost as much as the cane.

'She's her father's daughter all right. Both of them obsessed with punishment.'

'Except that her father liked to administer it and she prefers to be on the receiving end.'

It was Dervil who had spoken this time, his voice drily amused. His hands dragged up the rubber skirt to display her buttocks, no doubt still raw and glowing red from the spanking he had given her earlier.

'Just look at this if you don't believe me,' he continued loudly, standing back so that every guest in the room could also witness the shame of her scarlet buttocks. 'These marks won't fade for days. Yet you should have heard the slut moan while I was handing out the corporal punishment; she loved every second of it!'

'What are you going to do with her now?' one of the younger men asked, his voice eager.

'Give her a good whipping,' someone suggested.

'How about the cane?'

'Let's do what Helmut said and fuck her up the arse.'

'No,' a woman cried from the back of the room. 'Tie her hands behind her back and force her to lick out all the women until they come.'

'Be quiet, Lavinia, you horny bitch!'

There was more raucous laughter as the other guests crowded round her, pushing and shoving in order to get a better look.

Indigo felt strange hands on her body and tried to wriggle away, though without much conviction, half eager for these people to hurt and humiliate her, half embarrassed by her own sluttish behaviour. She felt tell-tale fluids begin to leak from her pussy and groaned inwardly, wishing she did not have such a high sex drive. Nothing good had ever come from this need to keep climaxing after everyone else had given up and collapsed with exhaustion. It was true she had felt in need of something extra after Dervil had finished with her earlier. Being manhandled by a crowd of drunken partygoers, however, would seem like a humiliating end to an unsuccessful evening.

Still, it seemed unlikely that she could escape her fate. So she might as well stop clenching her thighs together and enjoy it.

Dragged to the edge of the sofa, Indigo opened her eyes to find a swollen and purple-headed penis being shoved against her lips. She looked up to see that it belonged to Wolfmann, whose face was a mask of lust now that he had stopped caning that unfortunate redhead and was determined to come. In her mouth, by the look of it. She dutifully opened her lips and took him inside, sucking on the bulbous head as though it were a lollipop, cheeks hollowed and her neck tilted back to receive his thrusts. The old man tasted oddly of aniseed, sweet and sharp against her tongue.

Someone lifted her to her knees while she was sucking, gentle hands supporting her while several other guests fingered her breasts in the tight rubber corset and pulled down her thong until the shiny black material was biting into her thighs. The same hands slipped beneath her belly and found her pussy, to pinch and rub at her clitoris until it stood erect. Could this be Dervil, planning to fuck her at last?

Eagerly, she glanced over her shoulder to see old Gunter fumbling as he tried to find the best position to mount her. She was disappointed but did not protest. Taking anyone up there was better than having an empty pussy and an untouched clitoris. He was a long-term acquaintance of her father's, a Swiss book-seller she had known for many years and first met when she was a gawky teenager, and it was strange to think he might soon be inside her. Seconds later, Gunter muttered something she did not catch and slid up the moist channel of her sex, grasping her hips with a grunt of triumph as he began to thrust.

It was filthy and humiliating and glorious, she thought, one old man in her mouth and another in her cunt, both thrusting in and out while other hands roamed over her body, tormenting her nipples and fingering the tight sphincter of her anus.

Staring past the guests, she caught a sudden glimpse of Heinrich. The old man was standing by the door, partly concealed by a long black hooded cape. She frowned, surprised to see him. Why had he decided to come to the party if he despised this sort of thing? Perhaps she was confusing him with someone else. But no, it was definitely Heinrich: she could see the flash of those fang-like teeth.

Wolfmann seized her head and held it still, forcing her to continue sucking. 'Keep your mind on the job,' he growled. 'If I'm not satisfied with your work, I could still have you whipped.'

Not entirely unhappy about the situation, Indigo sucked his penis even deeper into her throat. He was rigid now, his frequent grunts a sure sign of impending orgasm. A hot tide of pleasure washed over her and she groaned, wiggling her bottom to encourage Gunter's thrusts as he ploughed her from the rear. She loved feeling so helpless and submissive, down on her knees with a man using her at either end. Especially when there was an audience like this, dozens of people not only witnessing her public humiliation but joining in, pinching and fondling her body in the tight black rubber outfit.

Shaking her head free for a second, Indigo gasped up at the ring of avid lusting faces, 'Spank me, someone!' before sinking back onto Wolfmann's cock with a moan of satisfaction.

Immediately, several pairs of hands began a determined tattoo on her bottom, slap after slap taking her closer to orgasm. As if sensing what was required to tip her over the edge, a gentle feminine hand curved beneath her belly and located the taut peak of her clitoris. Tugging and pinching at her flesh without any mercy, those clever fingers soon had her writhing and groaning on the penis in her mouth. Almost ready to explode, Indigo concentrated on the sheer filthiness of what was happening to her: encased in tight rubber and ridden at both ends by two dirty old men; spanked so hard it felt as though the breath were being knocked from her lungs at every slap; fingers squeezing her rubber-covered nipples and milking her erect clitoris; her whole body swinging back and forth under their thrusts, eager for the spunk to begin pumping.

Jerking his pelvis against her face, Wolfmann gave a final tremendous grunt and emptied his balls into her mouth. As she gagged and instinctively recoiled, unable to swallow such a load, the book dealer jammed her head between his two strong hands and forced her to hold still.

'What's the matter? Don't you like the taste?' he taunted her as his penis continued to pulse thick sperm down her throat. 'Just keep swallowing. This is what you get for being a thief: a bellyful of sperm as a lesson in manners.'

Gunter's thrusts had become erratic, his breathing laboured as he hung on a few minutes longer than his friend. But the sight of Indigo gagging as she swallowed the other man's spunk must have proved too much for him. He gripped her hips and pushed helplessly up inside her cunt to shoot his come. Making a noise like some prehistoric beast as he enjoyed the last throes of his climax, Gunter finally collapsed on top of her, his balls pressed hard against the sweaty backs of her thighs.

'That's it, fill her up with your spunk!' Wolfmann encouraged his friend, withdrawing from her mouth then using her hair to dry his damp penis. His tone was strict as he looked down at her flushed cheeks and rocking body. 'I'm glad your father's not alive to witness this public shame, young lady. Mortimer was a man of integrity. The way you've behaved tonight would have shocked him to the core.'

Listening to the old man's words of condemnation, Indigo arched violently into orgasm, her vision red and her mouth stretched wide. The unseen fingers massaging her clitoris had done their job well. She experienced the orgasm in every fibre of her body, an incredible tingling glow that spread from her toenails to the tips of her ears, her belly heavy with pleasure and her heart juddering behind her ribcage.

No wonder the other party guests were staring at her in a mixture of amazement and disgust, she thought. Her chin and neck were sticky with spunk, the smell of it strong in her nostrils, with more come oozing from her used pussy to leave a creamy deposit on the sofa. Slithering into a sitting position, she licked the last

traces of spunk from her lips with a lascivious expression. Let them stare, she told herself defiantly. At least I
know who I am: a filthy cock-hungry slut, always ready
for one more slap. Not some weekend submissive in
cheap PVC, with a pair of plastic handcuffs and a
husband still tied to his mother's bra strap.

The woman who had been rubbing her clitoris, a
broad-shouldered blonde with a strong German accent,
was still crouched beside the sofa. She leaned forwards,
sliding one hand up her thigh. 'Poor darling, your pussy
looks all nasty and sticky with spunk. You want me to
eat you out?'

Indigo almost purred with desire, her thighs parting
by themselves at the thought of being felched by another
woman. 'What a disgusting offer. I think I'm going to
have to say yes.'

But Dervil Badon, who had been watching the entire
scene in impassive silence, abruptly unfolded his arms
and yanked Indigo to her feet. Apparently oblivious to
her look of fury, the dominant dragged her across the
room behind him like a doll, her bare buttocks jiggling
and her cheeks scarlet with humiliation.

'Sorry to interrupt, but you've had enough fun for
one night,' Dervil said firmly, thrusting her out of the
door. Turning to Heinrich's nephew, who had followed
her across the room like a bodyguard, he addressed the
young man without any attempt at politeness. 'You
brought her here tonight, didn't you? Well, now you can
escort Indigo back to her hotel and put her to bed. My
apologies if she's a little shop-soiled. But that's the risk
you run, bringing a slut like her to a party like this.'

9

The two of them staggered down the steps together, hearing the front door slam behind them. Christian helped her onto the dark street and glanced up and down for a taxi cab, but there was no sign of any vehicles. She swayed against him, feeling oddly light-headed, and his arm tightened about her waist.

His voice was low and unflustered. 'Badon was a little rough on you there. Are you OK?'

Indigo dragged the tight rubber skirt down to hide her crotch and flagrantly displayed bottom. Her hands were shaking and she felt horribly embarrassed by that public scene. How dare Dervil Badon treat her like that, especially in front of so many other members of the book trade? The man was an ogre. Nevertheless, he could not be allowed to dominate her with his male arrogance.

'Oh, he doesn't scare me,' she lied. 'I've faced worse than Dervil Badon in the past.'

Discreetly, the young man adjusted her rubber corset so the zip was fully fastened and her breasts were no longer spilling extravagantly over the top. For a moment she was irritated, thinking he was being prudish. Then she realised her mistake. He was genuinely concerned for her well-being, removing his leather jacket and draping it across her shoulders as they walked along the street in search of a taxi. She had not paid much attention to Christian before but now she flashed him a grateful smile, pulling the edges of the jacket closer for warmth.

Considering he was Heinrich's nephew, he did not seem too unattractive: clean-shaven, dark spiky hair, and a slight nervousness in the way he held himself, the sharp blue eyes darting constantly over her face as though unconvinced that she was OK.

'You were in that office for ages. I was getting worried. Did you manage to get a look at the book?'

Indigo shook her head, not bothering to hide her frustration. 'Dervil's far too clever for that. He did show it to me for a few seconds but it was wrapped up in brown paper. I couldn't even see whether it had the original boards or not. Then the bastard took the book and locked it back in his briefcase.'

'You must be very disappointed.' Christian saw a taxi cruising along the street towards them and flagged it down, then helped her inside with a solicitous hand at her back. 'So what happens now? I suppose you'll be going home to London?'

'In the morning, yes.'

He was nodding, his eyes lingering on her smooth bare thighs. She glanced down at herself in some confusion, wondering whether there were still traces of sperm on her skin. But there was nothing there, and when she looked up at him his eyes had already moved on, staring out of the window at the dark streets as they flashed past. Did he want her? The possibility surprised her: she had assumed from his manner and polite disinterest that Christian must be gay. But perhaps there was more to Heinrich's nephew than she had supposed.

When they reached her hotel, she smiled at him. 'Would you like to come up to my room? It's only just after one and we've barely had a chance to talk tonight.'

Christian flushed, looking away. 'If you're sure . . .'

'I absolutely insist.'

In the hotel bedroom she kicked off her high heels and poured them both a cognac from the mini-bar, handing him the glass with a wry grimace. 'Tiny

122

measures, huge prices. Still, anything's better than powdered coffee. *Salut!*'

He sipped obediently at the cognac, still watching her over the rim of his glass. '*Salut*.'

'You keep staring at me, Christian. Why?'

The young man seemed confused. He sat down on the edge of the bed and shrugged, staring into his glass. 'Because you're beautiful.'

Flattered, Indigo could not prevent herself from smiling as she lay down beside him. She rolled onto her side and stretched out, aware that the tight rubber skirt and corset made her look even slimmer than she really was; though the fact that both garments were covered in what appeared to be odd smears of sperm and sweat was perhaps a little off-putting for a boy like Christian. Unless that was what made her appealing, she thought. To any young man used to clean-cut teenage girls in white panties and soft sweaters, encountering a filthy punishment-loving slut like herself must be both a shock and an aphrodisiac.

'Am I?' She removed the glass from his hands and placed it carefully on the bedside cabinet. 'It must be hard for you, finding someone like me attractive. I expect you thought I behaved disgracefully at the party tonight. That I need to be punished.'

'No,' he quickly stammered.

She raised her eyebrows, rocking back on her hip so he could see all the way up her skirt to the sperm-drenched thong beneath. 'You don't want to spank me?'

'No . . . I . . .'

'Don't be shy, Christian. Tell me what you want.'

His face was suffused with colour, both hands curling into nervous fists in his lap. 'I want you to . . .'

'Yes?'

'I want you to spank *me!*'

Completely thrown for a moment, Indigo stared at him in silence. Then she started to laugh, putting a hand to her mouth as she realised he was serious. 'You're a submissive too?'

He nodded, not daring to meet her eyes.

'That's quite a problem, I'm afraid,' she said, then hesitated. She was still feeling horny, after all, and there was no harm in experimenting with the right sort of person. 'Though I suppose in the past . . . Well, it's not been unknown for me to switch.'

'Switch?'

'Act dominant instead of submissive.'

Christian stared as Indigo slid off the bed to stand in front of him, his blue eyes suddenly filled with hope. It was obvious from his expression that he did not often confide in people about his sexuality. Not that she blamed him. So few people outside the scene ever understood what it was like to feel that genuine need to submit.

His voice was not entirely steady. 'So you give it as well as take it. That's cool. Are you going to hurt me?'

'Do you want me to hurt you?'

'Yes, please.'

She slapped his face experimentally, noting how he flinched at the unexpected blow, his expression shocked but still excited, his face lighting up with desire as he realised she was serious.

'Drop your pants then.' Not needing a second invitation, the young man fumbled at the waistband of his trousers and let them fall in a puddle of dark material around his ankles. Playfully, Indigo struck him on the buttocks with the flat of her hand. 'Now bend right over. I want to see you touch your toes, no slouching.'

Again, he obeyed her instantly.

It felt odd, ordering a man around instead of taking the orders herself, but she enjoyed the unfamiliar sensation of being in control. Indigo giggled, but hurriedly muffled the sound behind her hand. It might feel strange, but Heinrich's nephew was hers to command for the next hour or so. She could make him trot naked around the room like a pony or perform press-ups until he was exhausted. His bare bottom, firm and smooth as a girl's, tempted her with its vulnerability. She could squeeze a little shampoo up there and ease her finger inside. Perhaps two or even three fingers. Or the shampoo bottle itself. He would not be in a position to argue about his treatment, having to bend submissively from the waist while she amused herself with his exposed genitals and bottom. It might do the young man good to have his anus filled to the point of discomfort.

Still touching his toes, Christian looked up at her eagerly as he awaited the next instruction. His penis was semi-erect, with full balls nestled against a scattering of pubic hairs. In spite of his nakedness, he did not seem particularly worried by how she might torment him.

For some reason, his lack of fear was irritating to her. She glanced about the hotel room, frowning. There was a copy of *Cosmopolitan*, which she had bought at the airport, intending to read in an idle moment, lying on the bedside cabinet. Indigo rolled the magazine into a tight cylinder and struck him hard across the buttocks with it. The blow was no longer playful but forceful, intended to sting. He jerked at the impact and let out his breath in a short gasp.

That's more like it, she thought, watching him with grim satisfaction. Now he knows I mean business. 'How long have you been a submissive?' she demanded.

'For as long as I can remember,' he said unevenly, his bottom reddening as she continued to spank him with the glossy rolled-up magazine. 'But it was only last year that I . . .'

'Came out?'

He moaned as the blows intensified, his eyes glazed with pleasure. 'Um . . . yes . . . I was at college and my girlfriend . . .'

'So you're straight?'

Nodding, Christian closed his eyes and breathed heavily, apparently unable to continue speaking for a moment. By the time he spoke again, his cheeks were darkly flushed and he sounded as though he were teetering on the edge of orgasm.

'I told her how I felt and ... she humiliated me. Dressed me in her stockings and underwear. Spanked me until ...' He was groaning now, his penis fully erect and bouncing against his stomach with every blow of the rolled-up *Cosmopolitan*. 'I came all over her knickers. She made me wash them in the sink afterwards and hang them up to dry. Like I was her maid. It was fantastic.'

'You enjoyed serving this girl, doing her bidding? She was your mistress and you were her slave, is that right?'

Christian barely managed a nod in answer to her questions, shifting his legs further apart as he fought to keep his balance, his breathing tortured under the rigorous spanking. His penis seemed unnaturally swollen, the bulbous tip purple and hugely enlarged as it jerked below his belly. It would not take much more for the poor boy to come, she realised, and she was tempted to reach out and squeeze his erection. But it would spoil the mood of the scene if she were to do that, acting so completely out of character. She was meant to be in control here, she reminded herself. To be a bitch and a dominatrix, not some self-effacing submissive.

Her voice hardened. 'I hope you're not going to make a mess like that here. The hotel might charge me for getting spunk on their carpet. If you come on the floor, I'll make you get down on your knees and lick it up. Every single drop, you understand me?'

'Yes, yes,' he groaned.

'Yes, *mistress*!'

He corrected himself, wincing as the rolled-up magazine caught him painfully between the thighs. 'Yes, mistress.'

Stepping in closer to his quivering buttocks, she wet her finger in her mouth until it was slick and running with saliva. Then she pushed it up inside his anus without any warning. His high-pitched cry made her smile. Now that was a sound she recognised. Cool and relentless to the last, she pushed her finger even deeper inside. His legs were trembling violently, his knees ready to buckle. With her other hand, she raised the rolled-up copy of *Cosmopolitan* and brought it down hard across his buttocks one final time.

Christian cried out in anguish, clutching himself, but it was too late. His penis stiffened and began to spurt. The spunk flew out at great velocity onto the carpet, and the stain spread rapidly.

Which was when the door to her bedroom opened and she realised they were not alone.

Dropping the rolled-up magazine in bewilderment, Indigo spun on her heel to see Dervil Badon and the sturdy Russian blonde from the party, right there in the doorway to her hotel room. Behind them both, his expression one of prurient fascination, stood one of the clerks from the reception desk with a bunch of master keys in his hand.

For a moment there was silence. Nobody moved. Indigo still had her finger deeply embedded in Christian's anus, her face rigid with shock. She could not understand what was happening. Then her cheeks flushed with pure temper. 'What the hell do you think you're doing? How dare you break into my hotel room like this? You've gone too far this time, Badon. I'm tempted to call the police and have you thrown in jail.'

'Exactly what I said,' he replied coldly, holding up his black leather attaché-case, 'when I opened this and found it empty.'

10

Wiping her hands on the nearest towel, Indigo dismissed
the hovering desk clerk with a furious glare before
kicking the bedroom door shut and turning to face her
unwelcome guests. So someone had stolen the Book of
Punishment from under Dervil's nose and he naturally
assumed it must be her. What a charming man he was.
First he called her a thief and chastised her for it in
public, and now he had bribed his way into her hotel
bedroom in order to humiliate her even further.

'Christian,' she muttered, shooting a look at the
young man's reddened backside, still thrust obediently
into the air. 'Pull your trousers up and sit down. You
look ridiculous.

'And as for you, Dervil Badon,' she continued,
rounding on the man as he tossed his empty attaché-
case onto the bed. 'What do you think I am, some kind
of cat burglar? You threw me out of that party,
remember? I didn't sneak round the back and shinny up
the drainpipe, if that's what you imagine happened.'

'I wouldn't put anything past you,' he replied, un-
moved by her irritation. 'You admitted it yourself, you
were desperate to get your hands on the Book of
Punishment.'

'Not that desperate.'

Dervil glanced at his companion, the sturdy Russian
blonde who had been so thoroughly paddled at the
party. Coolly, he told her to search the room. While the
blonde flung open drawers and peered under the furniture, the infuriating man withdrew a silver cigarette case

from his jacket pocket and glanced at her before flicking the lid back. 'Mind if I smoke?'

Indigo held her breath for a moment, struggling to keep her temper under control. 'Go ahead, make yourself at home. Though I don't know why your friend's bothering to search my room. She won't find anything.'

He smiled, lighting his cigarette. 'We found you, didn't we?'

'Yes,' she agreed. 'How did you manage that, if you don't mind me asking?'

'You'd be surprised what a few euros can achieve.'

'You disgust me.'

Dervil Badon raised his eyebrows, looking pointedly down at the whitish smears of spunk still clinging to her tight rubber outfit. 'I disgust you?' he murmured. 'Somehow I doubt that.'

God, she loathed this man. Unzipping the rubber corset, Indigo began to undress in front of them without a shred of embarrassment. What did she care what they thought? She pulled on a pair of faded hipster jeans over a clean thong and wriggled a close-fitting white sweater down over her chest. After giving herself a severe glance in the mirror, she rummaged for a hair-brush in her bag, and dragged it ruthlessly through her hair until all the flecks of dried spunk had been brushed out.

The blonde had finished searching her room. She sauntered out of the bathroom empty-handed and shook her head. His mouth tightening with frustration, Dervil stared at Indigo as she reapplied her make-up in front of the mirror.

'OK, where is it?' he demanded. 'I know you must have taken it. You were the only one who knew where it was.'

'Actually, I seem to recall you announcing to the entire room that the Book of Punishment was in Wolfmann's office,' she pointed out in acid tones. 'Hardly discreet.'

His eyes narrowed on her face for a moment, then he shrugged and dropped his cigarette into one of the brandy glasses, watching it flare for a second before it hissed out. 'Yes, that may have been a mistake. Nevertheless, I'm still convinced you're the key to the book's whereabouts. So I'm going to have to insist you come with me. At least until I get the book back.'

'Go with you where?'

'To Paris.'

She gave an angry laugh, shaking her head. 'Oh no. I'm not swanning off to romantic Paris with you. I'm due back in London tomorrow. Unlike you, I've got a business to –'

'On the other hand, we could always inform the Swiss authorities of its disappearance,' Dervil interrupted, his voice deliberately smooth as he glanced at Christian, who had been perched silently on the edge of her bed for the last ten minutes. 'The story would make interesting newspaper copy, don't you agree?'

Her teeth snapped together. 'You're in this up to your neck too, Badon. It would be just as embarrassing for you to have it splashed across the papers.'

'I'm merely a bystander, my dear. The unfortunate victim of a theft. And I'm sure the desk clerk will uphold my version of events. He must have had a pretty clear view of your friend when the door opened . . . and indeed of your finger, which was, unless I'm mistaken, inside his bottom at the time?'

'You bastard,' she hissed.

'I presume that's a yes, then.' He picked up her jacket and tossed it casually across to her. 'Come on, put that on and stop arguing. Natasha will help you pack. I've wasted enough time here already.'

While she threw her possessions irritably into her suitcase, Christian raised his eyes from his contemplation of the carpet and spoke at last. 'What's in Paris?'

'It speaks! I was beginning to think he was a mute,' Dervil said lightly before answering his question. 'Since you ask, I hope to acquire another copy of the Book of Punishment in Paris. Though I have reason to doubt the authenticity of that copy; even if it is a true first, it's unlikely to be in as good condition as the one you stole.'

'I told you,' Indigo snapped, 'I didn't steal anything. And I fail to see why on earth you need me to go with you.'

Dervil smiled unpleasantly. 'Perhaps because I'd like to get to know you better. We're driving and it's a long haul from Geneva to Paris by car. Many hours of boredom.'

'If you think for one minute . . .'

'It doesn't take much to get you excited, does it?' he drawled, dodging as she threw some lipstick at his head. 'So hot tempered! I'm going to enjoy bringing you to heel, Indigo. It's about time somebody did.'

As she turned reluctantly to the door, suitcase in hand, Christian grabbed her arm. To his credit, the young man seemed genuinely concerned for her safety, his blue eyes earnest. 'Don't worry, Indigo. When I tell my uncle what's happened, I'm sure he'll find a way to help you. You're not on your own in this mess.'

'Heinrich!' Dervil made a snorting sound of derision and pushed the young man back to the bed. 'Trust me, your uncle won't lift a finger to help her. Heinrich's only interested in his own perversions, and once they've been satisfied –'

'Look, I'll be OK,' she reassured the young man, managing to shoot him a brief smile as Dervil ushered her from the room. At least Christian had tried to help her, rather than merely abandoning her to whatever lay ahead. A futile effort, perhaps, but one she appreciated. If nothing else, it demonstrated to Dervil Badon that she was not entirely alone and friendless in this part of the world.

Dervil's car turned out to be an elderly white Daimler with fly-encrusted English plates, parked beneath a

131

streetlight a few blocks from the hotel. It was a little battered, with one of the wing mirrors cracked and the odd spot of chrome peeling from the bumpers. Nevertheless, the Daimler possessed a certain majestic dignity and Indigo felt strangely relaxed, sliding across the spacious back seats and enjoying the cool touch of leather. Having made sure she was safely inside, Dervil swung into the driver's seat and started the engine. The Russian blonde settled next to her in the back, a malicious smile on her face as the car purred away from the kerb. Indigo tried to ignore her, slipping off her high heels and digging her toes into the soft brown fur which served as a floor covering. It might be a long journey from Geneva to Paris, she mused, but at least she might catch some sleep in a car as luxurious as this.

Dervil nursed the powerful engine out of Geneva's central maze of streets with obvious restraint, following the road signs as he headed for the Swiss-French border. Pulling out into the fast lane, he glanced over his shoulder at them, the sinister gleam of his eyes visible even in the dark interior of the car. 'Comfortable?'

'Very,' she admitted.

'Well, we can't have that,' he murmured, turning back to the road as he accelerated past a slow-moving lorry. 'Natasha, make our guest a little less comfortable.'

The Russian's smile broadened. She unclasped her substantial bag and withdrew a broad leather strap and a pair of handcuffs. Pointing to Indigo's jeans, she spoke in a thick Russian accent. 'Pull them down to your thighs.'

'What?'

'Pull down your jeans,' the woman repeated impatiently, 'and kneel up on the seat.'

'But the car's moving! It could be dangerous –'

Dervil interrupted. 'Might I advise you not to disobey Natasha? Unlike me, she has a nasty temper and there's no predicting what she might do if she loses it.'

132

Irritable but unwilling to cause a scene, Indigo pushed her jeans down to mid-thigh and clambered up onto her knees. The blonde instructed her to turn round and face the rear of the car. She did so in silent protest, swaying as the car rounded a steep right-hand curve on its ascent into the mountains. Without her seat-belt on, she would be unprotected if there was an accident.

Forcing her wrist into the handcuffs, Natasha gave her a knowing smile and snapped the metal cuffs onto a coat-hanger rail above the door. 'Just in case you were thinking about jumping out. You're not going anywhere until we get to Paris, darling.'

Handcuffed in that position, staring out of the rear window as the Daimler ate up mile after mile of dark motorway, Indigo raged inwardly at the injustice of such treatment. Whatever Dervil Badon might believe, she had not taken the Book of Punishment. She had not even managed to get a proper look at it, for god's sake, let alone be in a position to steal the blasted thing. Meanwhile, the real thief was out there somewhere, gloating over his or her successful theft. In spite of her innocence, she was the one paying for the book's disappearance: kneeling here, robbed of all dignity, her bottom exposed for the strap like some naughty schoolgirl.

Some time later she was rudely awoken by the stinging slap of leather across her buttocks. She groaned and opened her eyes, belatedly realising that she had somehow managed to doze off in spite of the uncomfortable position. Staring out of the window, she tried to see what was happening. But to her surprise they had not stopped, the car was still moving at the same high-powered pace.

'Ow,' she muttered, using her free hand to rub at the sore spot. 'What was that for?'

'You must stay awake!'

She glared at the blonde through the semi-darkness. 'Are you telling me I'm not even allowed to fall asleep now?'

133

Natasha looked back at her with a cruel smile but did not reply. Instead, she laid down the strap and slid both hands up her thighs, drawing the little suede skirt higher until her panty-covered crotch was exposed. Twitching the black lace panties to one side, she slid a long finger inside herself and gave a satisfied growl. 'See this?' she whispered, leaning towards Indigo. 'Pure pussy.'

'Says who?'

Once again, Natasha raised her hand and the small leather strap bit viciously into the soft flesh of Indigo's bottom. 'Watch your attitude! I don't have to be nice to you, you know.'

So that was her being nice? Now her poor naked bottom stung even more than before.

Biting back an acid remark which was sure to get her into trouble, Indigo forced herself to glance down at the blonde's gaping pussy. Her hand still held those generous lips wide apart, displaying a sweetly hooded clitoris and pink fleshy labia simply begging to be kissed. What the hell, she thought wryly, unable to deny her own arousal. There was nothing else to do on a long journey like this but lick pussy.

'If you want me to go down on you,' she pointed out, 'you'll have to take these handcuffs off.'

'Don't even waste your time asking. I don't need you to touch me with your dirty little tongue, English girl. I want to watch your pain, listen to you moan. That's what gets me off.'

'Pervert!'

'It takes one to know one.'

Indigo could not help herself. 'Yeah, except I'm not the one with the strap in her hand.'

The strap came down hard across her bottom again and Indigo cried out, trying to stifle the noise against the leather seat as several other blows followed. But it was no use. However much she ducked and writhed, hoping to escape the worst of each whack, the Russian still managed to catch her squarely across the buttocks. And Indigo seemed unable to keep quiet about it. The long and sexually demanding evening was beginning to catch up with her, she realised, embarrassed to feel juices oozing out from her pussy to soak her thong.

Giving in to the pleasure of such humiliation was the last thing she had intended when the Russian first lifted the strap. Yet what could she do? Her defences were low, far too low to combat this sort of cruelty. There was something delicious about the ignominy of her position, handcuffed to the coat-rail on her knees, her bottom hanging out of her jeans for every passing motorist to see and this brutal girl bruising the hell out of it with a sturdy leather strap. She would have to be a saint not to give up the struggle to appear outraged and start enjoying it.

She put her free hand down between her thighs, pushed the thong aside and rubbed surreptitiously at her clitoris. It felt good, a wicked contrast with the pain in her buttocks.

Dervil's spanking had left her bottom sore, the skin there tight and aching, no doubt still reddened from his hand. She tried to imagine how her backside must look to the Russian blonde, mottled buttocks quivering under every blow of the strap yet shamelessly stuck out for more, her thighs spread wide to show a few tantalising wisps of pubic hair and, a little above that, the darker hole of her anus contracting and loosening in turn as her excitement grew. It must be a lewd sight.

Gasping with pleasure as the strap found the tops of her thighs and left them stinging, she rubbed her chest against the smooth leather upholstery and felt her nipples stiffen.

Indigo knew what that meant and rubbed harder at her clitoris, no longer bothering to hide what she was doing. Orgasm was only another few slaps away.

Suddenly, she felt Natasha's hand between her thighs. The other girl's fingers explored the gash of her wet open lips before moving up to pinch her clitoris. It was nothing like being touched by a man, Indigo thought, moaning as she leaned forwards to make her lower half more accessible. For a start, the Russian blonde seemed to know precisely where to press to send her blood pressure rocketing; and she knew how hard to press too, the cruel fingers relenting as Indigo squealed in pain. Not only that, but she understood how to scoop a little fluid out of Indigo's pussy every few strokes, using just a flick of that mobile wrist, to keep the taut bud of her clitoris slippery and rolling around under its sensitive hood of flesh.

'Keep hitting me!' Indigo heard herself whispering, cheeks pink with humiliation as she was forced to beg for the orgasm she knew to be so close now. 'Please don't stop.'

The strap whacked across her poor tortured buttocks again and again, sharp frequent blows keeping time with the fingers working in her pussy. The oiled flesh around her clitoris began to quiver with sensation, everything in her body tensing for an explosion of pleasure. When it finally came, sweet and sudden, she cried out and bit down hard on the leather headrest in front of her in an attempt to stifle the noise. She did not want Dervil Badon to know the extent of her degradation; that would be far too humiliating. It was bad enough climaxing while his girlfriend punished her without advertising her sluttishness to him as well.

She quickly added her own fingers to the blonde's, both of them pushing up inside her cunt to relieve the aching emptiness. Fingers were never as solid or satisfying as a penis. But with a little imagination and a few hard jerks of the wrist she could pretend it was Dervil's cock swelling inside her as he pumped shot after shot of thick spunk up inside her belly.

It was not over yet, she realised, moaning as another orgasm mounted almost before the first one had finished. Her bottom still writhed and trembled under the strap, both cheeks stuck right out from her puddled jeans, a silent invitation for the other girl to hit her harder. And why not? she asked herself defiantly. Each blow inflicted by the strap only served to intensify her pleasure. It would be stupid not to ask for more and harder strokes.

But the blonde was wielding the strap erratically, her hand moving between her own thighs as she too reached orgasm. With a hoarse cry, Natasha dropped the strap and pulled her knees up to her chest, shoving three or four fingers greedily into her cunt. It must have hurt but the Russian woman did not seem to care, rocking back and forth on the back seat, apparently lost in the throes of pleasure.

'Why don't you girls try to get some sleep?' Dervil called lazily from the driver's seat, a hint of mockery in his voice as he glanced at Indigo in the rear-view mirror. 'Don't worry, there'll be plenty of time for you to play at being lesbians when we reach Paris.'

Her cheeks flushed with embarrassment, Indigo leaned her face against the cool leather upholstery and stared out at the dark countryside as it flashed by at speed. Her mind was moving equally fast. That man was such a bastard. He knew exactly what to say to get under her skin. Yet she still harboured a desire to have him inside her. Why was that?

Probably because she found the idea of being humiliated by a man like Dervil Badon extremely exciting. A complex about authority figures, that's what psychologists would call it: she enjoyed being subdued and dominated by men like Badon, men who seemed to be in control of their lives and everyone around them. That was what her father had been like, after all. In control.

Ah, she thought furiously, but if she could get Dervil Badon to lose control, to do what she wanted for once; now that would be a triumph indeed.

With her fingers stuck firmly inside her pussy, Indigo closed her eyes and drifted into a warm erotic sleep.

It was the pale light of dawn on her face that woke her, plus the gradual awareness – filtering through a lurid dream which had featured herself, Natasha and a large German Shepherd – that the car was slowing down. She stirred, raising her head with a groan. Her body felt stiff and painful from maintaining such an unnatural position for hours, slumped forwards against the seat with one wrist still hanging from the coat-rail above the passenger door. There was classical music playing somewhere near her head, presumably coming from speakers behind the headrests.

Blinking out of the rear window, she realised the car was still on the motorway. But now the road signs were all in French and the terrain was no longer mountainous but flat and unrelentingly grey. 'And it's raining,' she muttered, stretching as best she could in her limited position.

The jangle of her handcuffs must have woken Natasha; the blonde gave a cat-like yawn, displaying both rows of sharp white teeth, then uncurled herself abruptly from the back seat and put a hand on Dervil's shoulder. She had not even bothered to adjust her skirt after their sex play during the night, her crotch still exposed and the full puffy lips of her sex clearly visible as she leaned forwards between the front seats.

Her Russian accent seemed thicker than ever. 'Are we stopping? Because I need to piss urgently, darling. Or there's going to be an accident.'

Dervil looked tired, his eyes heavy and bloodshot in the mirror. Nevertheless, he managed a laugh as the car pulled onto the forecourt of a petrol station. 'Yes, we're stopping here. The car's almost out of petrol and I'm starving.'

'Just in case you'd forgotten about me, I need to pee too,' Indigo threw into the conversation, deliberately antagonistic. If he thought he could just abduct her without paying a price for it, he was wrong. 'So you'd

138

better unlock these handcuffs. Unless you expect me to pee in the car. Though I wouldn't put that past you, Badon. You've got a perverted sense of humour.'

He shrugged, unpeeling his fingers from the steering wheel and stretching in a leisurely fashion. The engine began to tick beneath the bonnet as it cooled, rain beating a quiet but insistent tattoo on the roof and windows. She thought his voice seemed surprisingly calm; most dominants would have lost their temper by now, unable to handle her belligerent manner.

'There are times, Indigo, when your audacity leaves me speechless. You need a firm hand, I can see that now. Natasha's hobble is somewhere in my luggage. Perhaps I should force you to wear it in Paris, and find a gag for that mouth of yours too.'

'You see? Utterly perverted.'

Flushing with anger, the blonde pinched her thigh fiercely. 'How dare you talk to your master like that? It's disrespectful.'

'Dervil Badon's not my master!'

'He soon will be,' the Russian girl insisted, her tone vehement. 'We swop drivers here. I drive now, Dervil sits in the back with you. Then we will see who is master.'

'Oh, I can hardly wait.'

He shot her an ironic smile over his shoulder, combing his fingers through dishevelled greying hair. 'Oddly enough, I suspect that may be true. Now where's the key to the handcuffs, Natasha? Come along, stop messing around and look for it. Two girls dressed like cheap whores are conspicuous enough without adding bondage to the mix. This is a motorway service station, we don't want to attract that sort of attention here.'

It was not the most glamorous place to stop for a rest. For a start, there was no café, only picnic benches set amongst the trees in the rain. The service station appeared to sell nothing to eat or drink but chilled

139

drinks and sweets, and when they asked in French for the toilets, both girls were dismayed to see the leering young man behind the counter point outside. Teetering on high heels across the rain-slick forecourt, Indigo and Natasha followed his directions and headed behind the shop towards a cluster of thorn bushes. There they found the toilet block, divided into two sections. The women's block was primitive, a narrow, dimly lit row of cubicles with one flickering strip light overhead. The only mirror in the place was cracked and the sinks smelt odd. Nevertheless, it felt good to be walking about freely after hours of captivity, and Indigo took her time having a pee and reapplying her make-up.

She was trying to decide which lipstick to use, torn between a modest coral pink and a lush scarlet, when the door suddenly opened and a tall slim woman pushed her way into the toilets.

Dressed in full bikers' leathers and wearing a dark-visored helmet, the woman paused for a moment, staring at them as though surprised to see anyone else there so early in the morning, and then backed into one of the grim little cubicles, wisps of garish red hair sticking out from under her helmet.

Seconds later, they both heard the loud splash and tinkle of her pee hitting the metal bowl of the toilet.

'Sounds like she was desperate,' Indigo whispered, giggling as the sound of pissing continued for what seemed like an eternity. 'Wow, that must be a world record for peeing.'

The blonde frowned disapprovingly and snapped shut her large black handbag then slung it over her shoulder. She walked briskly to the exit. 'Hurry up, I don't want to keep Dervil waiting. He is not a patient man and I don't see why I should be punished just because you are slow to pee.'

'But I haven't finished my make-up!'

Natasha hesitated, still frowning heavily. 'OK, five more minutes. Then I see you back at the car. And don't bother trying to run away. You have unfinished business with Dervil, remember?'

Almost as soon as the metal door clanged shut behind Natasha, the biker chick with the wild red hair peered out of the cubicle, glancing cautiously up and down the empty block before taking a few steps towards her.

'Has she gone?' she asked in English, the words muffled by her dark-visored helmet. When Indigo nodded, intrigued, the woman removed her helmet and she was shocked to see not a stranger but Christian grinning at her from beneath the curly wig. Her jaw dropped as she stared at him in complete incomprehension. 'Surprise! It's just as well Dervil's driving such a distinctive car. I'd never have been able to find you otherwise.'

'Christian!'

11

The young man kissed her on the cheek as she leaped to hug him, his leather-clad body cold and damp from the rain. But his smile was warm enough. 'Hey, you don't sound particularly pleased to see me. You do want to be rescued?'

'I'm just a bit shocked, that's all. I wasn't expecting to see you, Christian. Where on earth did you get that wig?'

'Uncle Heinrich loaned it to me. Convincing disguise, huh? It's always useful having a relative in the film industry. The bike's one of his too. Much faster than a car and the last thing that bastard Dervil would expect to see following him.'

Indigo frowned. 'Heinrich came with you?'

'No, he was too busy. But I brought a spare helmet for you. Come on, my bike's just outside.'

'Hold on a minute.' Indigo shook her head, pulling away from him. She was thinking fast. 'OK, here's the plan. Dervil says there may be a second copy of the Book of Punishment in Paris. If I can get him to tell me who's selling it and then slip away sometime in the next couple of hours, we could get to Paris and grab the book before Dervil even arrives.'

Christian was staring at her, clearly perplexed that she was not desperate to leap immediately onto the back of his bike and escape her abductors. 'Let me get this straight. You're planning to get back into that car with him? Aren't you afraid of what he might do to you?'

'I can handle the likes of Dervil Badon,' she said scathingly. 'The Book of Punishment is more important

142

to me than the odd grope in the back of a car. I've come this far and I'm not about to pass up any opportunity to add it to my collection, however dangerous it might seem to you. Don't get me wrong, Christian. I'm very grateful to you for coming after me. But I can't leave them until I've found out who the vendor is.'

He frowned. 'OK then. But I'll be right behind you all the way, in case you change your mind.'

She patted his cheek with genuine affection. 'That's a good boy. Now put your helmet on and get back on that bike. We can't risk Dervil seeing us together. He's too intelligent, he'd work it out in a flash.'

Once her rescuer had pushed reluctantly through the outside door, shooting her one last uncertain look, Indigo snatched up the scarlet lipstick and smeared it across her lips with a few bold strokes. Pausing to check her reflection through narrowed eyes, she tweaked her hair into dishevelled peaks and licked her lips to make them glisten. Suitably whorish, she told herself with a nod of grim satisfaction. This was no time to act coy, after all.

Just before opening the door to the toilet block, she pinched her nipples so they stiffened and rubbed clumsily at her pussy in order to get the juices flowing. If Dervil was to relax enough to divulge the book's whereabouts, she would need him to think she was entirely his creature. And that would take more than a dab of lipstick.

It was full daylight outside, blustery grey clouds giving way to a brighter morning now the rain had stopped. As she approached the white Daimler, she heard the roar of a bike engine and glanced back over her shoulder to see Christian wheeling a Harley Davidson in a wide circle as he prepared to set off.

Pretending not to take an interest, she looked coldly at Natasha instead, who was lounging against the curved white bonnet as she smoked a cigarette. 'Ready?'

143

The Russian took a final impatient drag on her cigarette, oblivious to the DÉFENSE DE FUMER signs all around them, tossed it down and ground it beneath her heel. 'Get in the car. He's waiting for you.'

Still listening to the roar of the bike engine as Christian pulled away from the forecourt, Indigo slid into the back seat of the car and shut the door behind her with a gentle thud. Although she had been confident enough in the toilets, her heart was now beginning to race. Had she made a mistake, climbing back into the lion's den?

Dervil was leaning against the other door, arms folded and his eyes closed as though asleep. As soon as Natasha started the engine, however, his eyes snapped open and he looked sideways at Indigo. His gaze took in her freshened make-up and the outline of her firm high breasts under the sweater. Reaching out, he flicked lazily at one of her nipples.

'What were you doing in the toilets for so long?' he asked drily. 'As though I need to ask. Once a slut, always a slut.'

'Just your type, then.'

The dark eyes met hers, searching her face for a long worrying moment. Did he suspect something? Perhaps she ought to have made some sort of caustic comment, appeared less willing to fall in with his seduction. But it was OK. Dervil seemed to relax again, kicking off his shoes and unbuttoning his shirt.

'I'm afraid so. It's true that wide-eyed innocents have never held much appeal for me. There's only so much fun to be had with a girl in white panties and ankle socks. But someone as irretrievably filthy as you, my dear, is quite a different story.'

Her heart thudding, she kneeled up on the seat beside him, unable to look away as his hands dropped to his black jeans and began to unzip them. He was not wasting any time, she thought, surprised but not unwilling for the pace to quicken. She licked her lips to make the tacky scarlet lipstick even glossier and more sluttish.

'You want me to suck your cock?'

'Blessed with intelligence too,' he drawled. 'That's a combination I find irresistible.'

Extricating his semi-erect penis from his jeans, she caressed the thickening shaft with one hand and slid the other inside his shirt to pinch and stroke his nipple. He drew a sharp breath, watching her as though suspicious that she was playing a game with him. Dervil did not trust her any more than she trusted him. Though on this occasion at least, she thought wryly, he would find her reasonably compliant. After loosening the jeans a little further, she cupped a gentle hand under his balls and bent to lick them. Tracing the outline of each ball with her tongue, she sucked them deeply into her mouth and rolled them back and forth against the inside of her cheek.

It had not been entirely honest of her, telling Christian she needed to stay with these two in order to discover who was selling this second copy of the Book of Punishment. There was another reason why she had not been keen to ride off with her rescuer. A less business-like reason. Even though the man infuriated her with his arrogance and cruelty, she still found it arousing to imagine what Dervil Badon was planning to do to her over the next hour or so. If she had not chosen to stay, he might have become an itch she could never scratch.

Running her tongue around the swollen head of his penis, she allowed herself to savour its warm saltiness before beginning to suck properly. It had been enjoyable, in a painful sort of way, to be handcuffed on her knees to the coat-rail while Natasha punished her for being insolent. The blonde had a surprisingly heavy hand for a woman and her bottom was still aching from that stiff leather strap. But cock was cock, at the end of the day, and she was not going anywhere until she had fully savoured this one.

Natasha, who had been driving in disapproving silence ever since they left the service station, suddenly burst out, 'I can't stand it any longer. What's going on back there?'

'She's sucking my cock,' Dervil replied calmly. 'Be quiet and keep your eyes on the road.'

'I hate you!'

He laughed and pushed Indigo even deeper into his crotch, with a firm and insistent pressure on the back of her neck which made her nipples stiffen and her pussy moisten. 'Natasha, my silly little Natasha. Stop behaving like a schoolgirl with a crush and drive the car. You don't want to make me angry, do you?'

'No.'

His voice was like a whip. 'No, what?'

There was a brief rebellious silence from the driver's seat, then Natasha growled, 'No, sir.'

'That's better.' Dervil leaned back and opened his thighs a little wider. Instinctively guessing what the man wanted, Indigo fondled his balls as she continued to suck. He gave a low groan and began to smack her bottom with a firm hand. 'Much better.'

Indigo raised herself for each smack, thrilling to his dominant manner even as she loathed him for it. She ought to have been enraged by his arrogance, but instead she found the thick denim of her jeans a frustrating barrier between her bottom and his hand. Struggling to undo them one-handed, she was relieved when he helped her. Soon her jeans were being dragged roughly past her ankles. She kicked them loose, somehow managing to suck his penis without breaking rhythm, her bare bottom stuck wantonly in the air.

In a moment of wild embarrassment, she suddenly remembered it was broad daylight and every truck driver they passed must have an excellent view of her reddened buttocks. She wondered whether Christian

146

was close behind them on his bike and what he might think of her for behaving so sluttishly. Then she forgot all about the younger man, her buttocks jiggling up and down as the intensity of the spanking increased.

Stifling a cry of pleasure as she sucked, she drew her knees closer to her chest and raised herself even higher, feeling cool air across her naked bottom and thighs from the half-open window. Dervil Badon might be a contemptible bastard, she thought appreciatively, but he knew how to spank.

They both swayed to one side as the car careered round a tight corner at speed, accelerating past a slower vehicle at the same time. Indigo could not raise her head to see what was happening, but she heard the distant roar of a truck and the sound of hooting. Had she been seen *in flagrante delicto* or was the driver irritated by the blonde's erratic driving?

Dervil stopped spanking her for a moment. He sounded impatient. 'Slow down, Natasha. She's an old car, she won't take that kind of punishment.'

'Is that slut still sucking you?'

'Yes.'

'You haven't come yet? My god, how much longer? She can't be doing a very good job, that's what I think.' The Russian's voice became sly. 'I'll pull over at the next exit, so you can use my mouth instead. You know how I love to suck your cock.'

'Don't be ridiculous,' he told her coldly. 'And ease your foot off the accelerator. We're not meeting the vendor until tomorrow evening, remember?'

Indigo's heart leaped when she heard those magic words. So he had arranged to buy the Book of Punishment tomorrow night, not later today as she had originally feared. That gave her and Christian plenty of time to get there first and top his offer. Now all she had to do was find out who the vendor was. If she could succeed, this might not be a wasted trip after all.

Dervil gave a sudden yelp as she sucked over-enthusiastically at his penis, and yanked her hair painfully. 'Watch it, you little vampire. Didn't anyone ever tell you you're meant to suck, not bite?'

She raised her head at his reprimand, her cheeks flushed, her eyes shining and a glistening thread of saliva hanging down from her lower lip. Her jaw was aching and her knees hurt but she genuinely wanted to please him. After all, he might not know it, but she was going to take the Book of Punishment away from him soon. Sucking his cock seemed the least she could do in recompense.

'S – sorry,' she stammered, in what she hoped was a submissive voice. 'I got carried away.'

He motioned to her to turn around, kneeling up on the seat beside her. She obeyed, knees squeaking on the smooth leather, her heart beating fast as she guessed what he was planning to do.

Seconds later, she felt him move into position behind her. The large hands gripped her hips and dragged her closer. Then something extremely hot, hard and swollen nudged the moist lips of her pussy. She leaned forwards and spread her thighs wide to help him, eager as hell to feel that cock inside her. But he only slipped it in a couple of inches, just enough to dip himself in her warm fluids, before withdrawing. To her dismay, the head was then jammed against the tighter opening of her anus.

'Oh no,' she groaned, realising too late what he intended.

His laughter mocked her. 'Oh yes.'

She felt utter humiliation as her sphincter yielded with only the most cursory struggle, his cock sliding easily up inside her bottom in spite of its girth. Her cheeks were hot. There could be no doubt in his mind that she had been used there before, many times and with many different men. She winced, though, as he began to thrust, her rectum stretched to capacity and his balls slapping against her thighs with little regard for her comfort. It was not the gentlest act of sodomy she had ever experienced, she thought grimly. But it was certainly the most exciting.

Her face squashed against the door, fingers working between her thighs at the burning flesh of her pussy, Indigo stuck her haunches in the air and let each thrust take her closer to orgasm.

There was something so deliciously rude about her situation, it was hard not to come immediately. And she was only too aware of Natasha in the front, listening sulkily to every squeak and gasp and thud as they rocked back and forth on the leather seats, locked together like a pair of wrestlers. To add to her embarrassment, her thighs were slippery with the juice that dripped from the empty sack of her pussy. Nothing strange in that. She had expected him to fuck her, had been yearning to have him inside her ever since the spanking last night. But at least he was buggering her. And Indigo did love to be buggered. She was such a filthy trollop, she adored the sensation of a hard cock bloating her rectum. She could hardly wait to kneel up afterwards and feel his spunk dribble stickily from that forbidden hole.

It was true, there were few things she liked better than taking a man up her bottom. But surely not this man? Not Dervil Badon? He was such a consummate bastard, how could she perform such a messy, humiliating act with him and not hate herself for enjoying every second of it?

Her bottom was so accommodating, in fact, that he kept slipping out. Pushing his cock back inside with a grunt, Badon laughed. 'Not exactly your first time, is it? Feels like you've taken half the British army up your backside.'

'Bastard.'

'You want me to stop?'

Her cheeks scarlet with shame, she shook her head. 'Just get on with it. You didn't want a virgin anyway.'

'To be honest, I find it hard to believe you were ever a virgin.' He pulled out again to examine his penis, his voice deliberately insulting. 'My cock's filthy now, you should be ashamed of yourself. Don't you ever wash up there? Perhaps I should make you lick my cock clean. That would teach you a lesson.'

'No,' she moaned.

Ignoring her cries of protest, Dervil dragged her back onto her knees and pushed his penis into her mouth. Her lips had no choice but to accept him, right up to the heavy sac of his balls. The smell was disgusting, a foul grease coating her tongue and making her want to retch. Yet after a few half-hearted sucks, she felt her belly tense with pleasure and knew that her orgasm could not be far away.

How could she find such a degrading act exciting? First, taking his cock up her arse like some common slut in the back of his car; lorry drivers hooting as they caught a glimpse of her naked bottom in the air; now to be sucking his penis clean afterwards, her own bottom grease thick on her tongue; pushing her fingers up inside her pussy so she could pretend another man was fucking her while she sucked, eyes closed and her face dark with desire.

With a sudden groan, Dervil wrenched his penis free from her lips and sprayed his come liberally into her face. She tried to jerk away but he held her still. Powerful jets of whitish fluid hit her forehead, her eyelids and nose, streaming down her hot cheeks to her chin, dripping onto the leather upholstery below. She could see Natasha's eyes on her in the rear-view mirror, watching with every evidence of malicious enjoyment as Dervil shot his load into her face instead of inside her as she had hoped. No doubt if Christian was out there on his bike, he would be able to see all this too. Her humiliation was complete, she thought, hot tears of shame springing to her eyes as she realised what a filthy slut she was at heart.

'Good girl,' he muttered, dragging her towards him. 'Now it's your turn.'

Not sure what he meant by that, she felt him spread her thighs and reach for the damp fleshy lips of her pussy. He pinched her lips sharply a few times, then rolled the taut bud of her clitoris back and forth between his fingers until she gave a high-pitched cry and stiffened in his arms. Tiny electric shocks radiated out from her clitoris, followed by a series of bright searing explosions along her legs and spine that left Indigo gasping and flushed, her face buried against the strong wall of his chest.

As she flopped back after her orgasm, thoroughly exhausted, Dervil glanced down at his shirt with a rueful grimace. It was stained with his spunk, sporting several large damp patches where her cheeks must have rubbed against him during orgasm.

'Such a messy business, sex.'

'Sorry.'

'No matter, I brought plenty of clean shirts with me.' He tucked his penis back into his trousers and settled back with a sigh. 'So, do you perform as well upside-down? There's something in the Book of Punishment I'd like to try out on you. I think you'd look rather sweet tied to a wheel with a church candle sticking out of your bottom. Perhaps when we reach Paris –'

'You enjoy humiliating women, don't you?'

He looked at her, his eyes very dark as he examined the whitish spunk caked across her forehead and cheeks, drying now and beginning to flake as she rubbed at it.

'I'm not such an ogre as you would like to believe, my dear Indigo. I only humiliate women when they want me to humiliate them. Though it's true that you have stolen something of mine, something which cost me a

151

great deal of money and effort. And I intend to get my money back. Either by having you return the Book of Punishment or by making you work it off on your back, in time-honoured fashion.'

12

It must have been several hours later when a sudden jolt woke her. The Daimler had pulled up, though the engine was still running. She shifted slightly, eyes still closed against the sunlight, drifting back from the depths of an exhausted sleep. Natasha was muttering something under her breath, clearly irritated. There was a sharp click and rustling from the front seat, as though the Russian had opened the glove box for a map which she was now unfolding.

Had they arrived in Paris? Indigo wondered sleepily. Aware of an aching in her bottom, she turned on the leather seat to get more comfortable and slowly remembered the strap, the way it had left the skin there sore and probably bruised. This had been one hell of a trip so far, she thought. What else did they have in store for her?

Seconds later, she heard the driver's door open and felt cool air on her face. It took a few more seconds for the realisation to hit: Natasha had got out of the car and left her door open, which meant the central locking was no longer in operation.

Eyes snapping open, Indigo grabbed up her jeans and bag from the floor. Without thinking, she flung the passenger door wide open and threw herself from the car.

That was when she realised she was naked from the waist down, crawling on hands and knees in the middle of a busy street, car horns sounding and passers-by swearing effusively in French as she staggered to her feet. The loud roar of a motorbike reminded her of Christian's promise to help her escape. Staring over her shoulder, she saw a gleaming Harley Davidson pull up behind the Daimler and the leather-clad rider shout something from beneath his helmet.

Almost falling as she struggled to manoeuvre one of her legs into the jeans, Indigo hopped towards the bike. She straddled the black leather seat behind Christian, her bag slung hurriedly round her neck and both arms locked about his waist.

'Go, go!' she yelled over the throb of the engine.

'You can't ride naked!'

Indigo jerked her bare thigh away from the burning hot metal, belatedly realising he was right. Clinging onto him as the bike began to pull away, she pulled her left knee into her chest and prayed he was not planning to go round any sharp corners in the next few minutes. 'I'll deal with it. Just get us out of here, fast!'

Before she had even finished speaking, he had wheeled the bike in a tight circle and sped back down the road in the direction they had come. Glancing over her shoulder at the car, she saw Dervil staring furiously after her through the back window and Natasha standing helpless in the road as the bike disappeared from view, fists clenched by her side.

Bubbling with laughter, she squeezed Christian's waist and spoke into his ear. 'Well done! Now let's find somewhere quiet to pull up and I'll get my jeans on properly.'

A few miles further on, he turned the bike down a narrow sunlit side street, finding a high-walled alley behind a row of houses. There she leaped down from the bike and pulled her jeans up over her bare bottom and pussy, after hurriedly checking that no one was watching. The rough material felt odd and scratchy against her bruised skin, but there was nothing she could do about that. Her thong was still lying on the floor in the back of Dervil's car. She was barefoot too, her high heels having been kicked off hours ago. It was not the safest way to travel on a motorbike, but they did not have much choice.

'Where are we?' she asked, glancing up and down the alley. 'I'm absolutely starving, I must have been asleep for ages. Is this Paris?'

He shook his head. 'But we're not too far now, we should be there before dark. I'm glad you finally managed to get out, by the way. I've been desperate for a piss for the past couple of hours. But I didn't dare let the car out of my sight.'

'Be my guest,' she laughed.

Christian unzipped his leather jeans immediately and pulled out a long pale-skinned penis, which he pointed at the nearest wall. With a sigh of relief, he let go a high golden arc of urine. It spattered noisily against the brick wall, trickling down over a pile of torn cardboard boxes and green plastic bin bags which had been left at the base of the wall. He was not an unattractive boy, she thought, and licked her lips greedily. The heady rush of that escape had kick-started her system with adrenalin; now she felt ready for something a little naughty.

As he finished peeing, she came up behind him and slipped a hand inside his jeans to stroke his balls. Christian jerked and stared round at her, his face flushing.

'What's the matter?' she asked softly. 'Stop looking so worried. You deserve a reward for rescuing me.'

He was shaking his head, confused. 'You rescued yourself, Indigo. I just provided the getaway. There's no need, really.'

'Don't pull away!'

'Indigo, please . . .'

'Be quiet, you talk too much.'

Indigo smacked his backside in the tight blue jeans and heard the young man gasp. His penis grew suddenly

155

rigid in her hand. Of course, she remembered with a burst of amusement, he prefers to be dominated. Indigo gave him a few more brisk smacks on the backside, wondering how to play this. She had intended to kneel down and suck him off but it did not seem like the right choice any more; he was probably too submissive to enjoy fellatio. Perhaps she could make him lick her out while he masturbated? She could certainly do with an orgasm, to give her enough energy to get through the rest of this journey without collapsing.

'Come on, down on your knees,' she ordered him, pushing at his shoulders. As he complied, his face deeply flushed, she unzipped her jeans again and pulled them down until her pussy lips were exposed. One glance was enough to reassure her that they were alone in the high-walled alley. Then she pulled his head brutally into her crotch. 'Lick me out.'

His tongue flickered out with only the briefest of hesitations as he began to lick and suck at her pussy lips, making an odd groaning noise beneath his breath. With humiliation or pleasure, she wondered, then abruptly stopped caring as his tongue found her clitoris. Flicked backwards and forwards, then repeatedly from side to side, it was soon taut and erect, the fleshy lips below lubricating like crazy as her body dreamed of penetration. He was not bad at cunnilingus for such a young man, she thought, closing her eyes while she enjoyed his ministrations. It usually took men at least forty years to work out where the clitoris was and how to work it. But this one knew what he was doing. Seeming to sense her need for more, he nuzzled into her groin like a baby searching for its mother's nipple. His tongue burrowed deeper and lower between her sodden lips, finding the tight opening to her pussy and pushing inside.

She allowed herself a soft little moan at the intrusion and opened her legs even wider, balancing on her toes, eager to experience that tongue right up inside her. It felt like a miniature penis, working so hard down there she feared he would make himself sore. The hot sun beat down on her face as she tilted her head back, moving her hips rhythmically back and forth, letting his tongue fuck her.

'That's a good boy,' she muttered, stroking his short spiky blond hair. It bristled under her fingers, like a cat's fur stroked the wrong way. 'Now, start playing with yourself. Come on, get your cock in your hand, start tugging at it. But you'd better not come until I give you permission.'

He mumbled something unintelligible into her crotch and for a moment she thought he would refuse. Then she saw the padded leather shoulder of his biker's jacket rising and falling as his muscles worked, one fist clenched around an unseen cock somewhere below and that strong wrist jerking himself towards orgasm. The knowledge that Christian was masturbating while he licked out her pussy made the scene even more lewd and exciting. Sweat began to trickle down her forehead in the afternoon heat. Her legs were trembling so much she could hardly keep steady on her feet. She felt hot and oddly shivery at the same time.

Indigo was surprised by the pleasure she was feeling, perhaps even a little shocked. It was something she could really get into, this role of dominatrix. Though if she did it too often, she would probably begin to miss being the submissive one. There was only so much bullying she could do before she needed to drop to her knees and be bullied herself. That was her nature and there was nothing she could do about it.

She was suddenly aware that her bare feet were wet. She glanced down and half laughed, half groaned. 'Oh god, that's disgusting! I'm standing in your piss.'

Christian was shaking too. She could feel his body tremble as he kneeled before her, his tongue still working in her pussy. It would not take more than a few minutes for either of them to come, she thought, tugging fiercely at his hair.

How long did they have before Dervil caught up with her? Assuming that he could be bothered to pursue them at all, of course. This alternative copy of the Book of Punishment was in Paris. He would continue straight there to collect it, surely, rather than waste time chasing after a rival buyer. No doubt they would meet again, though, the antiquarian book trade being a relatively small world. Now he knew what a greedy submissive she was, a dominant like Dervil Badon would be unable to resist crossing her path again.

'Lick my clit again, lick it hard,' she gasped.

Groaning as his tongue slid obediently up the fleshy channel of her pussy to lick and suck at her clitoris, Indigo allowed herself to consider how Dervil might punish her when they eventually came face to face again. Hadn't he mentioned an illustration from the Book of Punishment when they were in the car? Some hellish-sounding torment with a wheel and a gag and possibly a burning candle stuck up inside her as she spun naked and upside-down. Just the thought of all that hot wax spilling over her thighs and breasts was enough to leave her trembling with excitement and fearful anticipation. Dervil was such a ruthless bastard, she felt sure he would remember threatening her with that punishment and force her to submit to it in the end.

She yanked the boy's head into her pussy and screamed, nipples stiffening and an intense cramp in her belly as the orgasm hit.

'Now let's see how well you can wank,' she said breathlessly, taking a quick step back and sticking her fingers up inside her pussy. The hot flesh sucked them inside, only too ready for a second orgasm. 'Show me what you've got in those balls. Come on, tug harder than that. I want to see your spunk all over the ground at my feet.'

She watched in fascinated silence as the young man masturbated to a climax as instructed, kneeling there in the alley, a frothing puddle of piss around his body and his face flushed with humiliated colour. The purplish head of his cock seemed to swell in his hand as his strokes became faster and more urgent. She knew how it felt to be watched like this, to feel your excitement mingle with a sense of degradation that only made each tingle of pleasure sharper and more piercing. Now he was experiencing that submission too and she was dominant for once. Indigo could never imagine a man like Dervil submitting like this, not in a million years. She tried to smile at the idea but could not manage it, rubbing so hard at her clitoris it felt almost sore.

His breath was coming faster and faster, his hand a blur on his cock, then he groaned loudly and spurted a copious stream of spunk onto the dirty ground, spattering across the stone and leaving her bare feet flecked with white. Indigo felt her legs tremble at the sight and closed her eyes as another orgasm began to scorch a path through her body. In her imagination, she saw Dervil standing over her with a leather whip in his hand. He brought it down across her exposed belly and crotch, telling her what a slut she was, how much he enjoyed punishing her, and that he would not stop whipping her until she crawled to him for mercy. As she stared into those dark eyes in her mind, she cried out with pleasure, two fingers stuck up inside her pussy as far as they would go and her thumb pressing hard against her clitoris.

The sound of applause from an upper window made them both freeze, and they hurriedly adjusted their clothes as they realised they had an audience. Indigo turned to stare up at the buildings behind them with one hand shielding her eyes from the sun.

But it was only a naked old man, a broad toothless smile on his wizened face as he pushed open the shutters and proudly waved his own semi-erect penis at her.

'Oh shit,' she muttered, not sure whether to be embarrassed or gratified by his obvious arousal.

Christian got to his feet, a dark colour in his face as he shook trickles of pee from his leather trousers. He handed her the spare helmet and began to put his gloves back on. Although his voice was a little uneven, he seemed remarkably in control. 'Better get out of here before grandad calls the police. I don't have any boots for you, but put the helmet on. That will protect your head at least.'

'Don't worry, we can stop and buy some boots. I'm more concerned about where we're going to stay. You said you had an aunt in Paris, is that right?'

'Heinrich's sister-in-law, Terese.' He swung onto the bike, and gestured to her to climb up behind him. 'You'll like her. She's in the trade, used to be a book binder. Retired now, though she still accepts the odd commission. I telephoned her from Geneva, told her to expect me sometime tonight. It's a small apartment just down from Montmartre but I should imagine she's got plenty of room for two.'

'That's excellent. My credit cards have taken quite a hit since the start of this trip and I wasn't looking forward to sleeping rough.'

He nodded, revving the bike. 'Ready?'

'I'm always ready.'

Indigo clambered up behind him with a laugh, though not before blowing the old man at the window a farewell kiss. His erection was beginning to wilt now and it felt cruel to leave the poor man with nothing but a memory of her half-naked body. Still, Christian was right. It would be incredibly awkward if somebody called the police.

She pulled the spare helmet down over her head; it was a snug fit but she managed to fasten the chin strap without too much difficulty. Linking her arms tightly around his waist, Indigo leaned into the warmth of his back as the bike roared away down the alley. Her bottom still ached from all the beatings and spankings of the past 48 hours and there was a damp patch at the crotch of her jeans, embarrassingly sticky as she shifted on the seat to get more comfortable. This was not exactly how she had envisaged her first trip to Paris, riding barefoot on a borrowed motorcycle, but at least she was not entering the city as Dervil's sex slave in the back of his vintage Daimler.

By the time they finally reached the suburbs of Paris, it was dark and she was exhausted. They had stopped to buy her a pair of blue leather biking boots, and had then had a meal at a roadside *relais* which Indigo devoured with hungry enthusiasm. She had lost weight since leaving London; the faded blue jeans hung loose on her hips and even her breasts felt smaller than usual. It must be all the sex, she thought wryly, not to mention the considerable amount of punishment she had been taking.

Not that she regretted a single moment of her adventures. She felt alive for the first time in months, her skin glowing and a naughty bounce in her step. The bookshop had become her life; it was her father's legacy to her and she would not let him down by selling it. But even she had to admit that dragging herself out of bed before seven o'clock most mornings and falling asleep by ten every night was a regime which left little energy for anything but work. Chasing the Book of Punishment halfway across Europe had not been her intention on leaving home. Yet she felt closer than ever to her father now, pursuing his dream with a passion reminiscent of his own obsession. Perhaps she was more her father's daughter than she realised.

After climbing two steep flights of stairs to the apartment in Montmartre, they knocked for several minutes without any response. Finally, Christian's aunt came to the door in a creased blue cotton house-coat, clutching the unbuttoned sides together and smoothing down her silvery hair as though she had only just climbed out of bed. But at least she seemed genuinely pleased to see her nephew.

A slender woman in her mid-sixties, Aunt Terese's mobile features expressed joy and warmth as she embraced them both and ushered them into her tiny apartment. 'Sit down, please, both of you. You must be dead on your feet, such a long journey. Please forgive my appearance, I was just taking a quick nap. Let me get you a drink. I always keep a bottle of Pernod in case I have guests.'

They crowded into her tiny and dimly lit living-room, removing their helmets and heavy leather biking boots with a sense of relief. The room was thickly shelved from wall to wall and cluttered with books, scattered across the floor, in precarious stacks behind the door, and piled untidily on every available chair and table. The whole place was an antiquarian treasure house, Indigo thought appreciatively, catching sight of a familiar title here and there amidst the chaos of spines and dusty calf-bound boards. There was a crowded bar-brasserie below the apartment, a hubbub of deep-voiced conversation and strains of music constantly drifting up through the floorboards. Hanging in the window was an ornate cage containing a scruffy and ancient-looking parrot, who gave an alarmingly strident shriek at their entrance and watched with deep suspicion as they tried to make themselves comfortable on her book-strewn sofa.

'*Merci, Tante Terese.*' Christian settled back on the sofa, one leg crossed over the other, and sipped cautiously at his glass of iced Pernod. 'Indigo is hunting for an eighteenth-century book of erotica. There may be a copy here in Paris but we don't know any of the dealers. We were hoping you might be able to point us in the right direction.'

His aunt draped a cloth over the parrot's cage, nodding with interest as she listened. 'Your friend is certainly in the right city for erotic literature. What's the name of this book she's searching for?'

'The Book of Punishment.'

Terese turned sharply and stared at Indigo, her blue eyes narrowed on her face. 'The Book of Punishment?'

'You've heard of it?' Indigo asked eagerly.

The older woman gave her an odd look, removing a pile of books to the floor so she could perch on one arm of the sofa. 'I've not only heard of the Book of Punishment, my dear. I've seen it.'

'Here in Paris?'

'Yes, right here in Paris. Though that was many years ago, when I was even younger than you are now. It belonged then to a dealer called Xavier. He had a basement apartment not far from the Boulevard St Germain. I was working in one of the hotels nearby and he used to invite me there during my lunch break so we could ...' Her face coloured and she paused, her manner suddenly confused. 'Well, one day there was another man there with him, an Englishman. I believe he was planning to buy the Book of Punishment from Xavier. But someone came into the apartment that day and stole it, right from under our noses. I don't think Xavier ever got it back.'

'An Englishman? Was his name Mortimer?'

'Yes, perhaps. Though I can't be sure now, it was so long ago. You know this man Mortimer?'

'He was my father.'

'*Was*?'

Indigo nodded. 'He died last year.'

'I'm sorry to hear that. I often remember that day; your father was an attractive man, he had real charisma.'

'Thank you.'

Christian's aunt nodded and smoothed the cotton house-coat over her bare knee. As the material shifted,

Indigo caught a glimpse of breast higher up, a large dark nipple hurriedly hidden behind folds of cloth. So the older woman was naked beneath that thin cotton wrap. What had she said on opening the door to them? That she had been taking a nap? There was a faint flush in the woman's cheeks. Pleasuring herself seemed a likelier explanation for her nudity; lying down on her bed and bringing herself to a climax in the sticky evening heat. What exactly had they done to her in that basement, Xavier and her father? Which dreadful punishments had they administered from the book before it was stolen?

When Terese spoke again, her voice seemed huskier than before. 'Now you search for the Book of Punishment just like your father. But are you sure it can still be found in Paris?'

Christian nodded, finishing his Pernod and placing the empty glass carefully on a pile of books. 'We've been told there's a copy for sale somewhere in the city. We were hoping you might know the vendor.'

'Oh, I'm not sure I can help you. I'm retired now, I don't know any of the new dealers in antiquarian erotica. But I suppose . . .' The older woman mused for a moment, her lips pursed. 'Well, there are a few places you could try along the left bank.'

'Near the Eiffel Tower?' Indigo asked, then shrugged helplessly. 'There may be some connection, maybe not.'

'*La Tour* Eiffel? But of course, how stupid of me!'

'What is it?'

'It must be Jean-Luc who is selling the book. Xavier's son. He's an odd character, though, has a penchant for submissive women.'

Christian grinned at Indigo. 'Sounds just your type.'

'That's not funny!'

'He has a shop on the outskirts of the city but some weekdays he runs a stall only a few blocks from the Eiffel Tower. I have his mobile number here somewhere.' Terese began hunting distractedly through the piles of books scattered about the room. 'It's too late to contact him tonight, he'll be pissed out of his head by now. But we could telephone him first thing in the morning, perhaps arrange a meeting?'

'That would be perfect,' Indigo nodded, ignoring the way Christian was shaking his head in mock warning. Whatever it might take, she told herself, she was not leaving Paris without another crack at the Book of Punishment. She had come this far unharmed; why not take a risk and push on a little further?

13

The next morning Indigo and Christian breakfasted early on croissants and milky coffees, then took the Metro out to the Eiffel Tower. They had agreed to meet Jean-Luc opposite the tower, in a bar crowded with tourists. He was waiting for them as they approached, a large broad-shouldered man in his forties, his skin swarthy and an unfiltered cigarette stuck permanently between his lips as he spoke. He had brought someone else with him, a much older man with dark watchful eyes and a persistent cough.

It was a windy day and the striped canopy fluttered and flapped angrily in the sunlight as they shook hands.

'So you are Mortimer's daughter,' Jean-Luc said, glancing at the older man beside him. 'This is my own father, Xavier. He knew your father very well.'

'Xavier?' Indigo stared intently at the older man, putting out a hand and feeling those thin bony fingers seize hers in a surprisingly strong grip. 'You must be the man who tried to sell my father the Book of Punishment in 1959.'

'*Oui*,' the old man croaked in a hoarse smoker's voice, nodding. His eyes wandered over her body; she was wearing the light summer dress which Terese had lent her. His grunt was expressive as he glanced at his son. '*Pas mal, pas mal du tout*.'

Christian summoned a waiter, and gallantly pulled out a chair so that Indigo could sit down. 'Shall we have a drink before we get down to business?'

'Only a very quick one,' Jean-Luc said, looking pointedly at his watch. 'My father and I are due to go up in a hot-air balloon within the hour. So this conversation will have to be continued another time. Perhaps over dinner at my place tomorrow?'

Indigo shook her head, frowning. 'I have to get back to London as soon as possible.'

The large man shrugged and stepped away from the table, throwing up his hands in an expressive gesture. 'My apologies if it's inconvenient, but we can't delay departure. If you want to talk to me, you will have to stay in the city another day at least.' He laughed, meeting her eyes. 'Unless you feel like sailing the skies of Paris in a hot-air balloon.'

'Go up in the balloon?'

'If you dare.'

She bit her lip, glancing from one Frenchman to the other and thinking hard. 'Before I make a decision, let's get one thing straight. Do you own a genuine copy of the Book of Punishment?'

Jean-Luc nodded silently.

'Is it for sale?'

'For the right price and to the right person . . . yes.'

'Then I'll come up in the balloon with you.'

Christian put a hand on her arm, a look of concern on his face as he leaned forwards to whisper urgently in her ear. 'Don't be stupid, Indigo. You hardly know these men. It could be dangerous.'

'I know they have a copy of the Book of Punishment. That's enough for me.' Indigo shook off his hand and pushed back her chair, standing up to face the two men. 'When do we leave?'

'Right away.'

Christian got to his feet too, staring aggressively at Jean-Luc. 'If anything should happen to her . . .'

'Then you will cut me into a thousand pieces and feed me to the crocodiles. Yes, I understand how it goes.' The large man laughed, his whole belly shaking as he stepped past Christian and seized Indigo's arm in a possessive grip. 'We will alight outside the city later this afternoon, beside the river at Mille Champs. Collect your friend there if you want her back. You know the place?'

'I'll find it,' Christian said sullenly.

'*On y va, alors.*'

Which was how, about an hour later, Indigo found herself staring down from the basket of a hot-air balloon as it rose steadily above the level of the roof-tops. The view over the city was breathtaking: streets, houses, people, all shrinking rapidly as the balloon rose higher and higher. Soon it was no longer possible for her to work out where they were, only the glittering ribbon of the Seine still visible as a marker of their position. Indigo clutched the edge of the basket and felt the whole structure sway alarmingly beneath her.

She steadied herself against the wicker walls, feeling much cooler now they had risen so high above the houses. Why had she not thought to bring a jacket? Not only was her light summer dress no barrier against the strong breeze, but she was wearing nothing beneath it and the chill winds were reaching her pussy now.

Though that was hardly her fault, she thought wryly. With no clean underwear that morning, she had been faced with two simple choices: going commando or borrowing some of Terese's old-fashioned cotton ones. Never a fan of those snug high-waisted panties, she had opted for the risky but more amusing bare-bottomed look. Now, though, she was beginning to regret her decision as the wind whipped so violently up and under her dress that she kept having to grasp it with both hands and force the flimsy material down.

Feeling dizzy and a little light-headed as the balloon rose higher, she turned to smile at Jean-Luc with a rush of enthusiasm. 'What an incredible feeling! Does the balloon belong to you?'

He shook his head, gesturing at Xavier who was adjusting the height of the flame in the burner. 'It's my father's pride and joy. He's been ballooning since he was a boy. Not scared, then?'

'Of you or the balloon?'

Jean-Luc grinned. 'I can see why your friend didn't want you to come up with us. You will get yourself into trouble, talking like that.'

'I usually do.'

The large man gave an abrupt laugh but, to her surprise, did not follow up on her unspoken challenge. 'Look, I have to help my father for a few minutes. Don't touch the burner and try not to rock the basket. Apart from that, feel free to look down at the city and enjoy the view.'

Naturally obedient, Indigo stayed where she was for a while, leaning on the hard edge of the wicker basket and staring out over the city as the two men behind her worked in silent unison. Soon they had managed to clear the city and were sailing gracefully over a sunlit patchwork of houses and tower blocks, the round shadow of the balloon clearly visible below them. Her heart was thudding in her chest as she remembered Christian's warning. She was alone up here with two strangers and could not possibly hope to protect herself in such a tiny space. But it was too late to do anything about it, she told herself; under the circumstances, she might as well try to relax and enjoy the ride.

Once he had finished helping his father with the balloon's ascent, Jean-Luc turned back towards her. He wiped his large sweaty palms on his jeans and put a finger under her chin, tilting Indigo's head back so he could examine her face. His voice was dry. 'As my father said, you're not an unattractive piece. Not bad at all. So what does a girl like you want with the Book of Punishment?'

'Probably the same as you.'

His eyebrows shot up in disbelief. 'You enjoy reading about how to punish and humiliate women?'

'Don't you?'

His eyes narrowed on her face, his expression thoughtful and speculative. He let go of her chin, his hand dropping to his side. 'The Book of Punishment is a classic in the world of erotic literature,' he said carefully. 'Ever since my father first told me about it, I've wanted to own a copy myself.'

'Ditto.'

A slow appreciative smile spread across his face. His eyes dropped to the high jut of her breasts, visibly outlined under the summer dress. The wind was so chill up there in the basket, both her nipples were already stiff, straining against the thin material in an impossibly rude manner. His smile grew broader as he eyed them. 'Cold?'

'Freezing.'

'Well, here's one way to warm you up.'

He stooped and caught the fluttering hem of her dress in both hands. To her shocked surprise, Jean-Luc pulled the dress up over her head in one swift movement, stripping Indigo of her only defence. Nude and shivering in front of the two men, she dropped her hands to her crotch, unsuccessfully trying to cover her sex. But it was far too late for such modesty. They had both seen her nakedness and the lust in their eyes told her what was to come.

Not wishing to admit how vulnerable she felt, Indigo glanced from one man to the other. 'I'm not sure how taking my dress off is going to warm me up,' she said tartly.

Jean-Luc's father, who had remained almost completely silent since leaving the ground, muttered something in his son's ear. Judging by the bulge in the old man's trousers, he intended to take an active part in whatever they had planned for her.

170

Jean-Luc turned to stare at his father, then glanced down at the looped pile of nylon rope in one corner of the basket. '*Bonne idée*,' he grunted appreciatively, reaching for the rope and winding a short length about his sinewy forearm as though testing it for strength and flexibility.

Her eyes wide with apprehension, she stared at the rope in his hands as he began to make a series of knots at regular intervals along its length. What on earth was he going to do with a rope like that? Could they be sadists, she wondered, planning to hang her upside-down from the basket? She took a hurried step backwards, only to find her bare bottom meeting the hard wicker sides of the basket. There was nowhere to run, she realised, her expression grim as she considered the unpromising situation in which she had placed herself.

'Come on, Jean-Luc.' Her skin was clammy, her heart beating fast as she tried to stay calm. 'Put the rope away. I came up here to talk about the Book of Punishment, not play dangerous games.'

'Any woman who talks about the Book of Punishment is already playing a dangerous game,' he pointed out. He gazed admiringly at her nudity, the cold pale sheen of her breasts and belly tautening in the wind. 'I believe you consider yourself an expert on fetishism. Do you know anything about Japanese rope bondage?'

'Not much,' she admitted.

He shrugged. 'It makes no difference. Now's your chance to learn.'

'Does it hurt?'

The old man laughed at her question and pulled her forwards so she was standing only a few inches from Jean-Luc. The wicker basket creaked under their feet, reminding her sharply that they were hundreds of feet up in the air. Xavier's voice was hoarse in her ear.

'Of course it hurts, mademoiselle. Why waste our time with it otherwise? But it is beautiful too. You will see.'

171

The knotted rope was looped gently around her back and pulled up into her armpits. Jean-luc then pulled the two loose ends down past her breasts and belly, and passed them under her crotch through to Xavier, who drew them up her back on the other side. She whimpered at the odd disquieting sensation of one of the smaller knots becoming lodged between her sex lips, first rubbing and then pressing against her clitoris. The old man ordered her not to move, his thigh nudging hers as he passed the two ends of ropes back through to Jean-Luc. He was clearly aroused by her discomfort and uncertainty.

She felt the hard bulge of an erection pressing against her hip and stared up into Jean-Luc's face, wondering if he too was aroused. But if she had hoped for mercy from that quarter, Indigo was disappointed. The smile had vanished from the Frenchman's face and been replaced by a frown of concentration.

Jean-Luc paid no attention to her whispered protests, working with rapid expertise as he wove the loose ends between the ropes dangling from her chest and passed them through to Xavier again. She stared down at her breasts and belly, feeling the large fingers brush repeatedly against her skin, the white nylon rope drawn taut as a diamond pattern began to emerge above her breasts and across her ribcage. And with each new pass of the rope, the knot between her exposed labia dug in even deeper, leaving her aching for more.

The Frenchman turned her in his hands like a doll, pushing one knee firmly into the small of her back to draw the knotted rope more tautly about her body. 'The Japanese call this the *karada*. You begin to see how it works?'

'Yes,' she gasped, staring up into a sky so blue it dazzled her eyes and left her half blind. The wind up there was so strong, her vision was soon blurred with tears.

172

He secured the diamond pattern with a more complicated knot than the others; she felt it bite into her spine and winced. His tone was concerned. 'Uncomfortable? Hold still while I adjust it.' His fingers quickly loosened it, retying the knot a little further to one side. 'Is that better?'

'Thank you,' she whispered.

He turned her to face him again, ignoring the lurch of the wicker basket beneath them and bringing the thin nylon ropes back to the front. Even though he had loosened that last knot for her, she was still finding it hard to take anything deeper than shallow breaths as he worked on creating another diamond, this time just below her ribcage. She was sweating now in spite of the chill wind. How far was he planning to take this game? The rope was beginning to hurt, her restriction becoming more complete every minute. Could she trust these men, or had she taken an appalling risk by putting herself in the hands of two strangers?

Some of that panic must have shown on her face because Jean-Luc paused, taking a few seconds to stroke the damp hair back from her face. That brief touch reassured her and she managed a smile in return, a restless heat between her legs as he fell to his work again and the crotch knot dragged against her sex with every tug of the rope. To her surprise, she could feel an orgasm beginning to build, her muscles tensing with pleasurable anticipation. Perhaps she should take her own advice and try to relax.

While Jean-Luc continued to loop the ropes around her ribs and back, weaving both ends in and out to create a series of tiny diamonds that ate into her flesh as the ropes tightened, his father found her nipples and played with the stiff peaks until she could not bear to stay silent any longer. A shuddering groan escaped her lips, her body almost too heavy with pleasure for her legs to support it.

173

As she sagged, the old man slipped his hands under her arms and held her upright. The basket swayed precariously and she cried out, suddenly afraid.

Xavier spoke close to her ear, croaking a stream of praise and admiration in his hoarse French. His voice gave her new strength and she stopped struggling, relaxing against his body. The nylon diamonds around her breasts and ribcage were in danger of constricting her breathing yet somehow she felt safe with these two men. Not only safe, but desirable too. She had been restrained before, of course, but never so thoroughly, nor with such loving attention to detail.

'Nearly finished,' Jean-Luc muttered, his hands working at hip level as he secured the ropes with a satisfied grunt.

Indigo could feel the nylon biting into her abdominal muscles, almost tighter than she could bear. The corresponding pressure at her crotch left her gasping and moaning with each additional twist of the rope. It was like being trussed up for cooking, she thought, every inch of her torso and pelvis aware of the cruel rope and how it restricted all natural movement. Her nipples were sore from the old man's fingers, her skin puckered in the windy sunlight as he stroked and flicked at their stiff peaks. She was inches away from climax the entire time, biting her lips to prevent herself from groaning and letting them know how excited she was.

As Jean-Luc completed the final diamond in his intricate pattern, that wicked knot which had been resting so unbearably between her labia was suddenly drawn up tight against her clitoris. She cried out in fierce helpless pleasure, her head back and mouth wide open as a powerful orgasm gripped her body. Her ribcage flexed against the ropes, trying desperately to inflate with air.

'Oh my god,' she moaned, staring wildly up at the vast billowing silk panels of the balloon. The roar of the

174

flame filled her ears and she almost fainted, her knees buckling weakly beneath her.

The large Frenchman caught her in his arms, turning her rope-bound body until she was kneeling with her face pressed against the wall of the wicker basket. Even though she could guess what he intended, she still felt helpless to resist, the criss-cross pattern of diamonds strapping her ribs down in a rope corset so she could hardly move.

His penis nudged against the exposed star of her anus and Indigo moaned, still flushed and breathless from her orgasm.

'Please,' she hissed over her shoulder, 'don't put it up there. Not up my bottom.'

But like Dervil before him, Jean-Luc paid absolutely no attention to her protests. She heard him spit, and felt something slimy being rubbed on her ring. She bowed her head and gritted her teeth, waiting for the inevitable moment of discomfort as he penetrated her. What was the attraction of that dirty little hole for men? Then suddenly he was inside her, the tight sphincter yielding to his erect penis with only the briefest flash of pain, and she stopped thinking. The sensation of something so thick and hard pushing up inside her rectum, while her torso was squeezed as though by a giant python, wiped everything from her mind except for an extremely urgent need to come again.

As Jean-Luc began to feed his penis into her bottom, his father knelt beside them and reached between her legs. She shook her head, trying not to respond; after all, they had tricked her into this little threesome. But she simply could not help her body's traitorous reaction. The old man found that small slippery knot which had lodged so snugly between her labia at the beginning, and rolled it back and forth across the aching flesh of her clitoris until she was forced to moan with agonised pleasure.

The basket rocked violently with each determined thrust. Yet even the fear of falling added to her excitement as she relaxed into an odd sensation of weightlessness, floating free above the roof-tops and fields in the hot-air balloon. Her taut nipples rubbed against the rough floor of the basket as she moved with his thrusts. Would the old man fuck her in the arse too, after his son had finished? Such a filthy mental picture made her moan even louder as she imagined the large man withdrawing, his cock still sticky with the thick oily grease of her bottom, and the older man fumbling to take his son's place inside her.

Indigo was panting now, the nylon rope cutting deep into the soft tender flesh of her breasts and belly. She was entirely at their mercy, she thought; they could do whatever they wished with her. The realisation made her gasp and writhe under Jean-Luc's forceful thrusts, her bottom able to accommodate even his thick length with ease. It was the second time in two days that she had been buggered, and the firm muscular walls of her rectum accepted his cock without too much discomfort.

'You need a little help, mademoiselle?'

Laughing when she moaned assent, Xavier abandoned her clitoris to slide several fingers up inside her empty sex. The old man stroked the thin wall between vagina and rectum, the sheer pressure of both holes being used at the same time driving her crazy, and did not stop even when she began to whine like a creature in pain. It took less than a minute of such intensely pleasurable friction for her to climax again, almost losing consciousness as the rope harness tightened about her torso.

When Xavier finally withdrew his fingers, fluid ran from her pussy, soaking the nylon knot and trickling down her thighs in a disgraceful display of wanton arousal.

With a guttural oath, Jean-Luc suddenly shoved himself up inside her rectum and unloaded his balls.

She gasped a few words of encouragement in French, pushing her bottom backwards until it collided with the hard wall of his thighs. His large hands gripped the rope around her hips and dragged it upwards, and she gave a sharp cry of pain and pleasure as the knot between her labia pressed even more deeply into her flesh. Then Jean-Luc withdrew, breathing hard as he rocked backwards on his heels. His spunk was expelled from her bottom in several bubbling spurts, coating her pussy lips in glorious slime as it dribbled down to mingle with her own juices.

Indigo put her hands between her legs to ease the discomfort but there was little she could do. Her anus stung and even her clitoris felt raw from the rope friction. She had been thoroughly bottom-fucked and she knew it.

Later she knelt for them again in the sunlight, red-faced and still finding it hard to breathe fully, as the two men released the knotted rope which had held her captive for the past hour or so. Even when the rope had been removed, however, Indigo could still see the deep imprint of its diamonds criss-crossing her flesh. They were nearing the site for descent and it would be inconvenient for anyone to see her like this. Most people would not understand the significance of the marks; but the three of them did. She looked down at herself, and saw that it was as though she had been branded by the rope, her act of submission leaving intricate marks all over her torso as clear as any beating.

'Beautiful,' Jean-Luc murmured, releasing the final knot and standing to admire the effect.

'Where did you learn to do this?' she asked huskily, fingering the strange weave pattern pressed into both sides of her breasts. 'It's amazing.'

'I'm glad you approve,' he smiled, handing the coiled thin nylon rope to his father. 'Most women dislike the constriction of rope bondage but I could see how much you enjoyed it. I was taught the basic layerings by a

177

Japanese master some years ago, in exchange for a book on Western bondage techniques.'

She managed a wry smile in return, reaching for her dress as the wind began to chill her again. 'So do I get the Book of Punishment in exchange for this?'

He shrugged. 'Why not?'

Taken aback by such a ready acceptance, Indigo stopped dressing herself and stared up at the dealer through narrowed eyes. 'You mean it? I can have the book without having to pay?'

'Well, you've certainly earned it,' Jean-Luc said comfortably, turning to help his father as the balloon began to descend again. Soon they were drifting down towards a stretch of green-gold fields alongside the river, a hilltop village in the near distance. He shot her an ironic glance as she stood beside them and gazed out over the rolling French countryside. 'I'm not known for my generosity, it's true. But your performance today was worth the Book of Punishment. So you might as well take it home with you.'

'It's here?' she asked eagerly.

Jean-Luc pointed to an old blue rucksack on the floor of the basket. 'The book's in there, wrapped up in brown paper,' he said briefly, before turning back to ensure a safe descent as the balloon neared the ground. His eyes were focused on the land below; they were planning to end up in a large grassy field beside the river where there was already a small crowd of people gathered. 'Go on, take it before I change my mind.'

She was winded by the sudden jolt as the balloon basket hit the ground, the silk canopy above them rippling violently in the breeze. Beyond the crowd she could see Christian standing beside a small car, his hand raised in greeting. So he had managed to follow Jean-Luc's directions to the landing site, she thought, with a growing sense of relief. Now at least she would not be walking back to Paris.

Smiling up at the two men, Indigo tucked the parcel containing the Book of Punishment safely under her arm. 'Thank you,' she murmured to them both, 'for an interesting ride.'

'Not at all,' Jean-Luc replied, his mouth twitching in a smile. 'I just hope you enjoy the Book of Punishment as much as this trip.'

'I'm sure I will.'

The old man kissed her hand, his lips dry on her skin. 'You are very beautiful, mademoiselle. Next time we meet it will be me who fucks you in the arse.'

'It's a promise,' she nodded.

As Christian drove her back to Paris in his aunt's hatchback, she put her bare feet up on the dashboard in the sunshine and tore open the brown paper parcel. Her hands trembled on the full leather boards, torn slightly along the spine and faded by the years, turning the eighteenth-century book over in her hands as she absorbed the weight and smell of it. It was not in first-class condition, but that was only to be expected for a book of its age. At least now she would be able to read it and see for herself the graphically illustrated punishments which had so excited her father.

Then Indigo opened the book and gave a cry of disappointment. 'I don't believe it!'

'What's the matter?' Christian slowed down, turning his head to stare at the book. 'Isn't it the Book of Punishment?'

'Yes, it's the Book of Punishment,' she said tightly. 'But not a genuine first edition. This one was printed in Paris, 1798.'

'So?'

Indigo closed her eyes, frustration gnawing cruelly at her as she realised how Jean-Luc had tricked her. Both her and Dervil Badon, probably. No doubt he had decided it would be easier to get away with double-crossing her than Dervil, who might go back and punch him in the nose once his deception had been revealed. God, she wanted to make him pay! But it was impossible. She had no time to take her revenge on the duplicitous Frenchman and his father. Not on this trip, anyway.

'The original Book of Punishment was printed the year before that, in London. But it was banned almost as soon as it hit the streets, burned by the authorities as a lewd work. So the basic text was copied by a enthusiast the following year and printed in Paris. But it wasn't even remotely the same as the first London edition. For a start, there were no illustrations and only a few of the original punishments.' She threw the useless book down onto the floor of the car, tears pricking at her eyes. 'This isn't the Book of Punishment. It's a travesty.'

There was silence as Christian absorbed that information, glancing at her with a sympathetic expression as he manoeuvred the Renault onto the crowded Boulevard Périphérique.

'Poor Indigo,' he said quietly. 'So what are you planning to do now? Don't forget I can give you a lift back to Geneva if you're heading that way.'

'I have to get back to London. The bookshop is suffering. I can't afford to be away any longer.'

'Not even time for one last evening in Paris?' His hand rested on her thigh for a moment, his smile provocative. 'I know an amusing little place where the ladies are all men and the men are all ladies.'

Unable to resist his charm, Indigo threw back her head and laughed. 'Christian, you are utterly incorrigible.'

14

Dervil slid back behind the wheel of the Daimler, his face tight with fury. His fists were clenched as he stared across the field to where the brightly coloured hot-air balloon stood, billowing in a light breeze, two men deep in conversation beside its wicker basket. Rage gripped him by the throat as he remembered what they had told him, their smiles as he swore impotently and paced the grass in front of the balloon. His chest hurt and he could hardly breathe. This was twice in a row that Indigo had stolen the Book of Punishment from right under his nose.

He could hardly believe this was happening to him. To him, Dervil Badon, one of the most feared and respected masters on the scene! He tried to envisage Indigo suffering a series of the vilest punishments imaginable, but none of them seemed painful or humiliating enough to do justice to his wrath.

He could feel Natasha's eyes on his face. Her voice was perplexed. 'What's the matter? Didn't they remember to bring the book?'

'Oh yes, they remembered,' he said tersely. 'They sold it to Indigo about an hour ago. Apparently she's already on her way back to London with it.'

'My god, I don't believe it!'

Dervil ignored her, his mind churning in turmoil as he considered his next move. That conniving little bitch! So far, she had managed to get hold of both available copies of the Book of Punishment and single-handedly make him a laughing-stock in the antiquarian book community. One day he would catch up with Indigo, he promised himself, and then he would make her pay for this embarrassing defeat.

He turned the key in the ignition and listened to the powerful engine purr into life beneath the bonnet. 'There's no point staying in France. The book's gone. Let's get back on the autoroute and try to make the coast before dark.'

Leaning on the ferry rail all the way back to England, staring out at the rolling sea, Dervil could not stop his mind playing back the humiliating events of the past week. How the hell had a girl like Indigo managed to get the best of him? He had thwarted her in Geneva by getting to the Book of Punishment first, and even though she had somehow stolen it from him at Wolf-mann's party, the pleasure he had taken in punishing her afterwards had almost been worth the theft. And now she had even taken the alternative copy as well, promised to him on the phone by Jean-Luc. He had been so sure the book would be his this time. To stand there and listen to their lame excuses – '*pardon*, mon-sieur, but she offered us something you never could' – and realise she was on her way back to London with the book at that very moment, no doubt laughing at him for a fool, had made Dervil feel physically sick.

In typical fashion, it started to drizzle with rain as they drove off the car ferry and back onto English soil at last. Though it was the early hours of the morning, the quayside was crowded, holidaymakers queuing in their cars for the cheaper night ferries across to main-land Europe. Dervil drove past them in silence, his mind still preoccupied. He turned the car towards London and set the windscreen wipers in motion, watching them sweep rhythmically across the glass as the rain began to fall in earnest.

Natasha glanced sideways at his profile, still angrily averted, and gave a long exaggerated sigh. 'Please don't look so gloomy, darling,' she murmured in an appeasing tone. 'It wasn't an entirely wasted trip. You did manage to pick up those erotic comic books from Wolfmann, and we spent such a romantic night in Paris.'

He laughed harshly. 'Romantic? I caned the soles of your feet before buggering you over a dirt-encrusted bathtub.'

'I enjoyed it.'

'That's because you're a complete masochist.'

Natasha smiled at him. 'Thank you.'

His fingers tapped the wheel restlessly, his mind still working hard as he remembered the mistakes that had been made, the opportunities missed. 'I would have done better to leave you behind. It was your fault she escaped with that idiot Christian. What on earth made you get out of the car like that?'

'I was lost. I needed to ask for directions.'

'How can anyone possibly get lost heading for Paris? The bloody road signs are everywhere.'

She was losing her temper as well now, the Russian accent thickening until her words became almost unintelligible. 'I took a wrong turn, OK? I forgot about the central locking. So I'm not perfect. What are you going to do about it?'

'Beat you until you scream,' he snarled back, clenching his fists on the wheel until his knuckles whitened. 'That's what you deserve.'

'Go on, then. I dare you!'

His laughter was furious. 'What, and play right into your hands? You'd enjoy it far too much. You probably let her go deliberately, just so you could trick me into an extra punishment.'

'You're a bastard, Dervil Badon.'

'And you,' he replied silkily, 'are a greedy, transparent, wet-cunted transsexual who loves nothing better than a cane across your backside and a cock up your arse.'

'Yes, yes!' She clutched his arm as he drove through the dark countryside at speed, her voice a persuasive purr in his ear. 'Darling, there's no other man in the world who knows me like you do. Let me come back and live with you again. No more silly games this time, no more lovers. I'll cook and clean and be a proper woman for you, I swear it on the Holy Bible.'

'And my clients?'

Natasha shrugged, pouting. 'You can do whatever you like in your own home. I won't interfere.'

His eyes scanning the road signs in the distance, Dervil shook his head with a slow ironic smile. He had heard all this before and he knew she was just day-dreaming. 'You talk a good master-slave relationship, Natasha. But the truth is, you can't handle even the slightest competition. As soon as my next client walked through that door, you'd be there in the hallway to scare them off; sabotaging my reputation just like you did last time.'

'I didn't understand last time. Now I realise it's just business. You hurt these women, you humiliate them. Then you take their money. It's not about pleasure. It's about making a living.'

'You think I don't enjoy it?'

She hesitated, frowning at him. 'Maybe a little bit. But it's always better with someone you love, surely?'

Dervil did not know how to answer that. He felt a muscle begin to jerk repeatedly in his cheek. It was nearly two in the morning and he had been behind the wheel ever since Paris.

Without saying a word, he pulled the car over at the next lay-by, a slip road hidden from the main road by a screen of high thorn bushes, and turned off the engine. There was an articulated lorry parked in front of them but the cab was in darkness, the driver presumably asleep. The engine ticked gently as he sat listening to the patter of rain on the car roof. It was his own fault, he thought grimly. He should never have let her back into his life, not even in return for information about the Book of Punishment. What good had it done him, after all? He did not have the book but Natasha was still here, talking to him in this disturbing way, badgering him to take her back.

'Get out of the car,' he said curtly, rubbing the back of his neck with a weary hand.

'What?'

'Stop staring at me and do what you're told. It's time we straightened this out the old-fashioned way.'

He opened the driver's door and went to the boot to remove her favourite leather strap from his suitcase. It was still raining but he ignored it, his sudden desire to hurt her too strong to resist. She followed him in confusion, her face pale in the darkness and her long legs bare below the tiny black skirt. Dervil tried to feel something for the woman, some spark of affection from the past, but he was too tired and numb to register anything. However, the thought of bending her over the white bonnet of the Daimler and giving her the strap made his penis stir with sudden interest.

Frowning, he tested the well-oiled leather strap against his palm. It made a satisfying thwack on his skin, tough but not too stiff. Perhaps he was making a mistake, turning away a willing sex slave and housekeeper. But he had got used to living alone now; it would only disrupt his life to take her back.

'Bend over the bonnet and pull up your skirt,' he ordered her, his tone almost bored.

She glanced around reluctantly. 'Here? But what about the lorry driver? We might be seen.'

'That's never bothered you in the past.'

After a moment's pause, presumably wrestling with an injured sense of dignity, Natasha stalked to the curved white bonnet of the Daimler and bent straight over it, raising her skirt to her waist as instructed. Not surprisingly, she was wearing nothing underneath; the smooth shaven lips of her sex were on full display, her buttocks gleaming in the headlights of passing cars.

'Get on with it, then,' she snapped.

Dervil felt an erection begin to press against the crotch of his trousers and raised the strap in retaliation. The beautiful transsexual squealed at the first stroke but stayed where she was, her legs still spread wide for him and her buttocks raised invitingly. He could see the pale bruises and scars of old punishments criss-crossing her bottom in a delicate lace-like pattern, clearly visible in the light from the moon. Why did he have to find her sexually attractive? She was nothing but a nuisance and a distraction.

He brought the strap down hard again, admiring the thick whitish mark it left behind, which rapidly flooded with red to leave a new bruise on her mottled skin.

'I'm sorry, master,' she gasped, writhing in pleasure against the car bonnet as he struck her again.

'What for?'

Natasha sounded bemused. 'I don't know. For being a bad slave? For talking to you like that? I'm sorry because you're angry with me and I don't understand why.'

This time Dervil aimed at the tender flesh just below her buttocks, leaving a thin cruel stripe across the top of her thighs. Her skin was wet with rain, shiny and slick as dampened rubber. The look of it pleased him and he felt his mood begin to soften. 'I'm not angry with you. I'm angry with myself.'

She moaned, swiftly rubbing herself before putting her hands back flat on the bonnet. 'Why?'

'Because there's no point in you coming back to live with me. I'd be no good for you, Natasha. You said it yourself, I'm a bastard.'

'I love bastards.'

He laid the strap on even harder, his breath coming in short pants now, his chest heaving. She was right, it was too public here. Giving her the strap was one thing. But if he wanted to fuck her, he would have to take her inside the car or find a spot in the bushes where they could not be seen. The matter was becoming urgent. As the skin on her bottom reddened and glowed in the moonlight, so the bulge in his trousers grew more and more uncomfortable.

'Sooner or later, we'd only split up again. It was hell last time; I don't want to go through that a second time.' He put a hand between her thighs, felt for the smooth lips of her sex and slid a couple of fingers inside. 'Let's just fuck tonight and go our separate ways.'

She raised her head from the bonnet, her pupils dilated with pleasure and her face darkly flushed. 'Hit me harder first.'

'You've had enough.'

'Please, Dervil. I need it.'

He grabbed her by the wrist and yanked her towards him. She seemed almost in a trance, blonde hair sticking to her face and her lips moistly parted. Her blouse was transparent from where she had been leaning on the rain-slick bonnet, nipples straining against the thin clinging fabric. He knew that look on her face; she badly needed to be fucked. His cock felt like a piece of wood in his trousers, it was so rigid.

'I said no. You've had your fun; now it's my turn.'

After pulling her into the thick cluster of bushes, Dervil pushed Natasha to her knees without any regard for her comfort and released his cock. It sprang free, hot and swollen in his hand, and he knew there was not much time left for playing games.

He had a sudden desire to rub himself between those large firm breasts, so lewdly visible through the sodden blouse, until he came. Yet it would be a pity to waste such an accommodating mouth or miss the lush depths of her arse, one of his favourite parts of her body. This might be their last time together, after all. He had

187

wanted the occasion to be a memorable one, not some fumbled quickie in a lay-by on the outskirts of Dover.

Though it was apt, he thought ironically, to be ending their relationship in the same crude and ignominious way that it had started.

'Remember the first time we fucked?'

She nodded, her eyes gleaming as she stared up at his erect penis. 'Back of a pub car park,' she said unsteadily. 'In the rain.'

'The Pig and Whistle,' he supplied.

'That was before you knew . . .'

Dervil stroked the damp hair back from her forehead. 'I didn't need to know. You looked like a woman, you felt like a woman, and you certainly fucked like a woman. That was good enough for me.'

Her hand snaked up around his cock to grasp it firmly and begin to slide the foreskin back and forth. He wanted to close his eyes, but equally he did not want to miss anything. Her hands were as expert and calculating as ever, knowing exactly when to slow down and when to speed up, when to squeeze and when to stroke him lightly, until he was going crazy with the need to spunk all over her fingers.

She looked so deliciously filthy, down on her knees in the bushes, her bare legs smeared with dirt from the ground, wet hair still stuck to her face, her eyes begging for it. Now that was the Natasha he remembered, the one he had fucked so violently in the car park of the Pig and Whistle. He would never have known she was a transsexual if she hadn't told him the very next morning. Not that it had ever made a difference to him. She had tits and a cunt, and a temper to match. If that didn't make Natasha a woman, he had no idea what would.

The rain started to slow and gradually came to a halt, leaving the bushes dripping all around them. He watched her masturbate him for a few more minutes, enjoying the sensation. He remembered how the skin on her buttocks had turned a fiery red as he brought down the strap, and those pathetic choked gasps in the back of her throat. Absolutely delightful.

Natasha was so responsive, such a reward to punish, it was amazing to him that her slender body was not a mass of bruises and weals. Just thinking about her submissive stance over the car, hands flat on the bonnet and her bottom raised high for each blow, excited him. The head of his cock was soon slippery with pre-come, the veins standing out engorged and purplish on his thick shaft.

She kneeled up without asking for permission and bent forwards, licking her lips. 'You want me to suck you?'

He nodded and was groaning even before her mouth closed obediently around his shaft. He had intended to play this with a cool mind, keep control of the situation, but the frustrations of the past week had left him ready to explode. Perhaps he ought to have given her the strap a little longer, he thought, strung out the punishment for another ten minutes. As it was, she was sucking him hard and he was going to come far too soon.

'Though not quite so eagerly,' he told her, yanking at the tousled blonde hair until her mouth relaxed its grip. 'I haven't decided yet where I want to come. In your cunt or up your arse. Do you have any particular preference or is that a stupid question?'

It was hard for Natasha to smile with his erect penis in her mouth, but she was clearly trying to do so.

'That's what I thought,' he murmured, extricating his saliva-covered penis from her mouth. It felt swollen and pleasantly tense in his hand. 'OK, you'd better turn around. Drop back on your hands and knees. Now spread your legs and stick your arse in the air.'

She kept herself clean up there, the smooth hairless skin between her buttocks always a revelation. His penis nudged the darker puckered ring of skin and felt it open like a camera lens, allowing the head of his cock inside her anus. Pushing further in, he gripped her hips and rested his weight against the back of her thighs as he began to thrust.

Her submissive moan at his entry and the sudden bowing of her head to the ground amused him. There was not much Natasha liked better than to be punished severely and then buggered in the most casual fashion possible. She enjoyed feeling like a sexual object, she had admitted to him in a drunken moment. Shunning her vagina for the relative tightness of her anus made penetration all the more pleasurable for Natasha, who liked to play with her unused sex while his cock stretched the walls of her rectum. Tonight, though, she had both hands planted firmly on the ground as though waiting for permission to wank.

'Go on, then, play with yourself,' he commanded her as he thrust, his words deliberately crude. 'Don't pretend to be shy. I know you love fingering your own cunt while you take it up the arse. You can't help yourself, you were born to be a slut.'

He watched Natasha reach enthusiastically between her thighs, listening to each groan with a genuine sense of pleasure. Her body began to shake, the reddish bruised buttocks pressing back against his body as though she could not get him deep enough inside. She was muttering something he could not catch, and he finally realised the words were in Russian. But he caught his own name occasionally and managed a smile as he forcefully ploughed her anus. Was the crazy bitch swearing at him in her native tongue or urging him on?

Dervil felt his orgasm begin to build and quickened his pace, eager now for it to be over. There was a thin spiky branch scratching his cheek with every thrust and he was kneeling in something unpleasantly damp. They still had a long drive ahead of them and he did not relish the thought of suffering damp trousers for the next couple of hours. To stimulate himself into finishing quickly, he stared down at her bottom in the pale light, a whitish mass of bruised skin between which his cock kept disappearing and reappearing, the puckered skin of her anus dragging backwards in an incredibly lewd fashion each time he withdrew.

It was a sight that never failed to bring him to orgasm. He felt his balls tighten inexorably and plunged forwards, shoving himself right up inside her rectum as his cock exploded in such a fierce outpouring of spunk that it left his chest heaving and his vision blurred.

Withdrawing with a grunt and hurriedly getting to his feet, Dervil brushed the filth from his trousers. 'Thanks, Natasha. That was exactly what I needed. But it doesn't change anything between us. I can't take you back and that's final. You understand, don't you?'

But Natasha was not listening to him any more. The greedy slut had rolled over and pulled her knees almost to her chest, pushing the heel of her hand down into her cunt, apparently oblivious to the dirt and fallen leaves that were leaving blackened smudges across her shaven sex. Panting hard, her face flushed, she stared up at him without really seeing him, still exhorting herself in garbled Russian.

Turning away to zip up his trousers and tuck in his shirt, Dervil caught a sudden startling glimpse of the lorry driver's face pressed against the window of his cab. The overhead light had been turned on inside, the shade pulled back just enough to watch what they were doing in the bushes, and the man even appeared to be wanking as the glass steamed up in front of his face.

'Cheeky bastard,' Dervil muttered, and saw the shade drop down to hide the man's furiously working hand even as Natasha's orgasmic cry rang out like an owl screech in the darkness.

15

The next morning, Dervil drove into central London early and parked in a car park off St Martin's Lane. He found himself a takeaway café serving croissants and coffee before heading off on foot through the narrow cluttered maze of streets. Indigo's bookshop lay down a narrow side street off Charing Cross Road, not too far from Leicester Square tube station. He stopped outside the shop for a moment, pretending to straighten his tie in the window. Although he kept watch over the interior for several minutes, there was no sign of Indigo. He could see a young plump-cheeked blonde behind the pay desk, her head down, scribbling in a ledger. Otherwise the shop was empty.

His gaze lowered to the window display, an assortment of popular second-hand titles marked a little below current London prices. She must be desperate to make sales, he thought, unable to resist a smile as he pushed through the shop door.

An old-fashioned bell jangled noisily above the door and the blonde looked up, her lipsticked mouth curving in an instant smile. She closed the ledger and stood up, revealing a substantial pair of breasts squeezed into a tight jersey sweater, her black skirt falling discreetly to her knees as she came round the desk towards him.

'Can I help you, sir?' she enquired politely. 'Were you looking for anything in particular?'

Dervil gave the girl his warmest smile, his eyes lingering on her breasts in a deliberately flattering manner. 'For Indigo, actually. Is she in today?'

'I'm afraid not. But she's due back from Paris this afternoon, on the Eurostar.' The blonde looked assessingly at his dark expensive suit and the sober tie he had chosen that morning. 'Is it a business matter? Perhaps I can help.'

'It's not business, no. I'm . . .' he hesitated, trying to think up a plausible lie, 'an old friend of Indigo's. Been abroad for a few years. I was hoping to surprise her. But if she's not here . . .'

The plump blonde took a hurried step forwards as Dervil turned to leave; she reached for his sleeve, and they nearly collided. She laughed nervously, her face a little flushed. 'Please don't go, Mr . . . I'm sorry, I don't know your name.'

He glanced down at the nearest bookcase and chose an author's name at random from the spines. 'Webster,' he lied smoothly, looking back up at her face. 'John Webster.'

'Indigo would never forgive me if I didn't take down your number, Mr Webster, so she can get back to you. And at least let me show you round the bookshop before you go.'

'John, please call me John. That's very kind of you, but I don't want to be a nuisance.'

Her interested gaze moved over him, parted lips shining with pink lipgloss or whatever cosmetic gunk it was she had plastered over her mouth. 'Oh, it's no trouble, honestly. I was bored out of my skull until you walked in. You're my first customer of the day; it's been dead in here all morning.'

Dervil assumed a sympathetic expression, sensing an opportunity to uncover some of Indigo's weaknesses. He allowed the blonde to lead him on a brief tour of the bookshop, glancing at the crowded shelves on either side as they wandered down the central aisle. 'Can business really be that bad? You seem in such a good spot here, I'd have thought –'

'Too much competition from the bigger shops, that's the problem,' she said quickly. 'If we were on the main road, we might make more sales. But stuck down a side street like this? I think she's just about managing to keep her head above water.'

'Poor Indigo. I had no idea.'

The girl glanced back at him over her shoulder, flustered. 'Perhaps I shouldn't have told you. You won't repeat that to anyone?'

'Your secret's safe with me.'

'Thank you,' she murmured gratefully, tucking a stray strand of blonde hair behind one ear. Her blue eyes were so innocent, he could scarcely believe she had ever been hired to work in a shop like this. Though perhaps Indigo thought such untouched innocence would draw the customers. If so, she was probably right. Even her voice seemed girlishly soft as she prattled on. 'I'm so awfully indiscreet. Indigo would be furious sometimes if she could hear what I was saying. I'm always blurting things out without the slightest –'

'Well, I think you're charming.'

She lowered her gaze at once, staring at the floor as though she had just seen something terrifying down there. 'Do you really?'

'Absolutely,' he nodded, smiling. 'Though I feel a little bit awkward. You know my name, but I don't know yours.'

'Chloe.'

He took her hand and patted it reassuringly. 'There's no need to be so modest, Chloe. You're doing a marvellous job. I'm very impressed with what I've seen so far. Talking of which, perhaps you could show me the erotica section?'

Her face still oddly averted, she led him up a narrow flight of steps at the back of the shop to a book-lined room marked ADULTS ONLY. There was a reading table placed discreetly behind one of the taller bookcases and the lighting was less harsh than on the ground floor, a gentle yellowish glow from spotlights set into the wall at intervals. He spotted a discarded white tissue on the floor under the table and smiled. Indigo's clientele were clearly allowed to read for some time without being disturbed.

Scanning the shelves in silence, he found himself having to admire the sheer range of erotica in stock. It was not only comprehensive but charmingly eclectic at times, the most bizarre hardcore titles rubbing shoulders with mainstream erotica simply because the books shared a fetish content. It was an arrangement which made for pleasant and highly unusual browsing. With a properly funded advertising campaign, he thought wryly, this place could be a real success story.

He drew out an illustrated history of erotic movies from one of the lower shelves. 'This any good?'

'I'm sorry, I've never . . .'

Dervil glanced up at her, his eyebrows raised in mock surprise. 'You don't read the stock, Chloe?'

'Not my thing, I'm afraid.'

He straightened with the book in his hand, his smile patronising. 'Dirty books turn you off, is that it?'

Chloe blushed, obviously confused and unsure how to respond. Her stammered explanation was revealing. 'No, you don't understand. I only work here when Indigo's away. I don't read that much myself. I'm dyslexic. Gives me a headache, all those lines of print.'

'But these are just pictures,' he pointed out calmly, taking the illustrated history to the table and laying it open for her. 'Photographs and stills from erotic films. These wouldn't give you a headache, surely?'

She looked over his shoulder, her blue eyes widening in shock at the photograph below: a middle-aged man entering a beautiful Thai girl as she hung upside-down from a bed. Her voice shook as Dervil continued to turn the pages, his browsing revealing ever more graphic images as he progressed through the book.

'I suppose not, no. Though . . . My goodness, what are those men doing to that poor girl?' Her cheeks had turned scarlet. 'Is that physically possible? I mean, doesn't that hurt?'

He tapped the still photograph of two men fucking a well-stacked and enthusiastic-looking brunette at the same time. 'Double penetration? It can be uncomfortable for the girl but perfectly possible. Besides, she's smiling. Hardly an image of torture, is it?'

'I guess not.'

Still looking distinctly uncomfortable, Chloe flicked through the glossy pages herself until she came to a photograph of two blondes licking each other out against the pine backdrop of a Swedish sauna. She paused in silence while her finger traced the image, just the tip of her tongue protruding from between her lips as she stared down at the lithe naked girls, their buttocks and thighs shiny with sweat.

Dervil considered her for a long moment, his eyes narrowed on her lips. His mind clicked slowly through the gears. 'Don't take this the wrong way, Chloe. But are you a lesbian?'

She jumped, startled, almost as though she had forgotten his presence beside her. The flush in her cheeks deepened.

'A lesbian?' she repeated, stumbling over the word. 'Of course not. Why on earth –?'

'Liar,' he said lightly, reaching out to stroke the high curve of her breasts. She stiffened at his touch but did not pull away. Her nipples grew hard, pushing against the tight jersey sweater. He flicked one of them idly, his smile ironic. 'It doesn't bother me, you know. One of my best clients is a lesbian.'

'Clients?'

He drew her closer, experimentally cupping her breasts in both hands as though weighing them to see which was heavier than the other. 'Didn't I mention that? I'm a professional master, a dominant. Women pay me to hurt them. Oh yes, don't look so surprised. Even a lesbian can sometimes enjoy the bite of a cane across her buttocks.'

'But you're a man!'

He looked into those wide blue eyes, gently stroking her nipples as he spoke. 'I don't fuck her, Chloe. I just administer the cane. That's what she wants, what she pays me for. She never tells her partner, of course. It's a little secret between the two of us, just one day a month when she gets to release all that pent-up desire to be humiliated.'

'That's awful. It can't possibly be true.' Chloe bit her lip so hard he could see a bead of bright blood breaking on the fragile skin. 'I don't believe you!'

It was not true, the girl was absolutely correct. But Dervil Badon was not about to admit that.

Raising an eyebrow at her aggressive tone, Dervil slid a hand down her belly until he reached the mound of her sex, a firm curve under her black skirt. When she gasped, trying to draw back, he let her go immediately but watched her with a knowing smile. 'What are you so afraid of, Chloe? The fact that I'm a man, touching you where I suspect no other man has ever done, or that you're actually tempted by the idea of letting me hurt you?'

'I think you're horrid,' she muttered, slamming the heavy book shut and bending to slide it back onto the lower shelf. 'You'd better go, Mr Webster. I need to reopen the shop before we lose business.'

He unlooped the black leather belt from his trousers and stretched it between his hands. He could feel his penis stiffen at the thought of initiating her into the world of male domination. But if she really was a lesbian, what were the chances of an innocent girl like Chloe letting him hurt her?

He decided to risk a slapped face and stepped in front of the blonde as she tried to leave the room. 'Come on,

197

Chloe, admit it. You have looked at some of these dirty books before. Maybe even overheard Indigo discussing them with her special customers. The ones who stay up here for hours and litter the floor with their tissues. You can't convince me you've never been tempted to try it yourself.'

'Try what?' she whispered, her eyes fixed on the belt.

'Pain.'

His blunt reply must have shocked her, for the girl suddenly shook her head and backed away, two spots of high colour burning in her cheeks. 'I told you, I'm not into that sort of thing.'

'How can you be so sure if you've never experienced it?'

Thrown, Chloe stared at him in silence for a moment. 'Erm ... I don't know ... but it doesn't –'

'Three strokes of the belt,' Dervil interrupted her, his voice low and persuasive. 'That's all I'm asking. Let me give you three strokes of the belt, and if you don't enjoy it we'll stop there and I'll leave you in peace.'

Her lip trembled. 'Promise?'

'Cross my heart and hope to die,' he said solemnly, and gestured her back to the table.

Yes, he thought fiercely, it would be the height of irony to teach Indigo's innocent young assistant a lesson about submission. He had fully expected to find Indigo herself at the bookshop, and had come here with the intention of making her an offer for the Book of Punishment. Not too high an offer, of course; he would have tried to use his belt as an added incentive. But now he knew her business was in trouble, there might be another way to get the Book of Punishment back into his own hands without needing to humiliate himself like that.

Still reluctant, but with an odd shine in her eyes, Chloe shuffled to the table and bent over it. The tight black skirt tautened over the full curves of her hips and bottom, outlining the crease between her buttocks in a pleasingly rude manner.

She was no fashion model, it was true, but Dervil always enjoyed administering punishment to well-padded women. Not fat-bottomed, but plump enough to wobble like suet under the cane or tawse. And to sink himself between those mottled fleshy cheeks afterwards was a delicious bonus, the women's little squeals of excitement and distaste as he buggered them never failing to bring him to orgasm.

'Now pull up your skirt,' he instructed her, winding the belt about his forearm to anchor it and leaving only a third loose, the narrow leather tongue at its tip sure to mark her superbly.

'Pull up my skirt?' Chloe repeated, surprised.

'I need your bottom bare if I'm to mark you properly,' he pointed out, giving her an impatient flick of the belt to speed up the process. 'Up with the skirt, off with your knickers, and spread those legs a little wider. Hurry up, I haven't got all day.'

Sniffing audibly, the blonde hoisted her skirt up over her sturdy thighs and the broad expanse of her bottom. Her panties were the old-fashioned type, high-waisted and hugging the curves of her bottom cheeks. Slowly, she hooked a finger under their waistband and drew them down to expose her buttocks, full dimpled cheeks with a deep cleft between. They came to rest mid-thigh, biting into her skin to leave a white-red mark under the elastic. Her pussy gleamed with gingerish hair, the lips gaping slightly as she bent forwards. And as those stout legs widened, even the dusky little hole of her anus was revealed, temptingly puckered and no doubt virgin.

His penis hardened at such an inviting sight. But it would not do to rush things; the girl was too inexperienced for that. Instead, he contented himself with taking up a suitable position behind her and testing the belt against the table with a few well-aimed thwacks. 'Three strokes, I believe we agreed,' he murmured, his tone cool and professional.

Chloe gave a nod, staring straight ahead at the wall, both hands gripping the table sides. Although she had not spoken, he could see her knuckles whiten and smiled, able to guess at the confused excitement flaring inside the girl as she prepared for her very first punishment. Dervil had chastised enough novices in his capacity as master to know exactly what she must be feeling, and reminded himself not to frighten the girl with too hard an initial blow.

'Ready?' he asked her gently.

She hesitated, not replying for a moment. 'I . . . think so.'

Silently, Dervil took aim and brought the leather belt down across her buttocks, hard enough to make her jerk with shock but not so fierce as to score the skin too deeply. The narrow mark he left behind showed instantly on those smooth white buttocks, darkening to a reddish bruise as he watched. His penis felt stiff and swollen, pressing uncomfortably against his trousers as he listened to her gasp and watched her fingers flex into claws before relaxing again.

Not wanting to push things too fast when it was her first time, Dervil waited a moment before enquiring, 'OK to go on?'

Her legs were trembling but she managed a nod.

'Good girl,' he said approvingly.

After his second blow, however, suddenly Chloe did not seem so sure of herself. Her whole bottom clenched as the belt came down and she jolted upright, clutching at her buttocks, a strangled cry in her throat. He had not held back that time, letting her experience the full weight of his arm. Clearly the pain had taken her by surprise.

Looping the belt over his forearm again, Dervil stepped backwards to give her some space. He had little sympathy for her suffering. It was just something his regular clients had always appreciated, a minute or two of privacy while the initial shock of the blow wore off.

'Smarting a bit now, is it?'

The girl stared round at him, cheeks bright red and tears in her wide-open blue eyes. 'It ... bloody ... hurts!'

'Of course it hurts,' he told her, frowning. How could she work in a bookshop like this and understand nothing about the art of submission? 'Your acceptance of the pain is what matters, Chloe. Do I take it you want me to stop there?'

Dervil had half expected her to say yes, and was surprised when the blonde shook her head and settled down again over the table for her third and final stroke. The gingerish hair covering her sex lips glinted damply, the labia parting as her legs spread even wider than before. Dervil paused to adjust the tight material of his trousers, his mouth dry with anticipation. He had not imagined she would enjoy her first beating this much, especially when she clearly preferred women to men.

'When is Indigo arriving from Paris?' he asked idly, raising the belt above her exposed buttocks.

'Just after two o'clock,' she whispered, her body tensed for the blow. 'She usually takes the tube into work. It's only two blocks from here.'

Dervil brought the leather belt down for the last time, watching it slice into her tender flesh with a smile of satisfaction.

The girl shrieked, her body writhing against the table-top with exquisite pleasure. Not for the first time, he wondered whether she really was a virgin.

Maybe he ought to find out, Dervil thought, quietly unzipping his trousers and producing his swollen penis. Glancing down at his watch, he saw that it was a little after twelve. There was still plenty of time to enjoy himself here before moving on to intercept Indigo from the train. Which was precisely what he intended to do, now that he knew when she was due to arrive. The Book of Punishment would not slip away from him again, he promised himself, and he smiled at Chloe's breathless moan as his cock nudged the tight lips of her sex.

16

Standing outside Euston station, Indigo stared gloomily up at the skies above central London. The clouds were grey and heavily laden, a chill blustery wind suggesting the early onset of autumn. It seemed unlikely that the rain would abate within the next half hour. Usually she walked into work from the station, but she had been to the hairdresser's that morning in Paris and had no desire to see her new style ruined in a downpour. Yet what choice did she have? She had already checked the change in her handbag and knew there was not enough for a taxi. Nor was there much point trying her card in a cashpoint. This abortive trip to mainland Europe had drained her slender resources and the bank account was dry.

Indigo tucked her bag under her arm and hurried out into the crowded rainy street, walking quickly to avoid drips from canopies and shop signs. She had gone less than a few hundred metres when a car horn sounded loudly alongside her.

Startled, she stared in disbelief at the man behind the wheel of a familiar white Daimler.

'Dervil?'

Badon pressed a button and the electric window slid down. Leaning forwards, he flashed her a disarming smile. 'You're getting soaked out there. Hop in, quick. I'm holding up traffic.'

Her temper rose instantly. 'Get lost!'

'Don't be like that,' he said calmly, patting the smooth leather seat beside him. 'Why walk in the rain when you could travel in style? Besides, Chloe's not expecting you back until tomorrow. I told her I was going to whisk you away for a romantic evening.'

'*Chloe?*'

Dervil Badon nodded, apparently unabashed by her furious expression. 'That's right, I met the lovely Chloe today. She let slip that your business was in trouble. I've a few suggestions that might help, if you're willing to listen.'

Barely able to keep herself from yelling at him in the street, Indigo stared at him with narrowed seething eyes. 'Do you have any idea how irritating I find you?'

'Get in and you can tell me in detail.'

The wind had risen, the rain increasing in intensity. She stood there a few more seconds, her hair being whipped violently around her face, then she opened the car door with trembling fingers and slid in beside him. God, she hated him. What the hell had Chloe told him about the bookshop? Nothing discreet, by the sound of it. She should never have hired that idiot in the first place. But if you only pay peanuts, she told herself grimly, you deserve to get monkeys.

With a triumphant smile, Dervil activated the central locking and pulled smoothly away from the kerb.

'Good decision.'

Indigo did not reply, staring ahead as the windscreen wipers dispersed the rain, which now cascaded down in a dark steady sheet. The car moved gradually along the street and turned up a cut-through, weaving through a series of narrow back alleys as he headed away from central London. Trying to keep track of their route, she wondered where he was planning to take her. Not for any romantic evening, as he had told that fool Chloe. Probably back to his place for a little retributory caning as a punishment for her escape in Paris.

'How was the return journey?' he asked lightly. 'Those fast trains throw you around a bit, don't they?'

'It was quite smooth, actually.'

So it was to be small talk first, was it? Followed no doubt by the cane or the tawse or whatever other vicious torment he had planned for her. She was not sure which version she found most unpleasant: Dervil Badon in a raging temper or Dervil Badon with a tigerish smile on his face, oozing sweetness and light. Not that it mattered, she thought wryly. Both made the hairs on the back of her neck prickle with ominous warning.

He glanced down at her bag, which lay on the floor at her feet. His voice was unreadable. 'Is it in there?'

'Is what in where?'

'Don't play games with me,' he snapped, then drew in his breath sharply. A long moment passed before he spoke again, carefully amending his question. 'Is the Book of Punishment in your bag?'

'No,' she said truthfully.

'But you do have it?'

She hesitated, not sure whether it would be wise to admit that she too had failed. Her position was more secure while he thought she had something he wanted. 'I don't have the book you think I stole from you in Geneva. But I did manage to get hold of another copy of the Book of Punishment. It should be mailed to me from Paris next week.'

He was frowning. 'Why?'

'It needed a little rebinding work. Christian's aunt is taking care of that for me.'

'Bad condition?'

She shrugged, looking out of the window again at the grey city skyline as the car accelerated onto an overpass. 'Not wonderful.'

'But still worth buying, I presume, or you would never have wasted your money on it,' he said silkily, making it clear he did not believe a word she was saying. 'I'll be searching your bag when we stop, you know. So if you've lied to me –'

205

'I'm not lying. Search all you want.'

Dervil made no attempt to stop and carry out his threat, however, his eyes narrowing on the road ahead as they continued to make their way out of central London towards the borough of Hackney. Gradually the rain stopped and a faint suggestion of sunlight broke through the heavy clouds. She wondered what he had done to Chloe, not feeling too much sympathy for the girl. If her assistant had kept her mouth shut, Indigo would be back at the bookshop by now instead of heading god knows where with Dervil Badon behind the wheel.

She should have been frightened. Perhaps she should have made more of an effort to escape. But it was hard to feel concerned when she was so tired, her eyes closing with the easy rhythm of the car. Her head was beginning to hurt. She had consumed far too much alcohol the night before. True to his word, Christian had taken her out on the town, and she had no desire to party like that again for some considerable time.

It was some time before she stirred again and straightened, gazing drowsily around herself. They seemed to be heading further east than she had expected, she realised as she saw a road sign flash past for Woodford. Indigo frowned, perplexed. She had thought Dervil lived in North London. Where was he taking her? It would be fatal to appear too passive in his company, she thought, deciding to act a little rebellious and see where it got her. Otherwise he might have her sold off as a sex slave or something equally unpleasant before she knew what was happening.

'Care to tell me where we're going?'

'Epping Forest.'

She stared at him, speechless for a moment. That was the last thing she had expected to hear. 'Epping Forest? This is hardly great weather for a walk. I thought you wanted to discuss the bookshop.'

'All in good time,' he replied, his manner annoyingly casual. 'First, I need you to do me a favour.'

Furious again, she gritted her teeth. 'A sexual favour, by any chance? I thought you'd had enough of those.'

His laughter made her even angrier. 'What a suspicious mind you have, Indigo. It's not a favour for me. It's a favour for some friends of mine. I belong to a little group that meets every full moon for a . . . well, pagan ceremony, I suppose you would call it.'

'Pagan?'

'In the past, I imagine some unfortunate female would have been sacrificed to the goddess at a gathering like this.' He glanced sideways at Indigo and laughed at her horrified expression. 'These days, of course, it's a rather more civilised affair. We still bring a young lady along most months, if we can find one who's willing. But we tend to fuck her instead of slitting her belly open and wrapping the entrails round the nearest oak tree.'

She shuddered at the mental image he had conjured. 'And you're intending to take me along this time? What on earth makes you think I'll agree to that?'

'From what I was able to glean from Chloe, your business appears to be in serious trouble. On the verge of closure, in fact. My financial support might provide a solution to your problems. Otherwise it could be *adios* bookshop.' His smile was chilling. 'You won't exactly be following in daddy's footsteps then, will you?'

'Bastard.'

'I knew you'd understand.'

'Lady of the Night, Mistress of Darkness, accept our sacrifice tonight. We, your humble servants, commit our seed to the loins of this girl and offer up her suffering in your name.'

The man in the centre of the circle moved closer behind Indigo, his dark robes brushing her thighs as she knelt on the forest floor, stark naked and with her hands tied firmly behind her back. His thin bearded face was lit up by flaming torches set at intervals about the clearing, a suggestion of fanaticism in the watery blue eyes.

'Teach her the meaning of submission,' he continued, 'as we lead your new servant in the Dance of the Full Moon.'

Indigo did not know which of these dark-robed and hooded men was Dervil Badon, though she knew he must be there, watching. So she kept her head high, not letting even a flicker of apprehension enter her face. Sod them, she thought belligerently. If they wanted to see her cry, they would have to hurt her first.

Almost as though he could read her thoughts, the man in the centre of the circle produced a whip from the voluminous folds of his robe. Her heart sank. He raised his arms wide to either side, turning slowly so that both he and the whip could be seen by every man in the clearing.

'If any man here knows of a reason to keep this girl pure, let him step forwards now and she will be spared.'

Indigo waited in desperate hope for one of them to speak. It was dark and freezing and she did not like the look of that whip. But there was silence from the assembled men, whose many pairs of eyes watched her from the depths of those dark hooded robes as she knelt before them, her bare breasts thrust outwards by the tight rope binding her wrists and her sex glistening in the light of the flaming torches.

The bearded man nodded slowly, unfurling the whip and cracking it down across her back with an expert hand. She cried aloud with pain, rocking under the force of his blow.

His voice was nauseatingly triumphant. 'The Goddess has claimed this girl for her service tonight. Let us obey her and worship with our hands and bodies!'

A great shout of excitement rang out in the forest and the ring of robed men rushed forwards, some of them carrying lit torches, while others reached for her arms and held them fast as she tried to shuffle away. A thick leather gag was placed between her lips and she was ordered to bite down. It would have been a pointless exercise to refuse, so she closed her teeth obediently on the gag and felt them fasten it behind her head.

Bound and gagged, she stared up at the circle of faces, searching them in vain for Dervil Badon. Then someone lowered a black cloth hood over her face and everything went dark.

Jerked unceremoniously to her feet, Indigo wondered whether it was worth undergoing these indignities simply to save her father's bookshop from closure. Yet even as that thought darted through her head, she felt a large male hand slap her bottom smartly enough to make her bare buttocks jiggle, and she was forced to acknowledge that she was not only doing this for the bookshop. Besides, her father would almost certainly have approved of tonight's event: sacrificing young women to a pack of lusting pagans was probably something he had fantasised about at least once. And it was not as though she had any innocence to lose.

The men holding her arms suddenly released her and she stumbled forwards, blind and disoriented.

Even through the hood, she could smell the sweet cloying scent of burnt incense and the musty stench of their robes, presumably unwashed since last month's gathering. Her bare feet stung on the rough ground as she fumbled her way through the circle. The men around her were chanting in some foreign tongue; she could not understand a word.

Without warning, one of their whips cut mercilessly into the back of her thighs, sending Indigo to her knees.

'Back on your feet,' the leader was shouting at her, 'and complete the ritual! You must circle the clearing three times before approaching the altar.'

She was seized from behind and forced back to her feet. From her left, a whip flailed across her breasts and

209

she yelped at the unexpected pain, her cry muffled by the thick leather gag. Before she had a chance to recover, another whip curled about her naked buttocks in an explosion of searing white heat. Driven forwards by whips on both sides, she broke into a tearful breathless trot, unable to see where she was going but steered by the robed men and their cruel lashes. She really ought to have been terrified, perhaps even afraid for her life. But to her immense shame, Indigo felt warm fluid trickling from her exposed sex and knew that she was aroused. The only woman there, she knew what to expect after they had finished tormenting her. The thought both appalled and excited her.

She stumbled again, catching her foot on a tree root, and felt one of the men grab at her. His robe brushed roughly against her breasts and she winced, the stinging mark from the whip still raw there. She heard the man laugh, and felt him reach out to squeeze and fondle her breast, apparently taking pleasure in her pain. His voice, low and intimate in her ear, was horribly familiar.

'Scared, Indigo?' he asked softly. 'Don't worry, this will all be over in about . . . what, maybe three hours?'

Dervil Badon! Her heart seethed with impotent rage at the sound of that voice and she longed to tell the bastard exactly what she thought of him. But the leather gag was too comprehensively in place for anything more than a furious grunt.

Presumably sensing her anger, Dervil laughed again and propelled her forwards so hard that she overbalanced and fell.

Unable to save herself, she crashed to her side in a drift of damp fallen leaves, choking with fury. He had done that deliberately! Before she could get back to her knees, though, the men seized her legs and dragged her along the forest floor for some distance while she struggled and moaned. Then she hit her head on something, perhaps a rock or part of a felled trunk, and lay stunned for a moment.

Opening her eyes, she felt the heat of a flaming torch inches from her breasts and smelt its acrid smoke, the flickering glare visible even through the thick black hood. Her instinctive response was to jerk backwards from the danger but one of the men blocked her escape, slapping her bottom with an impatient hand.

'Enough of this!' It was the leader again. She was beginning to dislike the sound of his voice. 'If the whore refuses to dance, let her be drawn through the forest instead.'

With barely a pause, one of the men clamped a thick leather collar around her neck and attached a chain to it, then dragged her forwards like a reluctant dog. To add to this humiliation, she felt rough male hands parting the cheeks of her buttocks and then the sturdy handle of what felt like a whip being inserted into her anus.

Half trotting, half stumbling, Indigo found herself being drawn around the clearing in a wide erratic circle with the derisive hoots and yells of the men ringing in her ears, tears in her eyes and her breasts bouncing painfully high with every step.

Her face was hot beneath the hood. She hardly dared imagine what she must look like to this rabble of pagans. The whip handle in her bottom slipped and she had to clench down hard to keep it in place, suspecting a severe punishment might follow if she allowed it to fall out. It felt utterly enormous, rigid and inflexible as it filled the narrow passage and left her anus stinging, a thin trailing lash flicking the backs of her thighs like the tail of a pony. The man in front kept yanking on her collar, making it hard for Indigo to keep her balance as she trotted, and every man they passed seemed to have a whip which they used on the aching flesh of her thighs and buttocks or, more cruelly, across her breasts.

Her sobs and grunts might have been stifled by the leather gag, but they sounded almost deafening to her

211

own ears. She was burningly aware of the heat between her legs and the taut peaks of her nipples. Her body knew precisely what it needed, even if her mind rejected its animal urges and wished she had never agreed to be a part of this ritual.

Indigo was exhausted by the time she had completed her third circuit, and she was allowed to drop in a shivering heap on the ground. Unable to prevent her muscles from contracting any longer, she grunted and pushed down until the whip handle in her bottom oozed slowly out with a revolting plop. If they wanted to punish her for that, she told herself wearily, then they could go ahead. But nobody seemed to care now that she had finished her run. Chanting quietly, the men had gathered about her in a tight circle, the gleam of their torches shining through the hood over her face.

Her senses prickled as the chain rattled, then it was carefully unclipped from her collar. So much for the ritual whipping, she thought grimly. Now it must be time for the sacrifice itself.

'Bring the girl to the altar,' the leader was saying, that fanatical tone in his voice easily recognisable. Hands seized her eagerly and dragged her to some sort of low wooden platform where she was forced to kneel, hands still tied behind her back and her body aching. 'Push her down. Tether her like a goat. It is time for her to feel the power of the Goddess.'

Like a goat? she thought furiously. Her knees were pushed apart and her thighs looped with lengths of rope that seemed to have been attached to the wooden platform. The men in dark robes were all around her; she could hear their loud breathing and the rustle of sandalled feet over fallen leaves. Was Dervil Badon among them, she wondered fiercely, or had he amused himself enough with her tonight? Erotic feelings of humiliation churned in her belly. The sight of her on hands and knees like this, helpless to resist, must please her rival immensely.

Once she was secured on the low platform, the men drew closer and began to explore her breasts and exposed sex. Indigo groaned against the gag, writhing and twisting, but was restrained too tightly by the ropes to evade their touch. It was embarrassing to know she was soaking down there, the full lips gaping moistly as the men's fingers stroked and entered. Even her nipples were aching, stiff and proud, begging to be squeezed.

These robed men had whipped her and humiliated her, and yet still it was not enough. Dervil had been right about her all along. She was nothing but a slut, a tramp, a common whore with no morals whatsoever.

Her body ticked with urgency, her warm pussy dripping juices like syrup as they fingered her. Would she be expected to satisfy every single one of them? Oh, she hoped so.

Then the hood was abruptly removed.

Indigo blinked up at the two torches burning in front of the platform and the tall robed man standing between them, his arms raised in a gesture of invocation. Her eyes stung with acrid smoke but she kept them open, glad to be free of the hot suffocating darkness inside the hood. The men who had been touching her stepped away and she saw them begin to unbelt their robes, her mouth dry as she watched each stiff penis appear from beneath the folds.

The long incomprehensible chanting came to an end and silence fell over the torchlit clearing.

'Servants of the Goddess, the moon is at her peak. Step forwards now and make this girl your living sacrifice.'

Indigo stared, her eyes stretched wide, as the priest came towards her with a long curving knife in his hand. To her intense relief, though, he merely slipped its shining blade between her cheek and the gag, cutting the leather as though it were paper.

Then he lifted his robe to reveal a sturdy purple-

213

headed cock which he pressed between her lips without further preamble.

This seemed to act as a signal for the other men to close in on them, as dark robes were thrown to the ground all around her and the fat shiny heads of penises pressed into her flesh from every direction. She felt one nudge into the slippery cleft between her buttocks and gave a muffled groan of protest, but it was no use. Seconds later, it was pushed up inside her bottom to the hilt.

She closed her eyes, the usual discomfort soon replaced by a sense of exhilaration. Her breasts were grabbed from both sides and the hard nipples milked, her body rocking back and forth as the men thrust in and out. Before long, she felt the warm generous splatter of come over her buttocks and back, and heard the men inside her groan as they too shot their loads and withdrew. She still needed to come herself, though, and longed for one of them to play with her clitoris, maybe rub and press it the way she liked best.

When a male hand finally slipped between her thighs, to find her clitoris and massage it hard, Indigo gave a grateful cry of pleasure and immediately climaxed against those clever fingers, her body shaking with the force of her orgasm. But when the man drew back, her smile faded as she looked up and saw it was Dervil Badon.

'You!' she exclaimed in disappointment.

Dervil smiled down at her in that arrogant way, hitching up his robe and presenting her with an impressively swollen penis. 'Yes, me,' he agreed. 'Now shut up and suck.'

17

It was nine days after the ritual in Epping Forest that Dervil finally received a text message from Indigo, suggesting they meet at her place that afternoon. So at last she was ready to talk, he thought with a smile of satisfaction, and he cancelled his four-o'clock appointment with Mrs Benwick to drive over there. Indigo had a basement flat, situated at the unfashionable end of the Old Brompton Road and approached via a flight of steps half hidden by overgrown shrubbery. Dervil raised an eyebrow at the dingy exterior of the Victorian terrace house but knocked at the door with an increasing sense of triumph. She would not have contacted him if she were not desperate; the Book of Punishment was practically in his hands now.

Indigo answered the door promptly, looking very smart in a severe black suit, the skirt past her knees and a tight white blouse under the tailored jacket. Her eyes flickered over him without emotion. 'You'd better come in.'

As he had suspected from the exterior, the flat itself was cramped, wallpaper peeling in the corners and a musty smell that signalled a problem with rising damp. The furniture appeared to be cast-offs from some elderly person's home, a sofa that sagged in the middle and two grim high-backed armchairs only slightly improved by the addition of colourful throws.

Dervil stood in the middle of the room, peeling off his leather driving gloves as he took in these surroundings with an expression of distaste. 'Highly salubrious,' he drawled. 'How long have you had the misfortune to be living here?'

'Nearly three years.'

'In this dump? My god. You could do so much better for yourself, Indigo. Talking of which, have you had a chance yet to think over what we discussed at our last meeting?'

Indigo nodded slowly and gestured to a parcel that lay partially unwrapped on the sideboard. He caught a glimpse of leather boards and a gilt spine beneath the loose brown paper.

'That arrived from Paris yesterday. It's the Book of Punishment, rebound but otherwise intact. Still interested?'

Dervil tried not to look as keen as he felt, though his heart was already beating a little faster at the thought of finally getting his hands on that rare and fascinating book. He had already parted with a substantial amount of cash in its pursuit and he had no intention of giving Indigo more than was strictly necessary.

'That was the deal, as I recall,' he agreed. 'The Book of Punishment in exchange for help in keeping your bookshop afloat.'

As she turned back to face him, he noticed for the first time how pale she was looking. Her eyes glittered and he disliked the acid tone in her voice. 'The deal's changed, I'm afraid. I've decided to cut my losses and sell the bookshop.'

'But your father —'

'Would have done exactly the same. He certainly wouldn't have struggled on like this until he'd lost everything. So thanks for the offer, Mr Badon, but I don't need your money any more.'

Dervil stared at her, rendered utterly speechless for a moment. This was not how he had envisaged their encounter this afternoon. Indigo should have grovelled first, telling him at length how much she admired and

216

feared him, then debased herself still further by sucking his cock in a slavish fashion until he came in her face; then they should have finished with an enjoyable bondage session, after which he had planned to leave her tied up for a few hours while he went out to dinner alone. Now she was ruining everything with this display of obstinate pride.

'Well, there's no need to make any hasty decisions,' he managed in the end, resisting the temptation to raise his voice. 'Are you still upset about that night in Epping Forest? I apologised at the time; how was I to know they would all want to use you? And it's hardly my fault you were so sore afterwards. You asked for it, flaunting yourself like that.'

'Flaunting myself? Your friends stripped me naked, gagged me and whipped me round the forest!'

He attempted to sound sympathetic, his eyes repeatedly straying back to the parcel behind her. 'Yes, I forgot to warn you about that part of the ceremony. Not a terribly civilised bunch. If it's any consolation, I won't be renewing my membership next year.'

Indigo drew a sharp breath, her voice shaking. 'Look, do you want the Book of Punishment or not?'

'Yes, I want it.'

'Good, because I'm still willing to sell it to you. But not for money.' She looked him directly in the eyes. 'If you submit to me for one hour, Dervil, you can have the book. But you'll have to obey every order I give you. If you refuse at any point, the deal's off.'

Stunned into silent disbelief, Dervil narrowed his eyes on her face, trying to decide whether or not she was joking. Then he gave an abrupt laugh. 'You really had me going for a minute there. That's funny, Indigo. Very amusing.'

'I'm perfectly serious.'

For once, Dervil Badon did not know what to say. His gaze flicked back to the half-opened parcel on the sideboard. It was an unthinkable proposition. He had handed out punishment often enough as a professional master to know he had no desire to be on the receiving end for once. Yet the girl was only asking for one hour of his time. Sixty minutes of humiliation in return for a book he might never again have a chance to own. On the face of it, was it such a bad exchange?

She was watching him, an intensity in her face he had never seen before. 'What's your answer?'

'I'll do it.'

'Scout's honour?'

'I was never in the Scouts,' he said drily. 'Will "cross my heart and hope to die" be good enough?'

Indigo nodded slowly.

He shrugged out of his jacket, not believing for a moment that she had it in her to order him about. Indigo was a submissive born and bred; she ought to leave the hard stuff to the men. His lip curled into a sneer when she still did not say anything. 'I'm ready and waiting. Where do you want me, mistress?'

'Take off your clothes and come here, slave.'

Dervil blinked at the speed with which her manner had altered, and turned to stare at her. Her voice was cool and matter-of-fact, her head tilted to one side and her hands on her hips in a dominant pose straight out of the advertisement pages in *Forum*. It might have been impressive if it had not been so annoying. If Indigo ever wanted a career as a dominatrix, he thought grimly, she would have no trouble establishing herself on the scene.

'My clothes?' he repeated.

'Every last stitch.'

With one eye on his watch, unwilling to hurry too much, Dervil slowly removed his tie, unbuttoned his shirt and stepped out of his expensive suit trousers, then draped them all carefully over the back of the sofa. He had no intention of returning home in a dishevelled state, whatever delights she might have in store for him this afternoon. It was rather more embarrassing to pull down his underpants and arrange them on top of the pile, especially since his penis had betrayed him by stiffening. He did not wish her to think this show of dominance had aroused him. Quite the contrary, in fact.

'Now put these on,' she instructed him, removing an armful of underwear from one of the drawers in the sideboard and throwing it to the floor in front of him.

He bent to examine the heap of frilly semi-transparent items with a mounting sense of disbelief. There was a lacy black bra and matching thong with red lace trim, a suspender belt and a pair of black fishnet stockings. She had to be kidding. His hands trembled as he fingered them, wondering desperately how to get out of this arrangement without looking weak.

'That's a pity. I don't think they're my size.' A sudden searing pain across his backside made him jerk upright with a yelp, dropping the lacy bra and clutching at his buttocks in wounded surprise. 'What the hell was that for?'

'This isn't a democracy, Dervil. Don't bother arguing, just do what you're told and put them on. Unless you want to feel this on your bottom again?' Indigo showed him the cane in her hand, smiling maliciously as she registered his shocked expression. 'You wanted to teach me about submission. Well, I'm a fast learner and now you're going to submit to me. Is that clear?'

'Yes,' he muttered, his teeth gritted and his face hot.

'Yes, what?'

Dervil struggled with his pride for a moment, only able to reply appropriately by remembering how much the cane had hurt and not wishing to repeat the experience. There was no irony in his voice this time.

'Yes, mistress.'

She laughed and sat down on the sofa to watch him dress, tapping the cane lightly against the cushions as though to remind him what punishment he could expect for further disobedience. In the severe black skirt suit and high heels, she looked every inch a dominatrix. Plus, the little bitch had a cane, and knew how to use it too!

His skin prickled at the thought of what might lie ahead. Why on earth had he agreed to this diabolical arrangement?

He wanted to put his own clothes back on and walk back to his car, perhaps giving her a good slapping on the way out. But it was too late to indulge a desire for revenge, however justified it felt at the moment. That would have to wait for another time. He had given his word of honour – he had agreed to become her slave for one hour. And that was precisely what he had to do now, like it or not.

Unable to bear the thought that she could see his face while he was getting dressed, Dervil faced the window-blinds instead. If she wanted to humiliate him, he thought, she could not have chosen a better punishment. Even though the bra was a 40 DD, it pinched his ribs terribly, barely stretching round his chest with its empty cups sagging. The black lace thong pulled painfully over his balls and hardened cock, cutting into the deep cleft between his buttocks as he bent for the suspender belt. But he could not make it fit, and had to wear the fishnet stockings without any support, holding them up with awkward fingers as he turned back to face her.

'This can't be your underwear, surely? The bra's too big for a start and I can't imagine you ever wearing these stockings. They're so . . .'

'Sleazy?'

He grimaced, hearing the laughter in her voice and knowing he must look ridiculous. 'Cheap.'

'They belong to the woman upstairs, if you must know. Oh, don't look so worried. I didn't tell her about you. She thinks I borrowed them for a friend. Which I suppose I did; just a male friend, that's all. Now why are you looking uncomfortable? They suit you, really.'

She was smiling behind her hand, her eyes flitting over him in the ill-fitting black lace bra and thong, one fishnet stocking slipping to his hairy ankle as he forgot to hold it up. He bent to retrieve it, wishing he could give her the caning she so richly deserved. His penis was fully erect now in the tight transparent pouch of the thong. It was purely a physiological response, he told himself. It had nothing to do with wearing women's underwear, so he could put that fear right out of his mind. Still, she was probably thinking something along those lines, and he could not blame her.

He felt an embarrassed colour rise in his face, his jaw tense with it. She gestured to him to turn around for her, to walk up and down a little, wiggling his hips like a model on a catwalk. His displeasure seemed to delight her. Then he had to wrap a long pink feather boa round his neck. The feathers scratched his skin and made him itch. He hated it, and wanted to slap her, ready to explode by the time she told him to bend over and display himself to her like a piece of rough trade.

'What?'

'Bend over and show me your arse,' she repeated slowly and loudly, as though he were stupid.

Clenching his fists, Dervil obeyed her and bent over but surreptitiously checked his watch at the same time. To his dismay, there was another 40 minutes left of this torment. He waited for permission to rise, his voice becoming terse when she did not give it. 'Seen enough?'

'Hang on there a minute,' Indigo muttered, approaching him from the rear in a disturbing fashion.

He felt something slim and hard nudge his anus, pressing against the sphincter. His head came up at once and he stared back at Indigo through narrow furious eyes, but she ignored him.

'Relax, it's only the handle of a feather-duster. Nothing scary about that. Is spit OK or would you

221

prefer me to use butter to make it easier? I don't have any proper lubricants, I'm afraid.'

'I hope you're not planning to stick –'

She giggled at his contorted expression as the feather-duster penetrated his anus and pushed straight into his rectum. He had the peculiar sensation of his bowels being pierced with a barbecue skewer, and his penis jerked in immediate humiliating response.

'Sorry. Did that hurt?'

'You bitch,' he ground out between his teeth.

'Oh, stop sulking,' she said, pushing the handle in a little further. 'I don't recall you stepping in to rescue me when I took half a dozen men up my arse the other night. And an erect penis is a good deal thicker than the handle of a feather-duster, trust me.'

He was panting, sweat breaking out on his forehead. 'Women . . . are better designed . . . to take it up the –'

'I beg your pardon?' The feather-duster was pulled out, then suddenly thrust back in without warning. His cry of anguish only seemed to make her laugh. 'I don't think so, actually. Women are just more stoical in the face of pain. Perhaps a little stretchier too, I'll give you that. It's a hormonal thing. Otherwise we wouldn't be able to have babies, would we?'

'No,' he agreed hoarsely.

'You know, I've often wondered why men are so keen on giving it to women up the bottom,' she mused, twisting the handle and listening with apparent indifference to his moans. 'I suppose it's tighter up there. What do you think?'

'Indigo, for the love of god . . .'

She hesitated, then laughed with mock surprise. 'Oops, sorry, did I forget to take the feather-duster out? Must have got carried away, thinking about all that anal sex I *didn't* enjoy the other week. But yes, you're quite right. Time is ticking and I haven't finished with you yet.'

222

Dervil fell to his knees as she tugged on the feather-duster handle and withdrew it from his anus, the skin there smarting and stinging as though she had poured alcohol on it. Visions of cruel revenge danced through his head before he managed to regain control of himself and staggered back to his feet at her brusque order.

Swishing the cane across his backside every few steps, Indigo dragged him through to the kitchen, little better than a glorified breakfast bar situated in a gloomy alcove, with a gas stove and a table-top fridge. She threw open the door of the fridge while he waited obediently beside her, both stockings puddled about his ankles now and his legs trembling from the shock of that painful intrusion. Dervil wondered bitterly what was coming next, his buttocks sore from the cane and his penis embarrassingly stiff. He knew she was aware of his erection too, her glance continually straying to its dark-skinned rigidity as though she were planning to do something about it.

What the hell was she looking for?

Mysteriously, she pulled out of the fridge a ceramic pot of *terrine de porc*, a tub of sour cream, and finally a half-empty tin of anchovy paste. She arranged these items on the breakfast bar and looked at him enquiringly. 'Which one would you prefer?'

What did she have planned for him now? he wondered bitterly. He recoiled at the anchovy paste, realising it must have been open several weeks, passed over the sour cream with a frown, but nodded at the *terrine de porc*. 'Is that fresh?'

'Opened it last night.'

He shrugged. 'That's what I choose, then.'

Perched on one of the breakfast stools, Indigo hitched up the severe black skirt to reveal a bare shaven pussy, the smell of her arousal tantalising as she dipped two fingers in the terrine and smeared its brownish meaty paste generously over her pussy lips and clitoris.

'*Terrine de porc*, by special request.' Her pale thighs spread wide, she beckoned him forwards and pointed to her sex. 'Lick it all out, there's a good boy. Oh, and pass me that cane first. I may need to use it if I don't get enough tongue.'

His face burning with humiliation, Dervil stared down at the floor as he struggled with a sudden desire to push her down and force his cock up her arse. How much did he really want the Book of Punishment? So far the bitch had made him dress up in women's underwear, stuck a feather-duster up his backside, and now instructed him to lick her out like a dutiful husband.

But a quick glance at his watch reminded him there were less than fifteen minutes to go until this ordeal was over. Surely it was worth forcing himself to submit for just another few minutes?

Presumably bored by having to wait, Indigo reached for the cane and swiped him across the backside. This time it was no longer a casual stroke but designed to hurt. His gasp of pain seemed to amuse her and she repeated the punishment, pushing his head down between her thighs with one hand as she cut into the flesh of his backside with the other. He jerked again but did not jump up, making himself concentrate on those pinkish lips smeared with terrine and the small hard bud of her clitoris. If he knew anything at all about this oversexed young woman, it would soon be finished.

Sure enough, Indigo was soon writhing against his mouth, firm thighs clasped around his neck and her bottom raised off the stool as though she too wanted the cane. Her first orgasm took them both by surprise, a grunting heated exchange of tongue and slick pussy. There was no terrine left by the time she spasmed for the third time, crying aloud as he pushed two fingers inside her at the same time and twisted them.

'Bastard!'

He laughed, pulling back and looking down at his watch. 'Time's up,' he said, ignoring the uncomfortable throb of his erection. His face sticky with pussy juice and a few remnants of terrine, he staggered back into the living-room without even waiting for her to recover. He had taken the punishment without protest, and now it was time for his reward.

After wiping himself with a tissue, Dervil ripped off the lacy black bra and thong, then stepped out of the fishnet stockings to leave himself respectably male again. The first thing he did was to shrug back into his clothes, tucking in his shirt and zipping up his trousers before she could claim that her hour was not yet up.

Indigo reappeared in the doorway, her skirt discreetly back in place. Her face was still flushed from her orgasms but her gaze was level enough. 'Is that any way to treat a lady? Who said I'd finished?'

He threw his tie loosely around his neck, ignoring her and picking up the parcel that contained the Book of Punishment instead.

'I'm taking this with me. That's what we agreed, right? One hour of submission in return for the Book of Punishment.'

She nodded, a slight smile on her lips as she watched him pull back the brown paper wrappings and uncover the book. He ran a hand over the smooth leather, glancing at the gilt letters on the spine. The rebinding job had been fairly well executed, though he still preferred to see original boards, regardless of their condition. He frowned, suddenly aware of her intent gaze on his face. What was wrong?

He opened the book and flicked through to the title page, holding his breath in sudden apprehension as he read the inscription at the bottom. 'Paris, 1798?' he exploded, lifting his head to stare at her. 'Paris?'

'Is there a problem?'

His teeth met with a snap, a red mist in front of his eyes as he realised she had duped him. 'You conniving little bitch, you know perfectly well this isn't the first edition!'

'Not the first . . .? But I don't understand. Jean-Luc assured me it was the genuine article.'

Dervil threw it down at her feet, and stumbled for the door before the urge to swing her over his knee and slap the hell out of her backside proved too much for him. His voice was hoarse, and he could barely get the words out. 'This isn't the last . . . don't think I'll forget . . . damn you, Indigo, I'll make you suffer for this one day.'

Her laughter was still ringing in his ears as he threw himself up the crumbling steps to the street, ignoring the startled glances of passers-by, his cock aching with frustration.

'I can hardly wait,' she called after him from the doorway, her voice infuriatingly cool. 'It's been a pleasure doing business with you, Mr Badon.'

Epilogue

Indigo poured herself a strong black coffee and sat down in front of the computer screen. Her pussy felt moist and relaxed, those orgasms still tingling pleasurably through her body. Yet although it had been amusing to tease Dervil Badon like that, she could not quite raise a smile. To sell her father's bookshop would signal the end of an era both for her and for many of her regular customers. It would also save her from incurring massive debts, of course, though that consolation did little to alleviate Indigo's sadness. What was there to smile about, after all? Not only had she failed to make a success of her father's business, she had also failed to hunt down his lifelong obsession, the Book of Punishment.

The list of her email messages appeared on the screen and she frowned. One of the messages had an intriguing subject: *Bound for Eternity*. The name seemed familiar but she did not recognise the sender's email address. Clicking on the screen, she quickly realised the email had come from Heinrich. His message was cryptic.

Interested in making another film for Sticky Fingers Inc.? This time a movie version of Bound for Eternity, *the SM classic about two vampires who fall in love. Ring me. I may have found what our mutual friend mislaid in Geneva. Yours ever, H.*

Indigo sipped her coffee speculatively, then clicked on the attached document. The window on the screen showed two images alongside each other: one a still photograph of herself from that porno film, peeing into poor Eloise's mouth, and the other, which made her nipples stiffen with instant excitement, was a facsimile of the frontispiece to the Book of Punishment.

Her heart thudding violently, she stared at the two images in stunned silence. So Heinrich had discovered her deception in Geneva, when she'd posed as a watersports model in order to get into his offices. But what did the rest of his message mean?

She traced a finger across the image of the marvellously lewd frontispiece to the Book of Punishment. Could it be possible that Heinrich was the thief who had snatched the book from Dervil Badon? It had all been so confused that night, but she suddenly had a memory of Heinrich's face amongst that crowd of drunken partygoers.

The wily old fox!

She had no idea how he had managed to pull off such a daring theft. But one thing was certain. Heinrich had a copy of the Book of Punishment in his possession and was offering it to her. In exchange for what, though? Presumably for accepting a role in this proposed film, *Bound for Eternity*, and becoming a porn actress again. In a flash, she remembered why the title sounded so familiar. *Bound for Eternity* had been the first erotic novel she had read, the book Heinrich had slipped her while she was still a teenager – the book that had sparked her obsession with sadomasochism.

Her nipples began to ache as she cupped her breasts in both hands, to squeeze them with her eyes shut and her lips delicately parted. Dreamily, she imagined herself in front of the cameras again, made up as a beautiful vampire, on hands and knees as some cloaked brute thrust forcefully into her anus. It was a tempting mental image. And in return Heinrich would give her the Book of Punishment. The real McCoy this time, not some worthless copy with half the original punishments missing.

Dragging up her long skirt, she slipped two fingers into her oozing shaven sex and closed her eyes as she began to masturbate.

It was slick down there, still aching from her orgasms. Dervil had done an excellent job of licking her out, she thought, remembering his furious expression as he realised she had tricked him. Oh yes, it would make her revenge all the sweeter to get her hands on a real first edition of the Book of Punishment, in addition to punishing Badon for his cruelty and arrogance.

Still masturbating feverishly, she reached for the phone and dialled the number at the bottom of Heinrich's email message. It rang several times before she heard his voice at the other end.

'Heinrich?' she said huskily, stroking her clitoris as she spoke. 'It's Indigo. I just got your email.'

'My dear, how lovely to hear from you again,' Heinrich replied, a note of wicked amusement in that civilised voice. 'Christian told me about your unfortunate misadventures in Paris. I trust you're fully recovered? No rope burns?'

It was hard to stop her mind drifting back to the possibility that she would be forced to perform filthy unnatural acts with vampires and beasts of the night in this proposed film. Indigo's face began to flush with heat, a soft keening noise issuing from between her lips. Her fingers worked between her thighs as she felt her orgasm approach, pinching and rubbing at the sensitive flesh down there.

'Yes, thank you,' she gasped, trying not to sound as though she were masturbating while speaking to him. 'Heinrich, are you serious about making this vampire film . . . in exchange . . . for the Book of Punishment?'

'Deadly serious,' he agreed.

'In Geneva?'

'That's right, my dear.'

'In that case, Heinrich, I would very much like ...'
Indigo climaxed with a guttural cry, dropping the phone
as she writhed and twisted in an explosion of trembling
pleasure, '*to come!*'

Also available from Nexus:

SWINGING

By Peter Birch

In *Swinging*, Nexus takes the theme of swinging sex a step further than usual, mixing up not only partners, but the sexes too. There's lots of variety between the eight stories, but all have one thing in common: girls are as likely to be with girls as they are with boys, as boys are with boys, in a no-holds-barred feast of uninhibited erotic story telling.

Authors include Monica Belle, with her boisterous tales of misbehaviour with lorry drivers, Zak Jane Kier with a story of what can happen with games of chance, and Paul Scott with all his usual enthusiasm for smutty suburban sex.

Available on ebook now

Also available from Nexus:

THE ACADEMY

By Arabella Knight

Miranda is a spoilt brat. Nothing Aunt Emma does seems to have any effect on her. There's only one thing to do: send the girl to the Academy, an educational establishment with a difference.

Under the steely direction of Mrs Boydd-Black, wayward young women like Miranda are taught how to behave correctly – and severe penalties await those who disobey...

Available on ebook now